PROLOGUE

Time to refresh everyone's memories...

Corbin? Dead.

Olivia? A damn, dirty traitor.

Sam? All healed up.

Me? Scared. Out. Of. My. Mind.

And why?

Because Anna thinks I may be pregnant. One quick bite later—which, yikes, let's never repeat that again—and I was speeding to the nearest grocery store to buy a test. Or two. Or three. Definitely four. Okay, five. I bought five.

Peed on the stick and everything.

Now, we wait. And wait. And wait some more...

Hold up.

Just wait a gosh darned minute.

Do those two lines... mean I'm pregnant?

1

Funny how two pink lines could completely upend your life.

Just two small, thin, pink lines.

Nothing more than that.

Except for, you know, the baby possibly growing inside of me. Like an alien just waiting to burst free of its squishy prison.

No, no, too graphic. It wouldn't be anything like that—*she said sarcastically*.

Maybe I was reading the stick wrong?

I glanced at the directions—which consisted of the finest print I'd ever seen—and squinted my eyes. Then I read the instructions over and over again. Remove stick from wrapper. Check. Submerge stick in urine stream. Gross, but check. Wait two minutes. Check and check. Heck, I'd even gone so far as to wait three. Then four. Just to make sure the stick didn't change its mind. I'd given it a mighty shake, too, as though *that* might erase the second line. Alas, they were both stuck on there, glaring up at me, all accusatory.

And according to the guide, two lines could only mean one thing.

Impregnato.

"This can't be," I whispered as I stared at myself in the bathroom mirror. I'd holed myself up in here after returning home with a gallon of water and an armful of pregnancy test boxes. All the instructions suggested it was best to do the tests in the morning, but I couldn't wait that long. I needed to know what I was facing right now.

And boy, did I now know.

A twist in my gut nearly had me dashing for the toilet, but with a fist pressed to my mouth, I managed to tamp it back. Hurling wouldn't accomplish anything. Not that I could control it like that. It wasn't as simple as mind over matter.

As much as I wanted to, I couldn't argue with the results. Anna herself had proclaimed me pregnant. And no one disagreed with vampires when it came to blood. According to my best friend, the bloodhound, I smelled different. Then she'd taken a nip of my blood to confirm her suspicions. Afterward, she'd suggested I go to the grocery store to pick up one of these darn tests. Of course, I'd grabbed five. You know, to be sure. False positives were a thing, yo.

Except... all five had come back positive. One even had a little smiley face staring up at me. For those who were hoping to conceive, a smiley face was a good thing. But that was a category Sam and I did not fall under.

It wasn't like I didn't want kids. I loved kids. What I didn't love was the vulnerability that came with them. Especially now.

My life was a hot mess. Imagine the worst-case scenario, and that was my life to a T.

My sixty-year-old mother had recently become a vampire—for which, she was utterly ungrateful. My stepdad was only starting to recuperate from a brutal attack that had nearly killed him. My sperm donor was dead—murdered, actually. And my half-sister wanted me dead.

In the past few months, I'd nearly died more times than I could count. Well, not quite. I could count much higher than three. But that didn't sound nearly as dramatic. After all that, though, a girl was bound to wonder if this was the best time to have a kid.

I scrubbed a hand down my face, then sat on the bathroom floor, my back pressed against the wall. I gripped the five pregnancy tests, all the while glaring at them as though they'd been the ones to make this happen. No, that blame rested with me and Sam.

Man, my mom was right. Sex truly did only lead to trouble.

I mean, pleasurable, sure. Orgasmic, some might even say. But then this occurs, and you're left staring at a plastic stick, wondering what the heck happened.

Sam's dick happened.

That thing needed to come with a warning label. *Warning: will knock you up. Proceed with caution.*

Sighing, I leaned forward and rested my elbows against my knees. Nausea churned in the pit of my stomach—a feeling I assumed I'd need to get used to. *Yaaaay.*

I had to pull myself together.

Step one consisted of leaving this bathroom. I couldn't hide in here forever. Not with Olivia out there somewhere, likely stirring up trouble. It'd been a month since I'd caught any whisper from her, but I had to imagine our problems with her were far from over. Especially considering I'd sorta kinda killed her mate when last we'd met. That wasn't something a werewolf forgave or forgot. In all fairness, they'd both been trying to kill me first, so fair's fair and all that. Doubt she saw it that way though. So I had to assume she'd added *seek revenge* to her to-do list. Hopefully that was one task she never crossed off.

Step two was telling Sam. Sounded simple, right? Except, the thought made my stomach churn again. It wasn't like he'd be mad. I knew that. The man wanted a family. And he loved me with every fiber of his being. Of that, I had no doubts. Still. Telling a man you were pregnant was a wee bit, well, terrifying.

I had a feeling Sam's wolf already knew something had changed. An instinct type thing. His protective nature had been working overtime these days. I hadn't given it much thought considering everything we'd been through lately. But now, I saw things differently. Hindsight and all that.

Perhaps I should have suspected something when he'd started working with my second in command, Cole. The two quite literally loathed each other. Fur usually flew when they were alone in a room. Yet, there they were, working together to canvass the neighborhood, patrolling for signs of a threat, all to protect me.

I was their alpha. I was supposed to protect them, not the other way around.

A gentle knock rapped against the bathroom door.

"Luce? You okay in there?"

I sagged at the sound of Anna's voice.

When I didn't answer, she jiggled the doorknob. "Can I come in?"

"Sure," I whispered, knowing she'd hear it.

The doorknob turned slowly, then the door eased open. She popped her head in, her long blonde locks flowing past her shoulders. Her hazel eyes creased with concern, her nose wrinkling. "How you doing in here?"

I lifted my hand and brandished the five tests.

Not a flicker of surprise crossed her face. Of course not. She'd tasted it in my blood, recommending the pregnancy tests for my peace of mind, not hers.

She stepped into the bathroom, then closed the door and leaned against it. Her gaze raked over the tests, and then my face. "Guess you guys weren't trying, huh?"

"Not even a little," I mumbled.

A smile graced her lips, but it didn't quite reach her eyes. "Try not to panic. Everything's gonna be alright."

"Nothing is going to be alright," I growled. "I'm in the middle of a freakin' blood feud with my sister. It isn't like she's going to stop just because I'm pregnant. If anything, she'll take advantage of this." My chest squeezed as the thought registered in my head. "Oh my god, she's going to take advantage of this."

"Luce—"

"She's going to use the pregnancy to hurt me." My hands flew to my stomach, even though it was far too early for me to be showing. My heart leapt into action, furiously thumping against my ribs, and my pulse thundered in my ears. "Anna, I can't—I don't— what am I... I-I don't know what to do."

Anna pushed off the door and crouched before me, her hands covering mine. "Shh. Take a deep breath." She pantomimed the movement, even though she didn't require air for anything but speaking. When my chest filled with air, she released her breath and indicated I should do the same. "One more time."

We sat there for a few moments, just breathing. Slowly, my body relaxed, but my skin broke into a cold sweat. Thoughts of everything Olivia could do to hurt me rolled around in my mind, taunting me.

"The timing isn't great, I'll give you that," Anna said, her voice uncharacteristically soft. "But that doesn't mean we'll let Olivia hurt you or your baby. You know we'll do everything we can to protect you. Sam, Vlad, me, Cole, your pack... We're all here for you."

My head jerked with a nod.

"What's important right now is remaining calm. It's hard, I know. Your nerves are probably shredded. But panicking isn't going to help you or the baby."

Right. Anxiety was bad for babies or something. Oh god, we were so screwed then. I was a walking ball of stress thanks to everything.

"Breathe, Luce," Anna urged me again.

I drew another deep breath, then focused on the color blue. Soothing, peaceful blue.

"Good." Anna squeezed my hands. "The most important thing right now is telling Sam."

I nodded. "And my mother too, I guess. Since she'll likely smell it on me."

Anna chuckled. "You have some time before she'll notice anything. Your mother is coming along nicely as a vampire, but she's still learning how to understand what her senses are telling her. She

12

might not notice your scent has changed yet. It's very subtle. Plus, Vlad's always said my nose is my strongest asset. Your mother's seems to be stubbornness."

I snorted a laugh, then sighed when all my tight muscles finally loosened. Stubbornness was my mother's number one strength, to the point where she still refused to accept she'd been turned into a vampire. Ignorance is bliss, and all that. But she'd even gone so far as to shun my dad—and, at times, me —since we'd been the ones who'd given Anna permission to change her. It made living with her only slightly awkward.

"Okay, how about we leave this bathroom and head into the living room? I'll whip you up a healthy smoothie or something. Then you can just sit and rest."

I inwardly winced. While I appreciated Anna's offer, her cooking skills had taken a sharp right-hand turn into Disgustingville after she'd become a vampire. Incredible sense of smell aside, she'd lost the ability to sample foods, and with that gone, it seemed so was her talent for cooking. I guess when one only drank blood, their taste buds withered and died.

Anna took my hand and gave a gentle tug,

pulling me up from the floor. I stood with a low groan, then turned and faced the mirror. I wasn't showing, it was too soon, but I felt so different already. Knowing there was this little nugget growing inside me. A part of me couldn't believe Sam and I had made something together, while the other part was still freaking the hell out.

"Come on, mama bear," Anna teased. "Let's get you fed. Sam and Cole should be back soon."

I trailed after her, my mind whirling as I headed toward the couch, while Anna deviated to the kitchen. A month ago, she wouldn't have been able to step a toe inside the room without the sun roasting her alive, thanks to all the massive windows. During the day, sunlight lit the kitchen up, which wasn't conducive to the vampire lifestyle. Vlad and my mother woke post-sunset, so they were never at risk. Anna, though, could be awake during the day, compliments of the ancient vampire blood she'd once ingested. The sun still burned her to a crisp, so we'd added a set of blackout curtains for her protection. It'd taken a while to convince her, since Anna craved natural light almost as much as she did blood, but I'd finally won that battle.

It bothered her though. She missed sunlight—and her humanity.

As a compromise, I'd equipped the living room with a few SAD lamps and bought her a pair of light therapy glasses. More than once, I'd found her sprawled on the floor with the bulbs all pointed toward her and the glasses covering her face, pretending she was sunbathing.

Seating myself, I listened as Anna moved about the kitchen, then heard the quick whir of the blender. A few moments later, she stood in front of me, cradling a chilled glass in her hand. I took it from her, but rather than drink it, I rested it in my lap.

"Come on, Luce," she urged, sitting next to me. "Drink up. It's good for you. All the vitamins and minerals a pregnant mama needs."

I forced a smile, appreciative of her efforts, then lifted the glass to my lips. The smell invaded my nose, and I sighed contentedly. My eyes closed as I guzzled it down, not pausing for breath.

"Whoa," she whispered. "There's more if you want some."

I drew in a refreshing breath and lowered the glass to the table. "Not yet. But thank you. I needed that."

Anna's wide eyes left my face, and she stared at the empty glass. "I'd say. You feeling okay?"

"I'm good. Just feeling a little anxious."

"Understandably. But you have nothing to be scared about. We both know Sam is going to be over the moon when he hears you're pregnant."

The words had barely left her mouth when the front door opened, and Cole and Sam entered.

My whole body froze like a deer caught in headlights.

"Shh," Anna quietly whispered, patting my hand. She lounged on the couch next to me and casually stretched out like she hadn't a care in the world. "Hey, guys."

"Anna. Luce," Sam greeted, his deep voice sending a shiver through my body.

I forced myself to lift my head and meet Sam's gaze. He stood in front of the door, his eyes on me as he removed his shoes and placed them on the mat. Cole stood behind him, gently closing the door.

"Hi," I rasped. I cleared my throat, then tried again. "Hey."

"Hi?" A smile curled his lips. "You okay?"

"Me?" My voice came out squeaky. Damn voice. I cleared my throat and tried again. "I'm fine. How are you?"

He lifted a questioning brow, and his mouth quirked into an amused smile. "I'm fine."

Small talk wasn't usually our thing. In fact,

normally by now, I'd have gone to him and welcomed him home with a soft kiss. If I did that, would he realize I smelled different? He hadn't this morning, so my fears were silly. But the thought still niggled in the back of my head.

"I don't think I've ever seen you drink a smoothie before," he commented.

I glanced down at the empty glass. Yeah, those were his thing. Part of his daily workout regime. "Oh, well, you made them look so good, I thought I'd give one a try."

He chuckled. "Glad to see you're broadening your horizons."

I forced another smile. Why was this so hard? It wasn't like this was *bad* news, per se. Just unexpected.

Anna nudged me with her knee, then tilted her head in his direction.

I released a shaky breath and nodded. Handing her the empty glass, I stood on shaky legs and shuffled toward Sam and Cole. "Find anything out there?"

"No. All's quiet," he said begrudgingly.

Hmm. It'd been this way for the past month, and it made me anxious. Along with everything else, it seemed. When last Olivia and I had met, I'd killed her mate, and she'd shot mine, nearly killing Sam in the process. After that, I'd expected her to retaliate, simply to avenge Corbin's death. Instead, it'd been nothing but crickets. No one had seen or heard from her since then. And while I would love to think that meant she'd smartened up and ditched this crusade of hers, deep down I knew better.

Where was she then? What was she doing? The not knowing was driving me batty.

"Maybe she realized she can't win and gave up?" I suggested.

"That's not what my intel suggests," Cole chimed in.

"Well, we can talk about that later, when everyone else is awake or whatever."

Sam stepped close, his hands rising to my cheeks. "You sure you're okay? You seem off."

"Do I?"

He leaned down and brushed his mouth against mine. The feel of his lips soothed me, and I instinctively leaned into him, my palm pressed against his chest. I couldn't help it. Touching Sam calmed me.

Once he drew back, I opened my eyes and steadied myself. There truly wasn't any reason to be scared. No way in hell Sam would abandon me, nor would he get mad. Why I was so nervous, I had no idea.

I wiped my damp palms against my thighs and met his gaze. "I-I suppose I do need to talk to you."

"What about?"

"Um." I glanced back at Anna and gestured to Cole.

"Right!" She hopped to her feet. "Come on, Wolf Boy. I need your help with something upstairs."

Cole blinked. "You do?"

Considering Cole and Anna rarely spoke, his confusion seemed valid. But this conversation definitely needed to be private. The two quickly vanished from sight, their steps retreating upstairs.

Strong fingers slid through my hair, pulling my focus back to the issue at hand. Sam swept my locks back from my face, then brushed his thumb against my cheek. My eyes fluttered shut, and I sighed, sinking into his touch.

"Lucy, what is it?" Sam asked.

I cupped his hands and eased them out of my hair, then pressed them against my belly. His fingers curled around my sides, his hands so large they nearly touched.

"Luce?"

I met his gaze and swallowed.

"Okay, you're scaring me," he said. "What's wrong?"

Two words. That was all I had to say.

Just rip the Band-Aid off, already!

My mouth opened, and I forced it out. "I'm... pregnant."

Silence rang through the house.

And not the normal, the-house-is-comfortably-quiet kind of silence. More like the deafening sort that made people's ears ring. Heck, the undead vampires sleeping in their bedrooms were making more noise than Sam right now.

Sam stood stock-still, his eyes unblinkingly wide and face a bit pale.

Had I startled him senseless with our news? I'd heard men could react a bit unpredictably when it came to pregnancy announcements. I'd even watched some hilarious ones on social media. But I'd hoped Sam would be different. A whoop of joy or an astonished laugh would have been nice. Maybe even a smile. Best-case scenario would have been him wrapping me in his arms and spinning me in circles.

Instead, he looked like a ghost who'd just been told he was about to be exorcized.

I gave Sam a few more minutes, all the while counting the many, many seconds in my head. Once I reached two-hundred-and-fifty, I sighed and jabbed him in the chest.

He responded with a slow blink. Just one. Then he returned to blindly staring.

Men.

"Sam."

No response. In fact, his gaze seemed to gloss over. I could only imagine the thoughts and questions circling his head. Especially considering our circumstances. It wasn't like this was the safest time for us to have a kid. Or for me to be pregnant. I had no doubt those realizations were ripping him to pieces.

Werewolves were a territorial bunch. Especially mated ones. Just imagine what that meant for a mated *pregnant* couple. Twenty bucks said his every instinct told him to cover me in bubble wrap and run away. Some place Olivia could never find us.

I waved a hand in front of his face. "Sam, come on. Say something."

After a brief pause, he cleared his throat and his now-focused gaze fell to mine. "Pregnant?"

"Pregnant," I said, nodding.

"You?"

"Um." I glanced around the room and shrugged. "I don't think there's anyone else in this house who could fit that description, considering we live with vampires."

Sam's head bobbed, as did his throat as he forced himself to swallow. "Right. Vampires."

"Are you okay?" I rested a hand on his arm. "You don't seem to be handling this all too well."

Although, I had to admit, he was handling it better than me. At least he hadn't locked himself in the bathroom. Yet.

"No, uh, I just..." He cleared his throat, then reached up and tugged at the collar of his plaid shirt. "You surprised me, that's all."

"Trust me, it surprised me too," I grumbled.

"Could you be mistaken?"

A humorless smile graced my lips. "I really doubt it."

His brows rose. "Why's that?"

"I didn't even suspect I was pregnant. The only reason I know is because Anna said she could smell it on me. Then she bit me—"

"She *bit* you?" Sam demanded, his voice deepening into a near-growl and his eyes flashing amber.

"Whoa," I whispered, stunned by his wolf's response. "She didn't *bite* me. She sampled me?" I gave another shrug. "She said my scent had changed, then she tasted my blood to see if her suspicions were right. To confirm, I went out and got a pregnancy test. Five actually."

Sam's whole body grew rigid. "Alone?"

Ah. Well. "Uh, yeah. Anna couldn't go out because of the sun, and you were out with Cole—"

Another low growl leaked past Sam's lips. "Lucy, need I remind you that Olivia wants you dead? Going out alone is too much of a risk."

"And need I remind *you* we haven't seen or heard from her in a month? I can't live my life in permanent fear, Sam. Besides, I wasn't exactly thinking clearly at that moment," I confessed.

"You need to. You can't take those chances anymore. If Olivia hurts you..." He shook his head. "No, she won't lay a finger on you."

It seemed pointless to remind him that Olivia had vanished.

"I know." I placed my other hand on his chest. "I'll be more careful, I promise."

"Good. Good." He released a heavy breath, then straightened to his full six-foot-five height. "I need to run out real quick. Don't go anywhere. You're not to leave the house. Okay?"

"What?"

His gaze jumped to the stairs. "Anna and Cole are upstairs, and Vlad and your mother should be awake soon," he said, more to himself than me. "Stay here where you're safe. Don't leave."

"What are you talking about?"

He cupped my cheeks, then leaned in and kissed me. "Do you trust me?"

"Of course. But is this really the right time for you to run some errands? I mean, I just told you I'm pregnant."

"I know. It's related, I promise. I won't be long. An hour at most."

I peered into his eyes, trying my hardest to understand what the hell was so important that he needed to leave right this second. "You aren't going to do something stupid, are you? Like go after Olivia all by yourself?"

"No, love." He kissed me again, this time lingering above my lips as though breathing me in. "I swear, I'll be right back. This is just something I need to do."

"Right now?" I asked.

He grinned. "Right freaking now."

The grin startled me, but I felt my lips tug upward in response. If he was smiling, then all had to be well, right? In fact, the more I watched him, the more excited he seemed. A flush had spread across his cheeks, and his eyes sparkled with happiness. Whatever he was running off to do, I had to assume it was a good thing.

Sam kissed me then. Except, it was more than a simple kiss. His mouth came down hard on mine, his tongue sweeping past my lips with an almost possessive edge to it.

Then he was gone, and I stood alone in the living room, staring at the damn door, wondering what the heck had just happened. What was so darn important that it couldn't wait until we'd at least had a chance to discuss things? My mate was no coward—far from it. So, logically, I knew he wasn't bailing on us. Soulmates were forever. They didn't bail on each other, no matter what. Besides, werewolves possessed strong urges to procreate. I bet his wolf was howling with bliss right now.

"What the freaking hell?" Anna hissed as she stomped down the stairs. "Where the hell is Sam? Did he actually *leave*?"

"He didn't leave," I murmured. "He just... left."

Anna whirled on the final step and stared at me, her brows vanishing into her hairline. "Leaving *is* leaving, Lucy!"

"Well, sure, but he didn't, like, *leave* leave."

Okay, this conversation was starting to get a little confusing.

"Oh, really? Then where is he?" she growled, her tone rising with every word. "He just learned you're pregnant!"

At the sound of approaching footsteps, I winced. She just had to yell that last part, didn't she?

"Wait, someone's pregnant?" came Cole's voice as he descended the stairs.

"Pregnant? Who's pregnant?" another voice, this one high-pitched.

Oh god. My mother. I'd hoped she'd stay asleep just a little longer. I wasn't in the right headspace to have this conversation with her.

"Lucy's pregnant?" came Vlad's familiar voice.

A quick glance at the grandfather clock revealed

the time. Seven p.m. Just late enough for all the little vampires to rise from their graves. And just in time to catch Anna's little tirade too. With ears of a bat, it would have been impossible to miss.

"Thanks a lot," I hissed at Anna.

She sucked her bottom lip into her mouth, her face knotted with worry. "I'm so sorry. I just got a little mad. I shouldn't have said that."

"You think?"

It wasn't that I planned to keep the pregnancy a secret, but I wasn't ready to tell anyone yet. Most couples waited until the second trimester to share the news. I'd always agreed with that choice—to keep the heartbreak to a minimum should the worst happen.

"Lucy?" My mother stepped in front of me and clasped my hands, her chilled fingers giving mine a squeeze. "Is this true?"

I groaned and closed my eyes. This really wasn't what I'd wanted to focus on tonight. I'd hoped for time to digest this information first. To let this info sit with me and Sam before the rest of the world found out.

"Sweetheart, are you pregnant?" my mom pressed.

Well, there was no point denying it anymore.

I managed a small head bob, but that was all it took to send the room into chaos. My mother clapped her hands over her mouth and practically squealed with excitement. Cole released a shocked "holy crap," while Anna hugged Vlad, as though this news meant the world to her. And perhaps it did, considering she was unable to have a baby of her own. Even Vlad wore a small smile, which was more emotion than he typically expressed.

"Oh, this is just wonderful!" my mother exclaimed. "Where's Sam? Does he know yet?"

"Sam knows," I said. "He had to go do something real quick, he said."

My mother shared a glance with me before pulling me close. Her strong arms wound around my back, holding me prisoner.

"Don't you worry about Sam. Men are weird creatures when it comes to babies. I was already pregnant when I met your father. We hadn't even slept together, and the first question out of his mouth was 'is it mine?'"

I burst out laughing. "How long had you two known each other when he asked you that?"

"About five minutes," my mother said, chortling. "It's like their brains completely misfire when they hear someone's pregnant. Even more so when it's someone they love. When Sam gets back, you two will be able to celebrate properly."

I appreciated my mother's words, but they didn't stop me from remembering all the horrible stories I'd heard about men "going out for cigarettes" and never returning. I had no reason to fear that from Sam, but my damn brain wouldn't shut the eff-train up right now. I would have liked to blame that on pregnancy hormones, but I doubted I was far enough along for them to affect me yet. Not that I was an expert on anything remotely pregnancy related.

"It's been a long time since we've had a new baby in the pack," Cole said. He descended the last couple of steps, then clapped a hand on my shoulder. We certainly weren't the hugging type. More like beating the snot out of each other sort. He was the one who'd taught me how to fight, and we both seemed keen to keep it that way.

"Guess I won't be able to train with you anymore," I said sheepishly. We hadn't sparred much during the last month—which was probably for the best. But now that I knew about my little bun, we'd have to press pause. At least until after I gave birth.

Oh god. Birth.

I squeezed my eyes shut and forced my thoughts

away from that path. I so wasn't ready to venture there yet.

Vlad stepped up and embraced me next, his chilled breath tickling my ear as he murmured, "Congratulations. Would you like me to hunt down your mate and 'whoop his ass' as Anna would say? I'm happy to help in any way I can."

I choked back a laugh. Yeah, I just bet Vlad would love that. He and Sam didn't get along on the best of days. They'd tried convincing me it was natural for them to hate each other, but I'd quickly pointed out that Anna and I loved each other more than anything. So they couldn't pull that werewolf versus vampire crap with me. I'd then told them both to suck it up and learn to get along, because Anna and I had no intention of ending our friendship. And since they were our mates, they were stuck with each other.

Vlad leaned back as though awaiting my answer. I shook my head, but his question had brought a smile to my lips, which I appreciated more than anything.

"Oh, there's so much to do!" my mom crooned. "First, we need to call your father. He'll be beside himself!"

"And do you plan on being the one to share this

news with him?" I asked. My parents hadn't properly spoken in weeks. But maybe this would be the thing to bridge the gap between them.

My mother's expression hardened. "I'll leave that to you. I'm sure you'd like to be the one to tell him."

"Nope," I said, popping the *P*. "You can call him."

"Lucy—"

"Mom. Enough. It's been weeks. You've learned how to control your hunger and you're not a danger to humans anymore. So there's no reason not to call him. We know you're not happy about our choice, but it can't be undone. You need to stop punishing us."

All emotion drained from her face. "I'm not ready."

"Tough," I said.

"So, I think we should call a pack meeting," Cole interjected, interrupting the impending storm brewing between me and my mom. "It's important everyone is aware of this new development, especially considering current circumstances. You may need pack protection, so they should be in the know."

I wasn't sure I appreciated Cole referring to my baby as a development, but I understood his concerns. I didn't love the idea though. The pack and I had taken massive steps toward repairing our fragile relationship, but I wasn't sure we were at a point where any of them would want to play bodyguard to me. Especially when I was their alpha. Technically, I was their protector, not the other way around.

As though sensing my concerns, Cole guided me into the kitchen, forcing me to take a seat at the table. My entourage followed, but only Anna sat next to me. My mother and Vlad both headed for the fridge and began preparing their "breakfasts." Nothing like a steaming mug of blood to help wake an undead body up.

"I know you and the pack have some issues—" Cole started.

"Understatement," Anna said, chuckling. "Or am I the only one who remembers the recent challenges?"

"Challenge," I corrected her. "Marcus retracted his."

"But Bryn didn't. And now she's dead."

Thanks to me.

I returned my gaze to Cole. "It's not that I have any problems with the pack. I'm just worried about pushing them too far. Bryn's only been dead a month. Some are still a little sore with me. They're happy that Corbin's dead, but they're not happy about Olivia. And since she's my sister...."

"You didn't change her into a werewolf," Cole said. "And the pack knows that. No one holds you responsible. And don't forget, the majority of the pack supported *you* instead of Bryn. Afterward, many came here with you to protect your parents. Besides, you won't be able to keep this a secret for long. Anna's already picked up on your changing scent. Soon, we'll be able to as well. So put your trust in us. The pack has your back, Lucy."

Warmth filled my chest. Cole was right. I'd made some great strides with the pack. And in the past month, I'd fostered those developing relationships. I'd reached out individually to each member to open a line of communication with them. We'd also thrown a few small pack events—ones that hadn't ended with any dead pack members.

The entire purpose of me coming here was to find someone to take my place so I could step down as alpha. But that didn't feel like an option anymore. With every passing day, I grew more attached to the pack. I missed New Orleans, and I greatly missed Sam's family. They'd taken me in and immediately accepted me. But the Mississippi Pack—my pack—needed me. I wasn't sure I could walk away from that anymore. Sam and I hadn't spoken about it recently, but we'd need to, and soon.

"Look, all I'm saying is you aren't alone. We may need to take some precautions and ask a few to help out, but they aren't going to resent you for it. In fact, they'll likely appreciate it. The strongest packs are the ones who work with their alphas."

I thought about Adrien and the New Orleans Pack. They were the strongest one I knew. Mind you, I'd only ever seen the two. His and mine. But his seemed like the ideal example of a healthy, well-functioning pack. Adrien treated his people like family. He was strong and protected his members, but when Corbin murdered Adrien's daughter, his pack had been there to help. They'd supported and cared for the family in their time of need. That was what I wanted.

"Okay," I finally whispered. "Let's do it."

"Yeah?"

After a slight hesitation, I nodded. "Yeah. I refuse to let something happen to me or the baby simply because I had too much pride to allow others to help."

"Good." Cole briefly touched the back of my hand before reaching for his phone. "I'll arrange the meeting."

My mother leaned against the kitchen counter, her mug of blood in hand, but she beamed at me, clearly approving of my decision. My gaze jumped to Vlad, who gave me a single nod. Even Anna seemed appeased by my answer.

Clearly, I'd made the right choice.

I JUMPED UP FROM THE COUCH THE INSTANT I heard Sam's car pull into the driveway. It'd been two hours since he'd left—longer than he'd estimated—and my nerves were frayed.

Anna slowly stood next to me, then gave me a gentle hug. "I'll give you two some privacy."

I appreciated that. With three live-in vampires and two shifters, plus a third who visited daily, privacy wasn't something we came by easily. But tonight, everyone seemed to understand it was needed. Vlad had long since retreated to his and Anna's bedroom—to conduct business, he'd said. Not that I had any idea what that entailed. My mother had also sequestered herself in her room, claiming she wanted some time alone. Personally, I suspected it had more to do with her avoiding my demands that she call my father. Cole had kept to the kitchen with the promise of giving me space, but had planned to stay until Sam returned.

Needless to say, I felt so protected, I could scream. Not that I did. These people were my family, and I loved them. Overprotectiveness and all.

"Thanks," I whispered to Anna before turning my complete focus on the front door.

My pulse leapt when Sam finally opened the door and stepped inside, letting in a breath of fresh nighttime air with him.

"Hi," he said, beaming at me.

"Hi," I echoed, studying every inch of him. Not a hair or piece of clothing out of place, so he hadn't gone after Olivia, thank goodness.

Without another word, Sam marched toward me and snatched me into his arms, hugging me so tightly I thought I might break.

"Uh, Sam," I wheezed. "Can't breathe."

"Oops," he said, chuckling.

His grip loosened, and I sank into the embrace, the last vestiges of fear melting away. I didn't realize I was trembling until Sam started smoothing his hands up and down my back, all while whispering a soft, "shh," and promising me everything would be okay.

I drank in his promises and held them close to my heart. With him at my side, everything *would* be okay.

When my tremors passed, Sam leaned back and cupped my cheeks. "I love you. So much."

My bottom lip quivered, and a massive weight lifted from my shoulders. I closed my eyes and rested my head against his chest, breathing in his comforting scent. "I didn't realize how badly I needed to hear that."

His arms tightened around me, and he pressed a kiss to the top of my head. "I'm so sorry. I didn't mean to worry you."

I reveled in the feel of his arms around me. When Sam held me, everything felt right. I'd never felt as safe with anyone as I did with him. He was my heart, my life, my home. Once upon a time, it'd terrified me to make a commitment to him. Hell, I'd even run away just to escape the thought of being his mate. But that all seemed so foolish now. Guess our hearts truly did know things our heads didn't. Even now, the thought of us taking care of a little person terrified me. But with Sam at my side, we could do anything. I just needed to believe in us.

"Are you going to tell me where you went?" I asked.

Another smile. "Where's everyone else?"

I gave a vague gesture toward the rest of the house. "In their rooms. Trying to give us some privacy." Not that they could. Supernatural hearing and all that. Everyone in this house could hear every word we said, but we'd all grown used to that.

"Perfect."

I arched a brow, silently wondering why that was so *perfect*.

Taking my hands in his, Sam gave them a squeeze before pulling them upward and resting them on his chest. "In a perfect world, I would have taken you out tonight. We would have gone to dinner at a fancy restaurant to celebrate our news, then I would have taken you for a walk in the moonlight. We would have shifted and run free through the woods. And once we'd shifted back, I would have made love to you under the stars."

I shivered. "That sounds wonderful."

"It does. And when we've put all this behind us, when we've handled Olivia, we'll do just that." He lifted one hand from mine and brushed my hair back from my cheek. "I know we didn't have the easiest start to our relationship. We've faced many obstacles, but we're here together. We've survived more challenges than a normal couple. Faced separation and death. Grief and loss. And we've come out of it stronger than ever. I know, as do you, that you're my soulmate."

A smile touched my lips. That was one thing I knew without a doubt.

"I've known since the day we met that we were destined to be together. And I know that we'll be together until our dying days." He dropped a hand into his front pocket and withdrew a box.

At the sight of the black velvet, my heart slammed into my ribs. "Sam—"

"Now, before you start panicking, I want you to know that I've been working on this for a few weeks now."

"Working on what?"

He eased open the lid, and my heart stopped dead at the sight of the most beautiful ring I'd ever seen. My breath whooshed past my lips, and I clapped my hands to my mouth.

"Would you believe I got the call this afternoon that this was ready to be picked up?" he asked, chuckling. "Providence, I say. I'd planned to pick it up tomorrow, but then you told me you're pregnant, and I just couldn't wait any longer."

Speechless, I stared at the gorgeous ring, glimmering up at me from inside its velvet case.

"The band is from my grandmother's wedding ring," Sam said. "And the first gem, this one here"— he pointed at the moonlit black diamond—"is from my great-grandmother's wedding ring. I had the jeweler add an accent diamond for every person we love to symbolize the joining of our two families."

Tears stung my eyes. "Sam..." My voice came out hoarse. "It's beautiful."

It was more than beautiful. It was downright stunning. The entire piece reminded me of the night sky, sparkling with countless stars surrounding the full moon. To think that he'd done this, that he'd been working on this without my knowledge, robbed me of breath.

"My mother gave me the original ring when she first met you," he said, his voice full of warmth. "She said she knew the second she saw us together that we would be eternal. I asked if I could change a few things, and she loved my idea."

Still stricken speechless, I tore my gaze from the ring and stared up at him, tears sliding down my cheeks as I did.

"Lucy, I love you more than anything. You're all I want, all I'll ever want, and all I'll ever need. Fate knew exactly what it was doing when it brought us together. You're the reason my heart beats, the reason I smile, the reason I live. No matter the obstacles we face, no matter what happens in life, I will always love you." He sucked in a deep breath, then stared deeply into my eyes. "Will you marry me?"

Sniffling, I wiped the tears from my cheeks and nodded.

"Yes?" Sam asked.

"Yes," I breathed. "Of course, yes."

Relief breezed past Sam's lips. He pulled the ring from the box and slid it perfectly down my finger, as though he'd had it measured. I gave a watery chuckle as I realized he probably had. He said he'd been working on this for weeks, after all.

"I... have no idea what to say," I murmured. "Other than I love you so much."

"And I you."

I wrapped my arms around Sam's neck, then hauled his head down to my level. Our mouths came together in a heated clash, our tongues quickly tangling as we both hurried to taste one another. I kissed him like I never had before, pouring every ounce of emotion and feeling into it, showing him with actions rather than words what he meant to me.

I couldn't believe this man belonged to me, and every inch of me vibrated with excitement as I realized he was not only my mate, but now my fiancé. Much like he'd said, I was his everything. And he was mine.

"Oh, wow," came a quiet voice.

Breaking from the kiss, I lifted my ring hand to my mouth and pressed my fingers against my trembling lips. If Anna hadn't spoken, that kiss would have delved into something much naughtier. And while I was ready and eager to climb into bed with Sam, now, unfortunately, wasn't the right moment.

The sight of Anna and my mother hovering in the hallway, their heads peeking around the corner, made me laugh. Sneaky little vamps, eavesdropping on mine and Sam's moment. I was so happy right now that their nosiness didn't bother me. Especially considering the expression on both their faces, their eyes shimmering with blood tears. It wasn't often I saw Anna cry. Once she'd been turned into a vampire and learned normal tears were a thing of the past, she'd made a vow to never cry again. An unrealistic promise, obviously.

Quickly swiping at their eyes, Anna and my

mother came toward us, the joy in their faces contagious.

"Damn, Sam. That was so beautiful," Anna rasped, her own voice gruff with emotion. "And that ring..."

I'd once thought Anna's ring was the most beautiful I'd ever seen. But in my mind, it ranked second now. As I stared down at mine, my heart flipped. It encapsulated everything about me and Sam. And the thought that he'd designed it especially for me was astounding.

My fingers curled inward, and I pressed my fist to my heart, knowing I didn't need actual wedding vows to promise myself forever to Sam. Mates were forever, so in my heart, we were already married. But the feel of his ring on my finger, the knowledge that we would soon wed and share our relationship with everyone we loved, made me want to squeal with happiness.

Anna fanned her face to dry her tears before they fell. "Man, this has been one hell of an emotional day. First, you're pregnant. Now, you're engaged. I don't think my undead heart can take much more."

My mother wrapped an arm around Anna's waist and pulled her close.

"Is it safe to come out now?" Cole called to us from the kitchen.

The four of us burst out laughing.

"Come on out," I said.

Cole wasn't the only one to venture toward us. Vlad appeared next to Anna, wearing his own smile. "Congratulations."

Sam bobbed his head in thanks.

I stared at the faces of all my loved ones and my heart filled with so much joy, I thought it might burst. Our lives were far from perfect, and things could change today or tomorrow, considering we lived under constant threat of death. But these people were my family, and this was my home. No one could tear that away from me.

THE NIGHT WAS STILL FAIRLY YOUNG, SO WE
decided to celebrate.

After considering ordering in alcohol, we
realized only Cole and Sam could partake and
decided against it. Seemed silly to order booze for
two people. Instead, we'd settled on pizza for the
three of us that could eat food and blood for the other
three. Vlad and Anna often went out at night to feed
themselves, and sometimes my mother tagged along.
But tonight, they'd opted to stay in. Once everyone
had finished their meals, we all grabbed a seat in the
living room and watched *Teen Wolf*. Even though
Anna couldn't eat popcorn, she and I laughed and

chucked the kernels at the screen. It was tradition, after all.

Halfway through the movie, my phone lit up with an incoming call.

The second I saw my father's name on the screen, I snatched up my cell and stood. My mother was too busy chuckling at the screen to notice who was on the line, so instead of answering it myself, I hit "talk," then thrust the phone at her before retreating to the kitchen.

Without thinking, she grabbed the phone and placed it to her ear. "Hello?"

The silence on the other end was deafening.

Guess my father hadn't been expecting her to answer.

"Hello?" my mother asked again, still half-distracted by the movie.

"Barbara?"

My mother shot to her feet. "Richard?"

"Ohhh, you're gonna get it now," Anna said as she trailed after me into the kitchen. "Your mom isn't ready to talk to him."

"Too bad," I said. "She can't keep ignoring him. She isn't ignoring me anymore, so it's time to forgive him too."

Anna studied me, her teeth scraping her bottom lip. "I'm just not sure that was the right move."

I shrugged. Maybe, maybe not. Guess we'd find out.

Grabbing an empty glass, I filled it with water, all the while straining my senses. I could hear my mother pacing toward her room, her voice soft as she spoke to my father. Soft was good. Soft meant she wasn't yelling at him.

"I think it'll be good for them. She needs to decide whether she can move forward with him."

"And what if she decides she can't? Lucy, keep in mind that your parents have been together your whole life. And now she's immortal, and he isn't. He's going to continue aging while she's stuck at sixty. She'll have to watch him grow old and die without her."

"I know," I whispered, tears thickening my voice. "I've thought about that. But she can't make a decision unless she speaks to him."

"And if she decides to move on?"

"Then so be it," I said, even though it absolutely broke my heart to think of that. I loved my dad—even though he wasn't my biological father. But that didn't matter to me. It didn't matter when I'd first learned that delightful tidbit, and it didn't matter now. He would forever be my real father. And he deserved to know whether he still had a wife. A month of not speaking couldn't be good for either of them.

"There's another option," I spoke quietly. I shot Anna a quick glance, then returned my focus to the water in my glass, swirling it gently. "He doesn't *have* to grow old without her."

Anna's mouth fell slack. "You want us to change him as well?"

"I don't want you to do anything. I just want him to know he has options."

"But is it the *right* option?"

"That's not for us to decide," I said. "Whatever he chooses, I'll support them both, but don't you think he deserves to be made aware of all his choices?"

"I suppose..." Anna drummed her fingers against the counter and fell silent, likely contemplating the idea I'd just pitched. "If that's what he wants, I'll do it. But he needs to be sure. Your mother's situation was different. She would have died if we hadn't done anything."

"I know."

"Have you suggested this to him yet?" she asked.

"No. I was waiting for my mother to speak to him first. I don't want to pressure anyone into anything. If she decides they can be together until he dies, then there's no need to suggest anything. If she decides she can't go through that, then..." I didn't finish the sentence.

"Okay," Anna said. "Guess we'll see what happens first."

I strained my ears once more and still heard the soft whisper of my mother's voice. I didn't listen any closer, though, wanting to give them privacy. But at least they were speaking. After a month of silence between them, I couldn't ask for more.

I brought the glass to my lips, about to down the contents, when I heard Sam's phone ring. Abandoning my drink, I ventured back into the living room.

Sam sat on the couch with his phone in hand, staring at the screen with a goofy grin stretched across his face. The sight of it took me aback. My mate didn't often show emotion to anyone other than me. He loved his family, but even with them, he could be a bit quiet.

I stepped closer, only to find his mother's face peering back at him on the screen.

"She said yes!" Elena screamed at someone behind her. "Adrien! Our boy is getting married!"

When she turned back to Sam, her face was pink

with excitement and her eyes glowed with happiness.

"What's going on?" a deeper voice called across the line. Adrien came into view, his head bobbing behind his wife's.

"Hi, Dad," Sam said.

"Sam. You're looking well, my boy."

"Of course he's looking well! He's engaged!" Elena practically shouted.

Both Sam and his father pulled away from her, but Adrien beamed at his son through the phone. "Is that right?"

"It is," Sam said. He glanced my way, then turned the phone toward me.

I held up a hand. "Hi!"

"Ahh, there's my future daughter-in-law," Elena cooed. "Oh, you're so beautiful. And so strong! Look at you. We haven't seen you in forever, and you look so different."

I stared down at myself, afraid that my stomach had suddenly sprouted and I was showing. But no, my belly looked the same. The only difference being that Elena and Adrien hadn't seen me since I moved here. And in that time, Cole and Anna had conditioned me into a strong fighter. Sometimes, when I looked in the mirror, the differences in my face even astounded me. What little roundness I'd once carried was now cut into straight lines. My "chubby chipmunk cheeks," as my mother had once called them, were gone. And my frame had grown narrow and firm. I hadn't been curvy before, but the difference between then and now was still rather dramatic.

"Well, now. Don't you look like an alpha werewolf ready to lead her pack," Adrien said, pride brightening his gaze.

With the phone still facing me, Sam caught my eye and mouthed, "Can I tell them?"

I hesitated. We hadn't even seen the doctor yet, and it made me nervous to share our news with other people beyond those who lived in the house—and even then, they'd only learned of the pregnancy because of Anna. But Elena and Adrien were family too. Mine already knew, so why not include Sam's parents? If the worst happened, they would support and grieve with us.

So I nodded.

"How are you, my dear?" Elena asked. "Are you handling things well? Sam's been keeping us informed. This whole situation sounds rather grim."

My mouth twisted. "It isn't fun, but we're handling it. Hopefully it'll be over soon."

"Lucy and I have some other news too," Sam said, turning the phone back to him.

"Oh?"

The elation that spread across Sam's face melted my heart. "Lucy is pregnant."

A literal *scream* erupted from the phone. I winced and playfully covered my ears with my hands. To say Elena was excited was an understatement.

"You're *pregnant?*" she shouted. Then came the questions, dozens of them, all fired off one after another. When did we learn we were pregnant? How far along were we? How will this affect my position with the pack? And so on.

"Mom," Sam tried to interrupt her. "Mom, stop."

But more questions kept rolling in. When can she come see us? When will we come see them? Will we marry before or after the baby is born?

"Mom!" Sam shouted, laughing. "We just found out today. How about you give us some time before you pester us for all this information."

"Pester," she repeated. "Hardly. I just want to know what's happening! Oh, I'm so excited. A wedding and a baby. What more could we ask for? Other than you coming home, of course."

My mother entered the room then, thankfully saving me from having to answer that question.

A quick glance told me the conversation with my father hadn't gone well. Red streaks highlighted her pale cheeks and rimmed her eyes. When her gaze rose to mine, I flinched. She didn't look angry, per se, but nor was she happy.

"Let us figure out some of that stuff for ourselves first, and then we'll let you know," Sam said, his voice distracting me from my mother.

"Okay, sweetie. We're just so excited. Lucy, you call me anytime!" Elena chirped. "We can chat about things, and I can coach you a little on giving birth."

My mom's head snapped up at that. "I'm here too," she said. "I can help her with that."

"Oh, Barbara!" Elena gushed. "Sam, let me see her so I can say hi. Turn the phone."

My mother shook her head sternly, clearly not excited about letting anyone else see her like this.

"Barbara just left," Sam said, reading her emotional state correctly. "But I'll pass on your love to her."

"Thank you, dear. But do have Lucy call me. We can chat about babies and birth and all that fun stuff."

I grimaced. That sounded *super* fun.

"Of course," Sam said. "We'll call you tomorrow, alright?"

"Okay. I love you both so much!" Elena blew Sam kisses, then disconnected the call.

Silence crept into the room, and all eyes turned to my mother.

"I don't want to talk about it," was all she said before grabbing her jacket, storming outside, and sitting on the porch.

At least my parents had spoken. And hopefully now they'd be able to move forward. I made a mental note to ask her tomorrow, then returned to the kitchen to find Anna.

She sat at the kitchen table, typing away on my laptop, a perplexed expression twisting her features.

"Anna?"

"Hmm?" She glanced away from the laptop. When she saw me, her face cleared, and she closed the laptop lid. "Sam's mother sounds excited."

I grinned. "Yeah. What were you looking at?"

She pressed her lips together, her eyes lighting up with laughter. If vampires could blush, I would have bet her cheeks would be pink right about now.

My eyes narrowed as I studied her. "Out with it." Clearly she'd been doing something naughty.

"Okay, so I was curious..." She flipped the laptop

back open. "I googled *what to expect when you're expecting.*"

My eyes shot wide. "Why on earth would you research that?"

"Uh, cuz we need to learn about this? Do *you* know anything about being pregnant?"

Probably about as much as Anna did. I frowned at the laptop. Maybe even less so now if she'd been researching it.

"Well, what'd you find?"

Footsteps approached from behind, and before I could glance back, Sam leaned down and pressed a kiss against my cheek.

"Well, there are some recommended essentials." Amusement brightened her face, which concerned me greatly.

"Like?"

Anna turned the laptop toward me. "Did you know you'll need nipple cream?"

"What?"

"Nipple cream," she repeated.

"Okay...," I hedged, reaching toward the laptop. "I'll bite. What the heck is nipple cream? What does it do, and why do I need it?"

Anna snickered, which didn't comfort me at all. "This website says that it'll soothe your nipples while breastfeeding your little monster."

"Oh yeah, I've heard of that," Sam said.

My head snapped in his direction. He *had?*

He caught my expression and chuckled. "We've had a few babies born in our pack. And mothers *love* discussing these things." He shook his head, still laughing. "The things I've heard discussed during pack meetings... I remember someone mentioning once that breastfeeding dries out the nipple, and the skin will sometimes crack and bleed, so—"

"What?" I yelped, jerking my hand back from the laptop as though it'd burned me and cupped my breasts. "Crack. And. Bleed? You're joking, right?"

Anna snorted a laugh. "I mean, bleeding nips just comes with the territory, don't you think? That's not even the worst thing you'll face."

The heat drained from my face. "What? What could be worse than bleeding nipples?"

"Well, labor to start," Anna suggested, while oh so helpfully pointing at my crotch.

I batted her hand away.

"What, you think your baby is just going to magically appear in a puff of smoke and glitter? Sweetie, that baby is gonna rip and tear through your baby-cannon like—"

"Stop!" I shouted, barely refraining from crossing my hands over my crotch.

Anna shrugged. "It's normal. I'm sure they'll give you drugs—ohhh, right." She winced in sympathy. "Werewolves metabolize drugs too quickly. Guess it's *au naturel* for you, girl. Oof, that's gonna hurt."

I whimpered, suddenly terrified for my *baby-cannon*. Was *this* what Elena wanted to talk to me about?

Sam rumbled a thoughtful noise. "I remember the last time a pack member had a baby, the mother mentioned something she found quite helpful." He grabbed the laptop and after a few keystrokes, turned it back toward me where I saw the word *padsicle* typed into the search bar.

I scanned the results, and when I spotted the words *absorbent perineal ice pad*, I crossed my legs and made a choking sound. "What the hell is that?"

"Padsicles," Sam repeated, snickering. "Such an odd word, so it stuck with me. She said you crack them like a glow stick, and it'll release some sort of chemical that cools them. Then you put them—"

"I can guess where to put them!" I shouted, my face suddenly blazing with heat.

My god, we were *not* having this conversation. I wasn't even showing yet. I hadn't even seen the doctor! No way was I ready to talk about post-labor care and padsicles with my mate and best friend.

"Oh, hun." Anna patted my shoulder. "This is happening, so best to start accepting it all now."

I unleashed my most ferocious glare on my best friend, then shook my head.

"I need a bath," I muttered. Anything to get away from these two. They found this far too amusing for my liking.

"Oh, I read something about that as well," Anna said, snatching back the laptop and pulling up another site. "Says here you can still take baths, but the water can't be too hot. Hmm. It recommends using a thermometer. I'll pick one up the next time we're out."

Disbelief widened my eyes.

Anna shot me a quick glance. "Everything's about to change, my love. But don't worry. We'll be here to help you through this. In the meantime, though, no hot baths, hot tubs, saunas, sushi, alcohol, or caffeine."

Well, there went my Friday night.

"Try not to worry about this too much," Anna said, her voice softening. "You have lots of time. And you'll be ready for it all when the time comes."

Easy for her to say.

"Bath," I repeated, now desperate for a little alone time. "Then bed." I needed to get out of this room and away from this conversation. I'd only learned I was pregnant today, for crying out loud. I wasn't ready to think about nipple creams and padsicles. Overwhelmed barely described how I was feeling right now. Today had been a rollercoaster ride full of emotions.

"Oh, okay." Anna's voice dropped with disappointment. "Well, let me know if you need anything else tonight."

I stood from my chair and headed toward the master suite bathroom.

"Sleep well," Anna murmured.

Sleep well? I'd be lucky to catch any winks tonight. Right now, I had images of a Chucky doll exploding out of my baby-cannon while blood poured from my nipples. A more horrific image I'd never seen.

UNSURPRISINGLY, SLEEP ELUDED ME.

Hard to drift off when my mind wouldn't shut up. A never-ending narration spiraled through my head, asking me countless questions I didn't have answers to. And because I didn't have any answers, I couldn't relax. If the voice would just shut up, I might have been able to catch some winks. Alas...

"You okay?" Sam's gruff voice sounded beside me.

A loaded question if ever I'd heard one.

When I didn't respond, Sam draped an arm over my waist and pulled me closer, tucking my back against his chest. His hand pressed against my stomach, and the feel of his fingers stroking my skin nearly had me purring. Maybe *this* was what I needed to help me relax. Sam's touch had worked miracles before.

My pillow shifted under his weight, and he pressed his head against mine. "Talk to me," he whispered, his breath brushing the back of my neck.

I shivered and squeezed his arm. "Just can't sleep."

"I gathered that," he said, chuckling.

A smile touched my lips. He'd zonked out the instant his head had hit the pillow, but my restlessness must have woken him. It wouldn't be the first time. I didn't have insomnia, but I sure as heck struggled with sleep. Falling asleep was easy, staying asleep, not so much. More than once, Sam had woken in the middle of the night to find me watching TV or reading a book. Except, tonight, I didn't want to do either of those things. My brain was too loud for me to focus on anything other than my fears.

"Luce," he murmured. "What's going on?"

"I'm scared," I admitted.

"About the baby?"

I nodded. "Yes." Then shook my head. "And no."

His chest rumbled against my back. "I might need a little more to go on than that."

I rolled over and faced him, our noses practically

touching. The sight of Sam's sleepy face and tousled hair brought a smile to my lips. The man was drop-dead gorgeous. I'd often compared him to Superman with his straight cut jaw and sharp facial features. I'd never tire of staring at him. There was always something new and fascinating to find. Tonight, for instance, even in the dark, I could see the amber hue of his eyes, and count the flecks of brown within.

Sam inched closer and brushed his lips against mine. "You can tell me anything, you know that."

I did. I just didn't know how to voice my fears. My brain was a muddled mess. I wasn't an anxious person by definition, but I had anxieties. And me being pregnant fueled them.

Sighing, I closed my eyes and tried to center my thoughts. "I'm worried. This is possibly the worst time for us to have a child. Don't tell me you didn't have the same thought. I'd be concerned if you hadn't. Olivia isn't going to stop coming for me simply because I'm pregnant. If anything, she's going to latch onto that. I killed her mate, Sam. Corbin is dead because of me. And she knows that. She saw. When she learns I'm pregnant, she'll—"

"I won't let *anything* happen to you. Or our child," Sam said, his voice deepening into a wolfy growl.

I opened my eyes to find his were blindingly bright, glowing with the power of his inner wolf. Clearly, this conversation was triggering his protective nature, considering male werewolves were the most territorial creatures out there.

"I know that. But you can't guarantee that nothing will happen. Olivia is out for blood. *My* blood. And now, this..." I took his hands and pressed them against my stomach. "I'm scared, Sam. How could I not be? She wants me dead. Nothing's going to stop her."

"She can't hurt you if she's dead," Sam stated unapologetically.

I winced. Olivia was my half-sister. Before she'd revealed her villainous ways, we'd connected. Sort of. I'd been stunned, and a little excited, to learn I had a sibling. I hadn't known at the time that she'd been using that connection to spy on our pack while plotting her nefarious schemes.

But I didn't want her dead.

I just wanted this to be over and done with. I wanted a quiet, happy life. I wanted to enjoy my pregnancy without fear of my sister's shenanigans. But that wasn't the hand I'd been dealt, unfortunately.

"Luce, you are my life," Sam continued, resting

his forehead against mine. "You know I'll do anything for you. I've never loved anyone as much as I do you. And I'll love our child just as fiercely. You're both part of me. I won't lose either of you. Not to Olivia, not to anyone. I *will* keep you safe. No matter what that means."

Tears blurred my vision. "I love you."

"I love you."

I had so many people in my life who wanted to help me. A family who loved me more than anything. Anna and Vlad weren't werewolves, but that meant nothing to me. Anna had been my sister long before Olivia had come along. And Vlad was like the brother-in-law I never wanted but had grudgingly come to accept. My mother may now be eternally sixty years old, but she was still a vampire, and becoming a force to be reckoned with. Vlad and Anna had begun teaching her how to fight and live as one of them. It was strange seeing my mother throw punches and flash her fangs, but this was our life now.

Then there was Cole. As my second in command, he and I had made a connection, one I could trust without any doubt. And thanks to him, the Mississippi Pack—*my* pack—was accepting me as well. These were all good things.

"Sam..." I drew a deep breath and considered my next words. "When this is all over, I think I want to stay."

He lifted his head and blinked at me. "What?"

"I want to stay here, in Mississippi."

A small frown furrowed his brow. "You do?"

"I think so. I know we intended to find a replacement for me, but that hasn't happened. And I think that's because I don't want anyone to replace me. I feel at home here. Not to say I didn't feel at home with your family, because I did. I love your family. But I feel like I can make a difference here. Like I can lead this pack and make them better. And with me as the alpha, we can improve relations between the Mississippi and New Orleans Packs. Reggie never cared about that, but I do. I know you're slotted to take over your father's pack and you're the heir, but—"

Sam laughed, then stole a kiss, effectively silencing my rambling. When he pulled back, he stared at me, grinning. "I always know how important something is by how much you babble."

Heat flushed my cheeks. "That doesn't mean we have to stay," I said, needing to clarify this. "If you want us to go home to New Orleans, I'll completely understand. I would never force you to do something that makes you unhappy." My pack was important to me, but nowhere near as important as Sam. He came first, no matter what.

"Luce, this isn't about me."

"Yes, it is," I argued. "And it's about us. We're a family now. So we have to make these decisions together."

"I didn't mention this because I didn't want to put any pressure on you, but my father has already begun training Aimee as the replacement heir for his pack."

I jerked back. "He has?"

"When I last left New Orleans, I told him I wasn't coming back without you. My father, Aimee, and I sat down and agreed he would start preparing her to take over, if necessary. Nothing is set in stone yet, but my father wanted to be ready in case you decided to stay."

I had no words. Adrien had always astounded me. He'd taken me into the New Orleans Pack without batting an eye, simply because I was Sam's mate. They'd even forgiven me for abandoning Sam when I'd first been changed, claiming they understood how confusing my life had become. It was those sorts of things that made me love his family as my own.

It also made it rather difficult to make this decision. But the New Orleans Pack didn't need me. Not like the Mississippi Pack did. They'd been through so much in the past six months, and seen so much death, all because of Reggie's obsession with legacy. He'd been the one to change Olivia, simply because he could. He'd risked her life to turn her into a werewolf, and in return, she'd ordered her mate to kill him. Now, she wanted to take his pack as her own. It wasn't my responsibility to clean up Reggie's mess. Heck, I hadn't even learned about him until a few years ago. But I refused to throw his people to the wolves and walk away.

"Would you be okay staying here? We'd make some changes," I quickly added. "Ask Anna, Vlad, and my mother to find their own places. We could even buy a new home for us, if you wanted."

"Luce, I don't care where we are, so long as we're together."

I melted. "But what about your pack?"

"They'll be fine," he assured me. "They have my whole family there to take care of them. And my father has no plans to retire any time soon, so he has lots of time to train Aimee."

"Is Aimee okay with that?" I asked.

"Are you kidding? My sister is glowing with the

idea of taking over the pack. If this hadn't happened, I might have worried about her killing me in my sleep."

A joke, of course. Sam's family all adored each other. They wouldn't dare harm a hair on each other's heads.

"I haven't mentioned this to Cole or anyone else in the pack yet," I said.

"Good. Let's keep it that way until you know for sure what you want to do. For now, let's focus on Olivia. Once we take care of her, we can think about the rest of our lives."

That sounded good to me. I loathed the idea of killing Olivia, but unless she gave me another option, I didn't see any other way to end this.

"In the meantime," Sam murmured.

"Hmm?"

Sam grabbed the blankets and pulled them up over our heads. Then he locked eyes with mine as he slid down my body, his fingers caressing my sides as he moved.

I couldn't help but chuckle at the impish expression on his face. "What are you doing?"

"Whatd'ya think?" he fired back with a wink. "Our friendly neighborhood vampires won't be back for a while yet. We have the house to ourselves, so I'm gonna—" His words ended the instant his mouth found its mark—right between my thighs.

As soon as his hot tongue stroked me, my back arched off the bed. Sam had a talent for making me squirm. His tongue was a deadly weapon, one that often left me moaning and crying out his name. A talent he'd apparently decided to unleash upon me right now.

"Isn't this what got us in trouble in the first place?" I asked in a breathless voice.

"Mm," was all Sam said, too occupied to form words.

I reached down and grasped his head, my fingers digging into his scalp. I'd learned early on that Sam enjoyed that. I think it had something to do with me losing control, which he took great pride in.

With every stroke and lick, I came closer to the edge, teetering on that fine line. My breath quickened and my blood heated until fire coursed through my veins. Sam knew exactly what he was doing to me. He'd become an expert on pleasuring me in the few months we'd been together. To the point where it didn't take long at all to make me orgasm. Evidenced now when I cried out, my legs practically wrapping around his head.

"God, I love when you do that," Sam whispered, his breath brushing against a very tender area.

I trembled beneath him, my eyes practically rolling to the back of my head.

Sam ran a finger up and down my entrance, teasing me with the promise of more. Only when he had my body quivering did he deliver. I cried out when he slid in one finger, then two. Slowly—so slowly I thought I might scream with impatience—he moved them in and out, never quite delivering what I wanted. From between my legs, Sam smiled, and then he withdrew one finger and replaced it with his tongue.

My body damn near shot off the bed.

"So perfect," he rumbled.

His finger and tongue worked in tandem, each eliciting a rush of pleasure that had me fisting the bedsheets. I pushed my head into the pillow and bit my bottom lip to keep from screaming. The house might be empty, but now that I lived with vampires, I was unendingly aware of the noises I made. Who knew who else lived in the neighborhood. They didn't need to hear our sexy noises.

Heat spread through my center, and I uttered a quiet moan when a second orgasm scorched through me. So lost to the moment, I didn't realize Sam had repositioned himself until he thrust his cock inside me. Gasping, my eyes snapped open, and I found him above me, eyes aglow with his wolf. The amber light shone down on me, but I wasn't afraid. My eyes had likely done the same.

Sam's mouth ensnared mine, his tongue effortlessly slipping past my lips and moving in rhythm with his cock. God, the way he made me feel, the things he did to my body—it was no wonder I'd ended up pregnant.

We broke from the kiss, and I buried my head in his neck, breathing in his scent as my hips rose to meet his. I opened my mouth and laid my teeth against his skin. Not breaking the flesh, but not gently either. This was another thing I'd learned Sam liked—the feel of my teeth pressing against him, lightly marking him. A wolf thing, I imagined. No blood play, thank goodness. I wasn't sure I could handle that. But the threat of it was there and excited him.

Sam quickened his pace until all I could feel was *him*. He unleashed a low growl, one more wolf than human, and pressed his face against my neck. I'd never welcomed the biting thing, but tonight... tonight I wanted to experience it.

"Sam," I whispered, tilting my head to offer him more access to my flesh.

He didn't question me, and I nearly jumped when I felt his teeth land on my throat. The threat of them breaking through quickened my pulse, and this time, the growl came from me.

With a move I'd learned from fighting, I wrapped my legs around Sam and flipped us over. I barely broke stride as I started gliding on top of him, my hands braced against his chest.

Sam's eyes were wide, but his mouth quirked as he watched me shamelessly ride him. This was one of my favorite positions. Because I possessed every ounce of control. The alpha wolf in me rather enjoyed that. I wanted to be on top. Wanted to ride him and use his body to bring us both pleasure. To make *myself* come on his cock.

Reaching down, I gripped his hands and removed them from my hips. Then I pulled them above his head and pinned them there. I could see the wolf in his eyes, fighting to take control. Sam wasn't an alpha of a pack, but he *was* an alpha werewolf. And generally speaking, alphas didn't enjoy submission. But for me, he allowed it. For me, he submitted.

I did exactly as I wanted, riding Sam's dick until

my body shattered. While enjoying the blissful high, I took Sam's hands and used them to cup my breasts, moaning when his fingers found my erect nipples.

"Luce," he ground out.

He wasn't far behind me. I could scent it on the air. With every thrust, his own climax grew closer. I had two options. I could slow down and prolong his inevitable end, torture him just a little longer. Or I could blow his mind—and his cock.

Decision made, I released his hands and once again braced myself against his chest. Then I quickened my pace. Sam groaned, his eyes fluttering shut. I saw the struggle in his face, knew he desperately wanted to take back control. But it was too late for that. His cock pulsed inside me seconds before he finished, filling me with his release.

Sam grunted and his body loosened. I leaned down and brushed my lips against his, reveling in the feel of his dick twitching inside me. There truly was no feeling greater than bringing someone that much pleasure, feeling them lose themselves inside you, knowing you were the one to give that to them.

"Jesus," Sam whispered against my mouth. "Remind us to do that again."

"And again and again," I murmured back.

His eyes opened, but the glow had diminished

until all that remained were his human amber eyes. *Guess I'd screwed the magic right out of him*—a thought that made me chuckle.

"What's so funny?"

"Nothing," I said, kissing him again.

His arms came around my back and he pulled me onto his chest, running his hands up and down my back.

"I wish we could stay like this forever," he said.

That made me snicker. "How about a shower first, then we can cuddle?"

A gruff laugh slipped past Sam's lips, and he nodded. "Fair enough. Think you'll be able to sleep now?"

Oh yeah. My body was all loosey-goosey now, and his dick had turned my brain to mush. I'd definitely be able to sleep now. And what better way to fall asleep than in Sam's arms.

6

I woke to the sound of songbirds and neighbors chatting in their yards. Memories of last night came to mind and a contented smile curled my lips. Before I'd even blinked the sleep from my eyes, I was staring at my ring hand, admiring the giant rock now cradling my finger.

I still couldn't believe this was my life. Sure, it had its bad moments—aka Corbin and Olivia—but all in all, I was happy. Strange, considering a year and a half ago, I'd been on the run, hiding from what I'd become and dodging my mate, who now slept peacefully beside me. Now I was his fiancée, and we were expecting. Life truly had a way of working out.

The thought of our little munchkin-to-be had me

kicking back the covers and sliding out of bed. I winced when my toes touched the cool floor and grabbed a nearby pair of fluffy slippers—a staple in my life. Then I slipped on my robe and tied the belt at my waist, covering me from any neighborly Peeping Toms.

When my fingers grazed my stomach, I paused, and Anna's words from last night came back to me. *Everything is about to change.* Made sense—babies required a lot of change. But they were a good change, right?

Still smiling, I retrieved my phone from the nightstand and glanced at the screen. The time blinked up at me, showing me it was ten a.m., and above that sat a list of missed notifications. I went through them one-by-one, my eyes stinging with tears at the sight of all the messages. Sam's sisters, his parents, my father—all had texted me to wish me their congratulations and relay their excitement. Both for the baby and our impending nuptials.

My father's message gave no indication about his and my mother's conversation the night before, but he'd asked me to call him this afternoon when I was ready. I couldn't help but notice how he'd said this afternoon, not tonight. As though he wanted to speak to me without my mother overhearing.

Not a great sign.

Last was a missed call from Cole and a voicemail telling me he had plans to drop by later this morning. Pack business, most likely. It truly was never ending, especially as the alpha.

I pocketed my phone and strolled out of the room in search of breakfast. It wasn't until I stood in the kitchen, watching the coffee percolate, that I stopped and laughed at myself. No caffeine, Anna had said, thanks to her research. That was going to be a tough nugget to give up, but a sacrifice I was willing to make. I would do whatever I had to.

Though it smelled heavenly—and a bit too tempting—I left the coffee brewing so Sam could have some when he woke. I made a second mental note to pick up some decaffeinated drinks, then boiled some water for myself. For today, hot water with lemon would have to do.

I took my steaming mug and moved to the kitchen table, where my laptop waited. I sat and quickly went through my daily routine, such as checking my email, only to find that Cole had sent one out to the entire pack last night, informing them about tomorrow's meeting.

After confirming I would be in attendance—*ha!* —I tapped a finger against the keyboard and eyed the internet browser icon. Anna's research last night had left me reeling and quite unsettled, but it'd also made me realize that I had no idea how to even be pregnant. It wasn't like that was taught in high school. Sure, they'd given us a fake baby and told us to take care of it, but Anna and I had quickly learned how to hack the device in order to make the assignment simpler. I couldn't hack a real baby though.

Resigned to my fate, I clicked open the search engine and typed in *what to expect when you're expecting*, then hit enter.

Countless results populated. My eyes slowly widened as I started scouring the websites. Man, it felt like I was back in high school, researching some sort of health paper. Except, this was real life, and it was *really, really* happening.

Which meant it was time to get down to business. Nothing like researching birth first thing in the morning before even eating. Although, an hour later, I was relieved I hadn't eaten yet—I might have tossed my cookies if I had.

I nudged my laptop away, leaned back in my chair, and focused on breathing. I'd read too much. Gone too far. Seen too much. And there was no turning back now. There'd be no forgetting any of those images and videos I'd clicked. The internet was a fucked-up place that stored far too much information. And not all of it good.

To think we women had to undergo... *that*. It was like I'd watched a horror flick filled with blood, placentas, and screaming—and not just from the babies.

"Good morning," a gruff voice greeted me.

I lifted my head and stared at Sam with wide, unblinking eyes.

He froze in the doorway, then rushed to my side. "Luce? Are you okay?"

"Sure...," I mumbled. "Did you know there's something called afterbirth? I also just learned about episiotomies. I think... I might need to lie back down for a bit."

Alarm flashed across Sam's face. "What are you talking about?"

"That," I grumbled, gesturing to my offensive laptop. "Sam. I *saw* things. Things I can't unsee."

Understanding dawned, and Sam pressed his lips together to keep from laughing. "What did you do?"

"I... *googled*," I said.

"Probably not a wise idea."

Not a wise idea, he says. Well, where'd he been a

half hour ago, when I'd metaphorically been dragged kicking and screaming to a page focused on perineoplasty.

"It's a horror show," I murmured, my voice monotonic.

"It's natural," he corrected.

"There's nothing natural about that."

Sam rubbed my back and continued to offer soothing, comforting words, but I didn't really hear any of them. I just kept seeing images of forceps and clamps, scissors and sutures.

"Have you eaten yet?" Sam asked, his voice finally breaking through the endless loop playing in my head.

I shook my head.

"Do you want me to make you something?"

Food? Right now? The thought of eating nauseated me. Instead, I cradled my mug close to my chest and once again shook my head.

"How about we stay off the internet for a while?" Sam suggested. He grabbed my laptop and shut it down before sliding it farther back on the table.

I had to admit, that sounded like a pretty good idea right now.

"Maybe we could go for a short walk," he

continued. "Get some fresh air. Just around the neighborhood."

A walk? Outside? Fear lanced my chest. "No." I shook my head rapidly. "Olivia could be out there."

"Luce—"

"No," I repeated, my voice firm. "If she were to attack, if something were to happen..." I couldn't even finish that sentence, let alone think it. I couldn't risk either of our lives right now. Not for something as silly as a walk.

"Okay," Sam murmured, leaning in to kiss me. "Then how about a shower? Maybe that'll help you feel better?"

A shower I could do.

Still feeling a bit numb, I rose on shaky legs and handed Sam my mug.

"Um, there's coffee," I said, gesturing vaguely toward the counter.

"Thanks, love. Go enjoy your shower. And remember—"

"Yeah, not too hot," I commented.

"No, I was going to say remember to relax."

Relax. Christ on a cracker. That was easier said than done.

I took a shower, then a brief nap, needing to purge my mind of everything and hopefully start fresh. The nap didn't last long, thanks to all the voices coming from my living room. From the sounds of it, I had a full house. Cole, Dominic, Paul—our new IT guy and Jorge's replacement, thanks to Olivia—and Sam.

Groaning, I opened my eyes and winced at the sunlight blaring into the room. It felt like the light was stabbing me in the eyes. Someone had opened the curtains, and now I was paying for it. Sadly, that someone had also been me. So I was suffering for my own crimes. Funny how this morning, I'd woken bright-eyed and bushy-tailed, but now, I could hardly keep my eyes open. Was this what pregnancy would be like? Up one moment, down the next? Or, in my case, energized to exhausted?

I pushed up from the bed and stumbled into my closet in search of clothes. Fuzzy slippers and a robe wouldn't cut it this time. Not if we had pack members visiting.

I flicked through my scant selection and settled on a blue T-shirt emblazoned with a yellow happy face and a pair of black leggings. That was the extent of my effort today. At least I'd remembered to put on socks. That had to count for something, right?

The bathroom came next, where I ran a hand through my tangled hair. Apparently, I hadn't bothered to brush my hair after showering, and now a rat's nest sat atop my head, one that required detangling spray and a lot of patience. A few tugs made my eyes water, but I eventually managed to brush through my dark locks without a single tangle.

I deserved a cookie for that.

Someone knocked on our bathroom door.

"Lucy?" came Sam's voice.

"Yeah, I'm coming," I muttered.

"Okay. You need anything?"

About ten gallons of coffee. Who cut out caffeine cold turkey? Other than pregnant people, of course.

"Luce?" Sam repeated when I didn't answer.

My stomach still didn't feel ready for food, but I needed to eat. Talk about a contradiction of epic proportions.

"Some crackers maybe?" I asked, wondering if I'd soon find myself draped over a toilet.

"Sure, I can get those for you."

I listened to the sound of his retreating footsteps, then leaned my palms on the counter and stared at my reflection. To be perfectly frank, I looked like hell. Dark, puffy circles under my eyes, wan lips, and pale skin. I looked sick. That couldn't be right, could it? I'd felt fine this morning.

Yet another question for the doctor, who I needed to call. In fact, best to do that now before heading to the living room and getting distracted.

After splashing some water on my face and patting it dry, I returned to my bedroom and grabbed my phone. Then I walked into my closet and navigated to the back, hoping this small space full of clothing would provide a little privacy from the sensitive ears in my living room.

I sat cross-legged and pulled up Meredith's contact information. I clicked "call," then waited for her to pick up.

"Alpha," she said by way of greeting.

Good ole caller ID.

"Good morning, Meredith." Or afternoon. I honestly wasn't sure what time it was anymore. I hadn't looked before dialing. "I was wondering if I could book an appointment with you."

Her silence had me questioning my wording.

"Absolutely. What can I help you with?"

Alright. Here we go. "I trust you'll remain discreet?"

"Of course. That is my job, after all."

Right. It wouldn't do well if she blabbed all the

pack secrets. We'd oust her before she could apologize.

Drawing a deep breath, I grabbed a sweater and held it an inch in front of my face, hoping it would muffle the sound of my voice enough to keep Dominic and Paul from hearing. Yes, we had a meeting planned for tomorrow night, but I really didn't need them to know until the rest of the pack did.

"Do you remember my roommates? Anna and Vlad?" I asked.

"The vampires? Yes." She sounded moderately intrigued.

"Well, Anna suggested I might be pregnant, so I... I took a test. Five actually. And all came up positive."

A moment of silence passed, and then Meredith's light chuckle carried across the line. "Oh, Lucy, that's wonderful news."

"Thanks."

"Let's have a look at my schedule, shall we?" she said.

I heard papers flipping, and I bit back a laugh. Who kept paper calendars anymore?

"I have an appointment scheduled tonight at seven. I could fit you in afterward, if that works? We can do an ultrasound to make sure everything's progressing nicely. How far along do you think you are?"

"Oh, I have no idea."

"That's fine. We can work that out. When was your last period?"

"One second," I murmured.

I pulled the phone away from my ear and opened my own calendar app on my phone. I combed through the dates. It wasn't something I really kept track of. I'd always been able to tell when it was coming thanks to my PMS, but otherwise, I didn't track dates. It was currently mid-May, and if I thought back... it'd been a while since my last period. Mid-March, maybe? Sam had returned to Jackson at the end of March, and I hadn't had one since.

I placed the phone back to my ear. "I want to say around March fourteenth."

"Okay." I heard some typing in the background, and then, "That puts you around eight weeks with a due date of December seventeenth."

A Christmas baby.

"Okay, so, does tonight work for you?" Meredith asked. "How about around eight p.m.?"

The thought of leaving the house terrified me, but I also couldn't bail on these scans. Even I knew that. That didn't mean I couldn't take precautions. And a nighttime appointment meant I could bring more people, like all the resident vampires.

I blew out a relieved breath. A security team of three vampires and two werewolves—because I assumed Cole would be there—made me feel much better.

"Tonight," I confirmed.

"Cole knows where my clinic is." Meredith paused for a heartbeat. "Is this what tomorrow's meeting is about?"

"Yeah, he thought I should share the news with the entire pack."

"I think that's a wonderful idea. Something to celebrate for once. We're in desperate need of some good news."

She wasn't wrong.

Meredith continued speaking, giving me instructions on how to prepare for the ultrasound. I nodded along, then we said our goodbyes and hung up.

When I glanced up, I found Sam standing in the closet doorway, leaning against the frame with a bemused expression. I could only imagine the sight I made, sitting cross-legged on the floor with a sweater pressed against my face as I whispered into my phone.

"I found you some crackers," he said. "And Paul, Cole, and Dominic are waiting for us in the kitchen. They have some information to share with you."

I could only imagine it wasn't good news if the three of them were here together. Sighing, I offered my hand and waited for Sam to help me to my feet.

Once I was standing, he brushed a kiss across the top of my head. "Ready for this?"

"As ready as I'll ever be, I suppose."

"You got this."

I smiled up at my mate, so very grateful for his support, then followed him back into the trenches.

Paul, Dominic, and Cole sat around the kitchen table—their favorite place to congregate when visiting. Easier access to the fridge, I assumed. Werewolves had unending appetites, which had been playing hell on my bank account as I kept my house stocked.

All three glanced up as I entered. Cole smiled, but Paul and Dominic both shared a look of concern, their brows slightly furrowed. Huh. Maybe I didn't look as put together as I'd hoped.

Before someone said anything offensive, I took a seat and gestured toward Paul's laptop. "Alright. Let's hear it." Because there had to be *something* to hear. The three of them only ever came together when they had something they needed to share with me. The only question was *what* news did they have to share?

"We have an update on Olivia," Cole said.

Ah. So the *bad* news kind then.

One hand moved to my belly without thought, but I let it rest there. That simple touch soothed me. I only hoped it didn't look too odd.

Sam seated himself next to me and rested his arms on the table, his attention on Cole. "Okay. What do we know?"

"First, you should know that I reached out to my contact from the Alabama Pack last night."

I gave a slow nod. We'd had some communication with the Alabama Pack over the past month, ever since one of their members had defected to join Olivia's cause.

"He informed me they've lost more members."

My head snapped up and I glared at Cole. "What? How?"

"They abandoned the pack. While my contact doesn't know where they went, they obviously have their suspicions."

As did I.

"Motherfu—" I bit off the word with a deep growl. As much as I wanted to rant and rave and howl at the moon, we had to remain focused. "Okay. So the Alabama Pack is dwindling. And we suspect they've joined Olivia?"

"From what I can see on the web, she's ramping up her recruitment drive," Paul said. He spun his laptop around and tapped the screen. "She has multiple posts. And she's targeting members who might be unhappy with their packs. She's luring them in by promising to be a better alpha, to give them a home and a place within her pack. She's promising a *rankless* system. No firsts or seconds. Just one happy-go-lucky pack where everyone is respected equally."

I blinked. "What? Rankless? How the heck would that even work?"

"I don't know," Paul replied. "Alpha is a rank, and she's quite keen on holding that role. Maybe she means no seconds or thirds? Just a giant group where all are welcome?"

Yikes, that sounded disastrous.

"Unfortunately, her recruitment drive seems to be working," Paul continued. "Alabama isn't the only pack reporting losses."

Alarm shot through me. "How many packs?"

"Dozens," he said. "From all over."

My stomach sank. I sat up and rested my arms on

the table next to Sam's. "Then she's built herself a shiny new pack. Even after we decimated them last time."

"A safe assumption," Dominic chimed in. "We aren't sure about numbers. The posts we've seen mention one or two missing people. If we add those up, she'd have a pack of about twenty-two wolves."

The New Orleans Pack was the largest one I knew of, with approximately seventy members. My pack wasn't far behind with fifty or so. But not all my members were active within the pack. We had two circles: one for those who wanted to participate, and one for those who didn't. My active membership was around thirty. If she kept recruiting, who knew how large of a pack she could build.

"Twenty-five possibly," Cole chimed in. "If we include Scotia, Lincoln, and Laini."

I grimaced at the sound of my packmate's names. Corbin and Olivia had abducted the three of them five weeks ago. I'd eventually learned that Corbin had changed Lincoln and Laini, both of whom had then promised themselves to his pack. Unfortunately, we had no idea what'd happened to Scotia. My people had scoured the city for her and found nothing. It seemed likely she hadn't survived the change—though her family hadn't given up hope yet.

Guilt twisted my stomach, and for a moment, I thought I might toss my cookies. Here I was, calling a pack meeting to share the *wonderful* news that we were going to have a child when we had families still grieving the loss of theirs. I wouldn't be able to hide my pregnancy for long, thanks to our heightened senses, but it still felt wrong to celebrate.

Sam rested a hand atop mine, as though he understood where my thoughts had ventured.

I cleared my throat and forced my attention back to the topic at hand. "Okay, so Olivia is growing her pack and recruiting from all over the country."

"Not just this country," Paul said. "The internet isn't designed that way. Anyone who knows how to access the dark web can see this. She's disguised the posts so that a human might not understand what it's about, but any werewolf with access to the dark web can see this. That means Mexico, Canada, Europe, you name it."

"Fine," I replied, meeting the gazes of my men. "Then we know what we need to do."

Cole's brows winged up. "We do?"

"We can't take this on by ourselves," I said. "This is bigger than us. And it isn't just our problem anymore. These other packs are losing their members. That makes it their problem too. So, we need to spread word. We need to inform every pack in the world of Olivia's intentions. Spread the truth."

"And how do you propose we do that?" Dominic asked.

I gestured toward the laptop. "If Olivia can recruit people from the dark web, then why can't we do the same? We don't need to recruit, we just need to let everyone know what's going on. It isn't fair for us to keep the other alphas in the dark. They're likely looking for their missing pack members. What happens when that search brings them to our doorstep?"

Paul nodded, his eyes glued to the laptop as though considering everything I'd said. "So we start our own campaign. Not to recruit, but to destroy Olivia. We can tell them everything, starting with how she abducted our people and go from there."

I nodded. "Can we keep her from seeing the post?"

"No," Paul said. "Just like we can see hers, she'll see ours."

Concern wrinkled the corners of Cole's eyes. "Are you sure you want to do that?"

I drummed my fingers against the tabletop as I considered his question. "Secrets have ways of coming out," I said, talking through the problem. "If we don't inform the other alphas, they might hold a grudge against us. Put yourself in another alpha's shoes. Wouldn't you want someone to have enough courtesy to give you a heads-up? Besides, we really should be the ones to control how this information gets out."

"While I agree with you, a random post on the dark web doesn't give us much control," Paul said.

I considered that. He wasn't wrong. "We need a liaison. Someone we trust who can be named as a contact. Someone who can diffuse the situation rather than ignite it."

"My mother," Sam suggested. "As an alpha's wife, she's respected. She's also calm and clearheaded. We can ask her to do this for us."

"Can I leave the task of asking her to you?" I asked.

"Of course. I told her I'd call her today anyway. I can speak to my father about it as well. See if he's on board with our plan."

Adrien's approval didn't matter—not in the grand scheme of things. I didn't need his permission to do this. But it also didn't hurt to have it. A bit of affirmation that I was on the right track. This was all new to me, after all.

"We also need to ramp up our efforts to find Olivia," Cole added. "If her pack is growing, she'll need someplace to house them. These people are coming from all over the country. I doubt they're all squatting in hotels. She'll have somewhere for them. A complex-type place."

I thought back to the warehouse where I'd killed Corbin. He'd been able to hold their entire pack there. But that place had been chosen specifically to ambush us. I hadn't seen signs of them living there. And I couldn't picture Olivia stuffing them all in a random warehouse for an extended period.

So where the heck would she keep them?

"Check farms and acreages," I suggested. "And let's expand our search to outside Jackson too. Maybe the reason we haven't found her is that she isn't here. Plenty of farms are beyond the city limits. Check the state parks too. Who knows, maybe they're living out in the woods."

I ran my fingers over my chin as I contemplated our options. We needed to find her before she did something stupid—like kidnap another member of my pack. In the past month, no one had reported seeing her. Perhaps because her disciples were now flocking to her. She didn't need to resort to kidnapping if she could convince them to come willingly.

I had to wonder what she'd told these people. We knew she'd promised them some sort of Eden, a pack without a hierarchy, other than her leading it. Because of course she *had* to be the alpha. But realistically, that couldn't work. Could it? Werewolves weren't wolves, but they weren't human either. They required a clear chain of command. Marcus and Bryn made the perfect example. The second they'd sensed weakness, they'd made their move. I'd managed to convince Marcus to back down, but Bryn had refused. And look what'd happened. An unstructured pack seemed like it would only bring chaos and death.

But what did I know? I was human-born, changed into a werewolf by a psycho who'd thought I was nothing more than a chew toy.

Maybe I was the wrong one here?

Olivia would never forgive me for killing Corbin. Nor would she step down from her claim on my territory. Being one of Reggie's daughters, she wanted this land. Except, it already had a pack on it. *My* pack. And she couldn't have it. Or the territory. Those belonged to me.

It raised an idea though.

I hadn't *wanted* this. When Reggie first died, moving back to Jackson and taking over his pack had seemed like the worst-case scenario to me. I'd promised Adrien I would come, name a replacement, and return home to New Orleans. I'd promised Sam the same thing. They wouldn't hold that against me, I knew that. But what if Olivia was the solution? What if we could strike a deal? She gets the pack and the land, and I... go home. Never to step foot in Mississippi again. I had to consider the option, right? I was pregnant. I wasn't fit to fight this battle.

And yet...

The thought of handing all this over to Olivia raised my hackles. These people and this land didn't belong to her. Reggie had named me his heir. Not her. And he'd had time to change his mind too. He'd turned her long before his death. I'd pissed him off so many times, yet he'd never changed who he'd named heir.

There had to be a reason for that.

I refocused on the present conversation and listened for a moment as Cole and Paul hashed out which parks each would take. That certainly wouldn't be an easy job. There was a lot of ground to cover.

"You guys can handle that, right?" I asked.

Cole nodded. "We'll work it out. We just need to be smart about it." His gaze locked with mine. "We don't want to spread ourselves too thin and weaken the pack."

I could read between the lines. He didn't want to send too many people away and leave me vulnerable.

"Agreed," I said, if only to keep that part of the conversation from spiraling out of hand. I didn't need Paul and Dominic to learn about our pregnancy yet. Things were complicated enough. "While you're handling that, I want to see what I can learn about Olivia."

"Is there something specific you're looking for?" Dominic asked.

"I'm not sure. Probably won't know until we find it. We know who she is, but we don't know more beyond her lineage. Maybe there's something we've missed."

"It couldn't hurt," Sam said. "Any idea where to start?"

I sighed and leaned back in my chair. When I'd first moved in, Sam, Anna, and I had packed all of Reggie's things away into boxes without going through any of it first. While I'd lived with him for a year, Reggie had truly been little more to me than a sperm donor. I hadn't felt that father-daughter connection with him. Our conversations had primarily consisted of us chewing each other out.

However, his office had originally contained a great deal of personal information. Papers and documents that we'd stored in the garage.

"Reggie's personal documents," I said. "Regardless of how Olivia and I felt about Reggie, we were his daughters. Maybe I'll find some information about her in there."

"Reginald wasn't the journaling sort," Cole stated.

"I know. But it can't hurt to check, right? I can't just sit here doing nothing. I need to help."

"Doing nothing?" Dominic's gaze darted to my face. "Why would you think you're doing nothing?"

I flushed, heat splashing my cheeks. "No, I just mean, I need to help. Reggie was my father, so I'll go through all his documents and see what I can find."

"Very well." Cole rose to his feet, effectively signaling the end of the meeting. He'd done it purposely, to avoid any further questions.

Paul tucked his laptop into his backpack, then stood next to Cole.

"Maybe we should check Olivia's credit cards

again," I said. "Who knows? We might get lucky and find out she's been using them."

The corner of Paul's mouth tugged upward. "I highly doubt it. She knows we're watching them. But I can take another look if you'd like."

"Thanks, Paul. Can't be too careful now, can we?"

Cole walked Dominic and Paul to the front door, then held back as they left. With his hand resting against the frame, he turned to face me and Sam. "Do you need me for anything else today?"

"Actually, yes. I have an appointment with Meredith tonight at eight. She said you know where her clinic is. Can you come with us?"

"Of course. I'll be back around seven. Who's all coming?"

"I assume all of us," I mumbled. "But you'll have to stay in the waiting room during the appointment."

"A full house then. We'll need two vehicles."

That didn't bother me. In this case, less was not more. "I'll see you tonight."

Cole gave a quick salute, then headed out.

Releasing a deep breath, I turned toward Sam, gasping when I suddenly found myself in his arms.

"What are you doing?" I asked breathlessly.

Sam brushed a gentle kiss across my forehead,

then started carrying me toward the bedroom. "We have a few hours before Anna wakes up, and those little baggies under your eyes shows me how tired you are. I figure we can cuddle in bed, watch some TV, and forget about all this for a little while. Just be an expecting couple with no other problems in life."

If I didn't already love this man...

"You don't need to carry me. I'm quite capable of walking."

Sam caught my gaze and winked. "Now, where would the fun be in that?"

An hour before Vlad and my mother woke for the night, I started guzzling water as per Meredith's instructions. So much so that my damn bladder felt like it was going to explode. It was half past seven now, and we'd just set out for the clinic, but every bump in the road had me crossing my legs and whimpering. I hadn't been this uncomfortable in, like, ever.

I sat in my car along with Sam, my mother, and Cole. Anna and Vlad had opted to take their own vehicle in case they ventured into town after my appointment. My mother claimed to have no interest in going out to feed tonight and planned to return home with us. She'd been incredibly quiet since her conversation with my father yesterday, one that she refused to discuss. When I called my father this afternoon, he'd also refused to speak about it, and instead had kept the conversation centered on me, the baby, and the wedding.

I had a feeling my mother *needed* someone to talk to. But I also suspected that someone wasn't me —being that I was her daughter. She had plenty of friends to reach out to, but she hadn't spoken to a single one since she'd been turned into a vampire. She didn't want to tell them she'd been changed.

I understood.

Anna was the only person from my hometown who knew I was a werewolf—other than my family. The circumstances weren't quite the same, since vampires were public knowledge and werewolves weren't, but even if we were, I still wouldn't have spread that knowledge around.

I stared out the windshield and considered my mother's options. When Anna was first turned, her friend Camilla had taken her to their local Vampires Anonymous group. Thanks to the Queen of Vampires, Anna had only attended one meeting before she'd been arrested and dragged halfway across the globe. But still—maybe that was something I could look into.

I fished into my purse and withdrew my phone. A quick Google search later—one that was thankfully unrelated to the pregnancy—and I had a website. I perused the site and quirked a grin at the name, "Eternity for Seniors," a subgroup for the local Vampires Anonymous. According to their information, they specialized in people aged fifty-five and up who'd been turned into vampires. They focused on a litany of things, including accepting your new life. They even had hobby nights. Pottery, crochet and knitting, quilting, ukulele lessons, card games, you name it. My mother had always loved crafting. Her specialties consisted of quilting, making homemade soaps, and painting—all of which were offered on individual nights throughout the week. These people were dedicated, and I loved it.

It sounded perfect.

Now I just had to convince her to go. Maybe Anna and I could take her to her first meeting so she wouldn't be alone. She needed help. Perhaps help we couldn't provide. And who knew, maybe she'd meet someone who could help her with my father.

I screenshotted their information, then pulled open my ongoing text conversation with Anna and fired it off.

> L: Wanna check this out tonight?
> You, me, and Mom?

It didn't take long for the responding three dots to appear.

> A: Where did you find this?

> L: Google to the rescue. The
> meeting is after my appointment.

She didn't immediately respond. Likely discussing it over with Vlad. I'd have to do the same with Sam. It was far safer for the vampires to go out than us right now.

My phone chimed, and I glanced down at the screen.

> A: Maybe I should take her alone.

I considered Anna's response. I understood. But I wanted to be there to support my mother. I wanted to see her happy after all she'd been through.

> L: I'll talk to Sam and see what he
> says, but I'd like to go.

> A: I imagine he'll come with then.

Which wasn't a bad idea.

> L: I suppose we could all go. Better safe than sorry.

> A: Let's see if your mother is interested first.

Nodding to myself, I slid my phone back into my purse. When I lifted my head, I found Sam glancing my way before he turned back to face the road.

"Everything okay?" he asked.

Other than the fact that I had to pee like a racehorse? "Oh yeah. Just asking Anna's opinion about something."

His head bobbed. I didn't want to bring it up right this second, didn't want my mother to feel ambushed. And while Cole was a part of our little tight-knit community, he wasn't family. I could wait until Mom and I had a moment alone before suggesting any of this.

A few moments later, we pulled up in front of a small building lit with a warm amber glow.

"This is it?" I asked. I leaned forward and peered out the windshield. "There's no sign or name?"

"Meredith's practice isn't open to humans, so she likes to keep everything low-key. Our pack keeps her busy enough, and when she has time, she travels to other territories if another pack doctor needs help with something."

"Makes sense," I mused. "Shall we?" I popped open my door and stepped out into the humid night air, my bladder practically screaming in pain.

My entourage followed suit, the sound of car doors shutting echoing in the night. Sam stood on my right, Anna to my left.

"It looks cozy," Anna said. "I like it."

She wasn't wrong. I had to admit, I preferred this to a hospital. No labyrinth of hallways to navigate, no endless paperwork to fill out—I hoped—and no horrid chemical smell that seemed common in hospitals. Heck, the clinic looked warm and friendly. Welcoming, even. All plusses in my book.

Gripping Sam's hand, I led him up the sidewalk. With every step, my stomach twisted with nerves. I couldn't pinpoint exactly why I was so nervous, but I was. Goosebumps pebbled my skin and butterflies tickled my insides.

Half of me was excited to confirm the pregnancy and maybe get a sneak peek at our baby, and the other half dreaded it. Fear played nasty tricks on people, and I found myself imagining all the worst-case scenarios.

Sam squeezed my hand. I lifted my gaze to his

and forced a smile. The look of utter bliss on his face did little to soothe my anxieties. If anything, it made them worse.

"You okay?" Sam asked as we approached the front door.

"Yeah. Just nervous."

Smiling, he rubbed my knuckles, then lifted my hand to his mouth and kissed the back of it. "Everything's going to be great."

I loved his positivity, but it only added to the pressure weighing me down. What if everything *wasn't* fine? I wanted to trust it was, but I'd heard stories. I knew there was a great deal of risk when it came to having babies.

Sam opened the door, and we filed in, quickly filling the waiting room. Thankfully, there wasn't anyone else present, since we'd need every seat. The clinic wasn't large by any means.

Across the room was a long hardwood desk, behind which a woman sat. Her head rose as we entered, and she flashed me a warm smile. "Hi there! You must be Lucy?"

I nodded.

Her smile grew and she stood, striding around her desk toward us. "My name's Julia. I'm Meredith's assistant. It's truly an honor to meet you. When

Meredith said you would be coming in, I admit, I got a little excited."

My grip tightened on Sam's hand. Who the heck was this woman?

"Dora's told me so much about you. I feel like I know you already."

"Dora?" I questioned.

"My cousin?" she said, her voice lifting at the end, as though surprised I didn't know this Dora. "She's one of your pack mates..." Julia frowned, her gaze darting to Cole.

"Hi, Julia," Cole said. "Hope all's well?"

Her frown didn't ease, and her attention darted back to me. "Um, yeah. I just—"

"Right, Dora!" I said. Truthfully, I didn't know that name. But I had a ways to go still before I memorized every pack member's name. "Sorry, I just wasn't expecting anyone other than Meredith, so I was a bit thrown. It's nice to meet you, Julia." I offered my hand.

The shadows vanished from Julia's face—my transgression clearly forgiven. She glommed onto me like shaking my hand meant the world to her. I choked on a breath, startled by her reaction. Her handshake almost had my teeth rattling.

"I can't believe you're the alpha," she exclaimed.

"You're so... small."

I blinked, not entirely sure how to take that. Did I say thanks? Or just move on? I voted for moving on. Seemed safer.

"Um." I stared at my hand, still crushed in her grip. "Can I have my hand back now?"

"Right! Sorry!" Julia released me, then took three giant steps back, though she continued to grin maniacally. "My parents say I'm excitable. They aren't werewolves, so I'm just plain human. It must be cool, though, to turn into a wolf."

Excitable was an understatement.

"It's, uh, an experience," I went with, not wanting to offend her.

"Welcome, Alpha," Meredith's voice joined the fray.

My shoulders relaxed and I turned to face the good doctor. "Hi, Meredith."

"Julia, you should be good to go home now. I don't think I need anything else today."

"You sure?" Julia asked.

Meredith nodded. "Tomorrow will be busy, so get a good night's sleep."

Julia gave a single nod, then bounded behind the desk and grabbed her jacket. When she returned, it was with another of those bright smiles. For a moment, I thought she might hug me, but instead, she snuck past and dove out the door. I admit, I breathed a little easier once she left.

"Don't mind Julia," Meredith said. "She's a wonderful person."

"And she clearly knows about us?" I asked. There weren't many humans who knew about werewolves, but there were a few. A police officer here, a firefighter there.

"She and her cousin Dora were best friends growing up. Dora didn't shift for the first time until she was eight. A late bloomer. So her parents assumed she was human-born. After she shifted, they couldn't separate the girls, and they decided to stop trying. Julia's known about werewolves practically her whole life, but she's always kept our secret."

The story brought a smile to my lips, reminding me so much of me and Anna. It'd taken us until high school to develop our relationship, but we'd been inseparable ever since.

"Shall we?" Meredith said, gesturing toward the back half of the clinic.

I glanced at Sam, then nodded. "Ready."

"Let's do this," Sam replied.

The others seated themselves in the waiting

room while Sam and I trailed after Meredith. She led us to a single room equipped with an examination table, computer, and some fancy medical equipment.

Meredith shut the door, then took the seat in front of her computer, spinning to face me. "First, I want you to know that your scent has begun to change. It isn't obvious, but I've been trained to pick up on it, so I did notice. You're definitely pregnant."

Sam grinned, which made my stomach flutter.

"I suspect others will begin noticing in the next week or so."

Not a lot of time. But we were notifying the pack tomorrow night, so that was fine.

"Okay, Alpha—"

"Lucy," I said. "Just call me Lucy."

She smiled. "Lucy. I'll get you to hop up onto the bed, then I'll need you to tuck your shirt up under your bra and lower your pants down under your hips."

I did as asked, wincing when the paper started crinkling. I hated that sound and found myself grimacing at Sam. He grinned at my clear discomfort before seating himself on a second stool next to my legs to give Meredith room. He rested a hand on my knee, giving it a small, comforting squeeze.

"Okay, lie back." Meredith reached for an odd-looking device on her desk that reminded me of an upside-down stick of deodorant. "It's a portable ultrasound. Less bulky and they do the job just as well."

"Ah," I said.

She grabbed her tablet and started tapping on the screen. A few moments later, she scooted toward me on the stool, tablet and ultrasound probe in hand.

"Comfortable?" she asked.

"Sure," I said, chuckling. I couldn't think of a single person who'd ever said they were comfortable on an examination table.

She laughed with me, then reached for a tube of jelly, which sat in what looked like a warmer. With her hands hovering above my stomach, she asked, "Ready?"

"Ready," I confirmed.

She squirted the jelly on my belly, then pressed the wand down on top. "Now, this can sometimes feel a little uncomfortable," she said. "When you're only a few weeks along, I have to push a little harder in order to get some clear images. But I'll try to make it as quick as possible."

Her first push had me groaning. My bladder hadn't liked that one bit.

"Sorry," Meredith said, chuckling. "I know, it's

unpleasant."

"I just wanna pee," I grumbled.

"I won't be too long."

Famous last words. My bladder certainly didn't agree with her assessment.

"Alright..." Meredith showed me the tablet's screen and tapped a bean-shaped, black-and-white splotch. "There's your baby."

Sam leaned forward, his hand moving from my knee to my hand. Together, we peered at the screen, but I couldn't see much beyond shadows and squiggles.

I leaned closer. "That little bloop?"

"That little bloop." She laughed as she wiped off the probe, then returned it to her desk. "You're around eight weeks, exactly as we thought." She tapped another button and suddenly a faint thumping echoed throughout the room.

I gasped and stared at Sam, gripping his hand so tightly. A sense of wonderment filled me. "Is that...?"

"The heartbeat," Meredith answered with a warm smile. "We were lucky. Sometimes it's hard to hear it this soon. Your little nugget is happily tucked away in there, nice and comfy."

Tears sprang to my eyes. I laid back on the bed and covered my mouth with my hands.

"Luce?" Sam whispered, his own voice hoarse.

"Sorry. I'm not upset." I shook my head, the paper still crinkling, as tears slipped down my face. "I just hadn't let myself really believe this was happening."

"It's okay," Meredith said. "Hearing your baby's heartbeat for the first time is emotional for many first-time mothers."

"Can we keep that recording?" I asked.

"Of course. And I'll send you home with some pictures too. Whenever you're ready, you can get up and go pee."

Relief swept through me, and I nearly wet myself right then and there. Thankfully, I managed to tamp it back and, instead, sat up.

"The bathroom is down the hall, second door on the right."

After cleaning off the gel and fixing my clothes, I waddled my full bladder down the hallway, relieved myself, then returned to the examination room.

"Sam gave me your email, and I've sent you the photos and the heartbeat recording."

"Thank you," I said, still awestruck. I whipped out my phone and pulled up the first email, grinning at my little bloop.

"No problem. I'd like to see you back in four

weeks for a more detailed ultrasound. After that, we'll do one more at the twenty-week mark and then you'll be home free."

"That's it?" I asked. "Just two more?"

"Yup, that's all that's needed. Though sometimes people have one at the end of the pregnancy, right before birth. But we'll determine if that's necessary closer to your due date. In the meantime, no more fighting, hear me?" She gave me a stern stare. "Shifting is fine, but I don't even want to hear about you engaging in any challenges or brawling in parks."

"Yes, doctor," I playfully snarked, my gaze dropping to the first sonogram photo.

Sam wrapped his arms around me and pulled me close, staring down at it with me. Suddenly, I couldn't recall a time I'd ever been this happy.

"I'll leave you two be." The door opened and shut before I even realized it, too consumed with the sight of our baby.

"Wow," Sam said, his gruff voice making me tear up again.

"I can't believe we made that."

Sam kissed my head and held me tight. I could have stayed there forever, tucked in his arms, staring at our baby. The rest of the world be damned. This was the only place I wanted to be.

9

WE'D REORGANIZED OURSELVES FOR THE DRIVE home. Anna, my mother, me, and Sam in one car. Vlad and Cole in the other. The instant I'd told them Meredith had taken some photos and given us a heartbeat recording, Anna and my mother demanded I forward them the email. Every few seconds, the soft patter of my baby's heart played in the backseat, followed by the gentle sigh of a soon-to-be grandmother or aunt. They were certainly eager, and it brought tears to my eyes. This baby hadn't even passed into the second trimester yet and it was already so loved.

At first, I'd felt bad for submitting Sam to this, but he seemed equally, if not more, smitten, the smile on his face never faltering. I knew werewolves were predisposed to reproducing and having children, but I could see now that it went deeper than that. Sam was positively beaming with happiness.

I patted his thigh, then glanced back at my mother and Anna. They sat side-by-side, cooing over the images, pointing out what *they thought* were arms and legs. I had an app on my phone that told me the baby was the size of a kidney bean. I really doubt it had discernable arms and legs yet. But it was fun to listen to them.

Once they settled down, I decided now was the time to approach the idea of Vampires Anonymous with my mother. I pulled out my phone and reopened the website, then handed it back to my mother.

"What's this?" she asked.

"This is something I think you should do."

Her brow furrowed as she scrolled the page. "You want me to join a seniors' home?"

"What? No! That's a Vampires Anonymous location."

"It's for old people."

"Well..." I bit my lip. Technically, she was right. I had chosen one more suited to her age. "Anna?"

"Right." Anna sat back in her seat. "Barbara,

every vampire is required to attend Vampires Anonymous. Or we were back when the queen was in charge. Gabriel might have changed that rule when he took over, I'm not sure. I haven't heard anything about that. Technically, I had to attend it when I first turned too. I only managed one meeting, but still. It's a place we can go to voice our concerns and struggles. Help us adjust to this new life. Express our issues to those who might be suffering in the same way."

"So, it's like an Alcoholics Anonymous meeting."

"In a way. But obviously, it's suited toward adjusting to your new life as a vampire. I don't need to tell you it isn't easy becoming something that isn't human. Our lives are completely different. And these people help with that. There are psychiatrists, counselors, and much more. But the one Lucy found here offers more than counseling. You can do other fun events as well. Clubs you can join."

"Yeah, no," my mother muttered. "That's not happening. I want nothing to do with this."

Sighing, I glanced over my shoulder and unleashed the sternest glare I could muster. "You're going."

"Lucy—" Anna started.

"No, Anna. I'm tired of this. I'm tired of her

avoiding the truth and hiding from her life." I pinned my mother with another glare. "You hardly ever go out. You refuse to forgive or even willingly speak to Dad. You refuse to tell your friends. You refuse to go home to Perish. None of this is healthy for you. You *need* to talk to someone. Even if it's just another vampire who's going through what you are."

"Anna can—"

"Anna can't," I growled, cutting my mother off. "You need a connection outside of us. So, guess what? We're taking you there right now."

"We are?" Sam asked, briefly glancing toward me.

"We are. I've decided."

My mother unleashed a growl that should have raised the hair on my arms. Except I wasn't a little girl anymore. Nor was I human. So rather than let her cow me, I turned and growled *back*. Except mine was louder and deeper. My wolf had more bite than my mother's fangs.

"Okay, everyone needs to calm down," Anna murmured. "Let's not get upset."

"Oh, I'm already upset," I snapped. "And you know what? It's time to do something about it. So, Mother, you're going to this meeting. And you're going to sit there and listen. If you don't want to speak, that's fine." I softened my voice. "Though I hope you will."

True to my mother's typical behavior, she crossed her arms over her chest and stared out the window. The way her jaw clenched, I knew I'd pissed her off. But I'd had enough.

"To the VA meeting?" Sam confirmed.

"To the VA meeting," I echoed.

WE SAT PARKED IN FRONT OF ONE OF THE LOCAL community centers. Lights blazed from within, and through the windows, I could see someone organizing a bunch of chairs in a circle. From the looks of it, the nightly festivities had only begun. Which made sense, considering it was only nine-thirty—breakfast time in vampire land. Most were probably still in their jammies.

I unbuckled my seat belt and turned to face my mother. "Ready?"

Shock widened her eyes. "You're coming with me?"

"Do you want me to?" I definitely wanted to be there for her, but if she chose to do this alone, so be it. At the end of the day, I just wanted her to get the help she needed.

My mother's head swung back toward her window, and she peered out into the darkness. After a brief silence, she reached for the handle and popped open her door. She paused before stepping outside, then shot me a nervous smile. "I don't want to go in there alone."

My heart broke at the sound of her trembling voice.

Was I a terrible daughter for forcing her into this? Was it too soon?

Anna hadn't wanted to attend her first VA meeting either. She'd fought Camilla on it. But Camilla had stuck to her guns and forced her to go—much like I was doing now. Except Anna was stronger than my mother. More resilient. Perhaps pushing her into this wasn't the best way to go.

Neither Anna nor my mother had chosen this life, and it required so much change. Maybe it was wrong of me to force her into attending, but for crying out loud, she needed help. I just wanted her to be happy again.

I understood why she didn't want to leave. She felt safe here. Anna and Vlad were vampires, meaning she had people to share this life with. But she couldn't keep hiding in Jackson. She had to return to her own life or make a new one.

But did that give me the right to force this on her? Much like how everything else had been?

Crap. Maybe I *was* a terrible daughter.

Sighing, I reached into the back and touched her knee. "Mom, you don't have to do this if you don't want to."

"Funny, it didn't sound like I had an option," she grumbled.

I took that knock to the chin like a champ. No point pouting over the truth. "I know, and I'm sorry. I'm just worried about you. You know I love you. I only want to see you happy again. If you want to go home, we can do that. We can come back on a different day."

She considered my words in silence. I could practically see the gears spinning in her head. For a moment, I thought she might agree and tell Sam to take her home, but with a deep sigh, she climbed out of the car.

Anna and I followed suit.

"I can go in with her," Anna said. "You don't need to do this."

"How about we both go?" I suggested.

Anna glanced at the building, her fanged teeth

gently scraping over her bottom lip. "Do you think it's safe in there for you?"

"I mean... no less so than anywhere else," I said as I studied the dark parking lot. "I think it'd be weird if Olivia came looking for me here. And if she did... well, it's a building full of vampires."

"Who might stand back and watch the bloodbath," Anna teased. "Keep in mind, vampires and werewolves really do bear animosity toward each other."

"Yeah, but I have you." I nudged her hip with mine. "I'm sure you'd be able to convince them to help me. You are famous, after all."

"More like infamous," Anna grumbled before heading toward Vlad's car.

I circled ours and approached Sam's side. He opened the window and draped an arm out, smiling.

"Are you okay with this?" I asked. "If you don't want to stay, you could go home, and we'll call you when we're done."

His smile faded and his eyes flashed amber, like a burst of sunlight from deep within darkness. "I'm not leaving you here alone."

"I wouldn't be alone," I reminded him. "Anna and my mother are here." I didn't expect Vlad and Cole to stick around.

"I'm *not* leaving," Sam growled.

I lifted a brow. "Fair enough."

I had a feeling his overprotectiveness would eventually start getting on my nerves, but for now, I didn't mind one bit. I leaned into the car and kissed him, reveling in the feel of his lips. "I'll text you once I have an idea as to how long the meetings last."

"Usually an hour or so," Anna said, clearly eavesdropping on our conversation from their car. She stood next to Vlad, her hand resting on his arm through the driver's side window. He'd put the car in park and Cole had tipped his head back against the seat. Looks like Sam wasn't the only one planning to hang around.

Guilt crept through my gut. Everyone here had their own lives to lead, but because I was pregnant and in danger, they were sacrificing their night to sit in a freaking parking lot so my mother could attend a support group meeting.

A flood of warmth and love doused my guilt. This was my family. And I adored them all.

Pushing off the car, I straightened and reached for my mother's hand. "Shall we?"

She took it without hesitation and threw me a shaky smile. I squeezed her fingers in a show of silent support, then led her into the building, Anna close on our heels.

We'd only made it a few steps inside when a large hand gripped my shoulder and spun me around. I teetered on my feet, nearly losing my balance, even with my mother gripping my hand.

"No werewolves allowed," came a deep, ominous voice.

Before I could so much as blink, Anna snatched the stranger's hand and twisted his arm so hard, he dropped to a knee with a loud curse.

"Do. Not. Touch. Her," Anna threatened, her tone violent and menacing.

The other vampire grunted, then whipped his head up to see her, his long, dark hair obscuring half his face. When they locked eyes, his face went slack. "Hey, I know you."

"You're mistaken," Anna snapped.

"No, I do. You're her... *Dracula's* wife."

A dangerous smile curled her lips, one that reminded me of a lioness before she pounced. Her fangs flashed in the yellow hallway light. "I am. And if you know me, you should also know that if you lay so much as another finger on my friend, I'm going to eat you for dinner. And then her fiancé will piss on your remains."

I grimaced at the picture she painted. Sam wouldn't—well, he *had* marked one of Vlad's coffins before, but that'd been for revenge, and this... Right, okay, so maybe he would.

And speaking of my mate...

Anna shifted her weight to reveal Sam's hulking figure hovering in the doorway. His eyes burned with anger and his lips had thinned back to reveal his teeth, all nice and pointy. Anger and violence poured off him in waves. He must have shot out of our car the instant this guy touched me.

The vampire flashed me an alarmed glance. "Sorry. It's just that we don't allow werewolves at our meetings. Vampires only. You understand."

"Now, now, Joseph," another voice joined in. "Let's not be so discriminatory."

I repositioned myself so I could keep Joseph in view while taking in the new guy. He practically oozed *vampire* as he strode toward us, his movements more predator than prey. Yet, I didn't sense anything threatening from him. In fact, his calm expression and folded hands reminded me a bit of a monk.

"Welcome, friends," he said. "My name is Ben, and I organize these meetings."

"Hiya, Ben. Name's Anna," she said.

"Hello, Anna. Would you mind...?" He gestured

toward poor Joseph, still kneeling on the ground, his arm bent at a terrible angle.

Anna flicked Joseph a disapproving glance, then released him.

A relieved breath escaped Joseph's lips as he picked himself up, moving ever so slowly to Ben's side.

"I apologize for the dramatics," Anna said. "We just don't take lightly to strangers touching our friends."

"Understandably so," Ben said with a serene smile. He patted Joseph's uninjured shoulder and pointed him toward the meeting room. "Finish setting up for me, will you? I'll be right in."

"Yeah, sure, okay," Joseph grumbled. He shot me another contrite look. "Sorry."

His grumbled apology inspired a little bit of pity, so I smiled. "No problem, Joseph."

"It was...uh... well, I don't want to say nice to meet you. But it was definitely an experience." He grimaced, then vanished into the meeting room.

"Now then." Ben braved a step closer, his eyes flicking over my shoulder.

I didn't need to turn to know Sam stood behind me. I took a small step back and pressed myself against him, knowing the contact would soothe his troubled wolf.

"May I ask what brought you all here?" Ben asked, his gaze locking on Anna.

"We came for my mother," I said, drawing Ben's focus back to me. Sam's body tensed, so I reached for his hand, giving it a squeeze. I wasn't in danger, but his wolf likely wouldn't back down until he saw me somewhere completely safe. "She was recently turned into a vampire."

"How recently?" Ben asked.

"A month ago."

His dark brows shot upward. "It's required that all new vampires attend VA. Usually they seek us out after their isolation week."

I nodded, a bit of shame heating my cheeks. "We've had a, uh, hard month."

Ben studied my face, then turned his gaze toward my mother, who hadn't so much as made a noise since entering. "Very well. Welcome...?"

"Barbara," she rasped.

Oh, yeah. She was nervous. I wanted to reach out to her, but I had an angry werewolf to settle first. Thankfully, Anna rubbed my mother's back.

"And you are Anna Perish," Ben said. "I've heard of you."

I almost laughed. I wasn't surprised he'd heard of her. Every vampire probably had. Not only was she married to Dracula, but she was also a famous social media influencer, *and* responsible for the Vampire Queen's death. One didn't remain anonymous with such an impressive resume.

Ben's gaze returned to me. "Now, Joseph was correct. We don't allow werewolves to join our meetings."

"I understand," I said. I could return to the car with Sam and wait. I didn't want to rob my mother of this opportunity.

"But I admit, I'm intrigued. It isn't often we come across a family such as yours. A mix of vampires and werewolves?"

"My mother, Anna, and Vlad—whom I'm sure you also know of—are vampires. My mate and I are werewolves, and my father is human."

"Your father... ah." Understanding softened Ben's face. "Well, that's quite a complicated situation. I think for tonight we'll make an exception. While werewolves aren't allowed, I have a feeling it plays into your family dynamics greatly." He turned to me. "I'm afraid I didn't catch your name. Or your mate's for that matter."

"I'm Lucy. This is Sam."

Ben dipped his head in greeting. "Lucy, you are welcome to enter. But Sam, I must ask that you leave."

Sam immediately started vibrating against me, his body trembling at the thought of me leaving. What'd been fine only minutes ago suddenly wasn't, all because an unknown vampire had dared to lay their hands on me.

"Thank you," I said to Ben, then I turned to face Anna and my mother. "You two go on inside. I'll be right in."

Anna's expression turned sympathetic, but she led my mom into the room without so much as a word toward Sam. Ben quietly trailed behind them, leaving Sam and me alone in the hall.

When I finally faced him, my breath caught. Sam wasn't exactly home at the moment, his wolf was definitely in the driver's seat. There wasn't a hint of humanity left in his eyes. His face was nothing but hard edges and sharp lines, and every muscle in his body had coiled, as though he expected an attack.

"Sam."

His blindingly bright gaze dropped to me.

"Hey, everything's okay. I'm not in danger," I whispered.

When he didn't respond, I took his hand and rested his palm against my cheek. I nuzzled the curve of his hand and ran my lips along his skin. "See, I'm right here. I'm fine."

He gave a slow blink.

I kissed his palm and held his stare. The glow began to fade, diminishing with each additional blink, until Sam finally took back control.

"Lucy," he rumbled.

"Hi there. You okay?"

He gave a jerky nod. "He touched you, and I..."

"I know. It's all good. Anna took care of the problem for me."

"I don't know if I can let you go in there without me."

I rose on my tiptoes and brushed a gentle kiss across his lips. He pulled me close, his arms like steel bands around my waist. I had to remind myself that just because *I* was the pregnant one didn't mean Sam wasn't undergoing his own changes.

"As you can see, I'm perfectly fine," I repeated. "And you'll be able to see me through the window the entire time. I'll make sure of it. Not to mention, I'll have Anna with me. And she's just as protective as you."

A growly laugh slipped past Sam's lips. "True."

"Okay. How about you head back to the car then? And I'll see you soon."

His head dipped and he stole another possessive kiss—one I didn't mind in the least. Then his arms loosened, and I stepped back. With a calm smile, I blew Sam a kiss and headed into the meeting room.

I HAD TO ADMIT, I ENJOYED THE MEETING. IT WAS interesting to hear everyone's stories. It also made me realize there were advantages to being "out in the open" so to speak. The vampires had this wonderful support community set up for them. Werewolves had their packs but lacked these social programs the vampires had latched onto. It made me wonder if this was something I needed to set up for our people. In the past, we hadn't needed it due to all werewolves being born that way. But thanks to Corbin—and by association, me—things were changing. We had new werewolves being turned every day. This sort of support group would come in handy considering the transitions were equally as gruesome as vampires.

When it came to my mother's turn, her story captivated the entire room. They listened as she told them about her past—my sperm donor—and her introduction to the paranormal world. Some even leaned forward, transfixed as she told them about the circumstances surrounding her change. She hadn't held anything back, and I'd bowed my head in shame when she'd admitted that my father and I had forced her to become a vampire without her consent. While holding my gaze, she'd admitted to the entire room that she would have rather died.

My heart had shattered into a million pieces.

After she'd finished speaking, Ben offered a few comforting words, then recommended a psychiatrist. One who specialized in these types of situations. My mother thanked him, then fell back into silence as she listened to everyone else's stories.

For Anna's turn, she lightened the mood, spinning a yarn about her equally dramatic entrance into the vampire world. Everyone had so many questions for her regarding our overseas adventures.

Thankfully, I wasn't required to speak, so I waved Ben off when he asked if I wanted to share anything with the group. We were here for my mother. Not me.

But I knew without a doubt that I wanted to start a program like this for us changed werewolves.

By the end of the meeting, it'd seemed like a weight had lifted from my mother's shoulders. I knew it wouldn't be quite so simple, and that she certainly needed someone to talk to, but she'd looked less burdened and a bit happier. Especially when she connected with a friendly lady named Beth, who appeared to be the same age as my mother, both in human and vampire years.

Beth's transition hadn't been as dramatic. She'd welcomed the change as opposed to dying from cancer. But she claimed to understand my mother's point of view.

As we were leaving, my mother had stopped to sign up for the quilting club.

The sight of it had brought tears to my eyes. She'd always loved to quilt, and I couldn't wait to see her return to something she found joy in.

As for my father, I had a sneaking suspicion their relationship would take far more time to repair than he and I had initially expected. And I had every intention of warning him of that next time we spoke. We needed to be patient with her and stop forcing her to decide. Clearly, the meeting had been just as beneficial for me.

Anna, on the other hand, had signed her and Vlad up for a dancing class. The mischievous glint in her eye had me biting back laughter. I imagined he wouldn't love that, but he'd do it without question—for her.

At the door, Ben thanked us for coming and told me I was welcome back whenever I needed it. I stared up at him, wondering what he'd done for a living as a human. The man seemed to be a walking empath. The way he tuned in to other people's emotions astounded me. Even now, he placed a hand on my mother's shoulder and gave her a reassuring squeeze as she left the building. He didn't say anything to her. Just offered her a friendly smile and an encouraging nod.

My mother returned it with one of her own.

This would be good for her. I knew it with every fiber of my being.

***

It was well past midnight when we finally pulled into our driveway.

After the meeting concluded, our group parted ways. Anna and Vlad adventured out in search of fresh blood, and Cole asked us to drop him off at his place. My mother, however, had opted to remain with me and Sam. The three of us hadn't spoken much during the drive home, but I sensed relief from my mom, as opposed to irritation or anger.

Sam killed the engine, then leaned his head back against the seat and sighed. Shadows bruised his under eyes and his mouth pressed into a thin line. It was exhausting losing control of your inner wolf like that. It took so much energy to rein them back in. Which meant I wasn't the only one thinking of our bed. The darn thing called my name and was promising me a grand love story, one filled with pillows, soft blankets, and pleasant dreams.

This late-night stuff often got a little tiring, especially considering we woke far earlier than the vamps.

"I'm going to head inside," my mom said. She was likely as tired as us.

"Okay," I said around a yawn.

She stepped out and shut the door.

I turned toward Sam and smiled. "How you doing?"

"Better. That was... that was a rough one."

I reached across the car and squeezed his thigh. He immediately rested his hand atop mine, giving my fingers a small squeeze.

"Anna said there'd be a lot of changes. And not just for me. Your wolf is going to be more active for the next seven months, I think."

Sam's eyes closed.

"One day at a time," I told him. "That's all we can really do."

"It worries me," he admitted. "That guy barely touched you, and I knew Anna could handle it. But I couldn't stop myself. Nor control my anger."

I lifted his hand and brushed my lips across his knuckles. "We got this. Together."

He turned to face me, the corners of his lips tugging upward. "Together."

"Come on," I said, gesturing toward the house. "Let's get inside and get some sleep. I'm sure tomorrow will be equally exhausting, considering we have the pack meeting at eight."

Sam groaned. "Can't we have one night to ourselves?"

"Nope," I teased.

"Maybe we need to take a vacation. You know, before the baby comes. Just you and me. We could leave the country for a week. Go somewhere warm with a beach and a warm breeze."

"Mm. That sounds heavenly. How about for our honeymoon?"

His eyes brightened with excitement. "Are you saying you want to marry before you have the baby?"

"I want whatever you want. If you want to marry beforehand, we can do that. If you want to wait till after, that's fine too."

Sam leaned across the console and kissed me. "I love you."

"I know," I quipped.

"I want to marry before the baby."

"Guess I'll need a maternity dress then."

His laughter filled the car. "Or we could just elope next week."

The idea had merit, except—"I don't want to marry until we've resolved this mess with Olivia. I would hate for her to ruin our day or hurt someone we loved simply because we'd gathered for a wedding."

Disappointment darkened Sam's face, but he nodded. "I hear you. Guess that just gives me more incentive to find her."

Chuckling, I popped open my door and climbed out of the car. The cool night air brushed my face, and I drew it deep into my lungs, letting it reinvigorate me. May in Mississippi had its warm temperatures, but thankfully nothing stifling. Not quite yet anyway. It'd be a whole other story in a month. I was just grateful I wouldn't be heavily pregnant during the summer.

Sam came up beside me, took my hand, and led me toward the front door.

When my toes touched the porch, I paused and cocked my head.

"What's wrong?" Sam asked.

My nostrils flared as I drew in a deep breath. Then I shook my head. "Nothing. Sorry. Just thought I smelled something."

"Hmm. A skunk maybe?"

No, definitely not something that repugnant. Shaking it off, I opened the front door and stepped inside.

But the second I did, my wolf raised her hackles and came snarling to the front of my mind.

Words like *invader, enemy,* and *intruder* flashed through my head.

I barely heard my mother shout, "Lucy, watch out!" before Sam grabbed me and shoved me behind him, his towering height hiding me from whatever awaited us in the living room.

"Who the hell are you?" he shouted, the words edged with a vicious growl.

"Oh, calm down, killer," replied an unfamiliar voice.

My pulse slowed a notch when I realized it wasn't Olivia. Small miracles.

"I'll calm down when you tell me who the fuck you are," he snapped.

I gripped the waist of his jeans and held fast. His entire body shook with barely restrained rage, and I understood why. Someone had invaded our turf, our home. And we hadn't noticed until it was too late, thanks to how exhausted we were.

"Name's Maddie," she retorted. "And I'm just here to talk. Promise."

"Yeah, sorry, but I have no intentions of taking you at your word," he said.

"Up to you," she said nonchalantly. "I could have nipped this fangy lady in the butt without you even knowing. But I didn't because I'm here on friendly terms."

Mom. Panic sent my heart rate skyrocketing. She'd gone in first. Was she okay? Had this Maddie harmed her? From behind Sam's back, I couldn't see her. But that didn't stop me from asking, "You okay, Mom?"

"I'm fine—" my mom managed to say before Maddie interrupted.

"Not very trusting, are you?"

"I tend not to trust people who break into my house. Must be a fatal flaw of mine," I bit out.

"Like I said, I'm just here to chat. So, let's all calm down and chat like adults. 'Kay?"

"No, not *'kay*," I replied from behind Sam.

Then I stepped out from behind him. No way I'd have this conversation cowering behind my mate. I was the alpha, after all.

"Lucy...," he growled.

I rested my fingers against his wrist. "I got this, Sam."

My gaze clashed with Maddie's. Hmm. Couldn't say I knew anyone by that name. I studied her face, but no recognition bells chimed. Long, blonde locks framed her face in loose waves that hung below her shoulders, and unnaturally bright blue eyes appraised me. Her scarlet red lips curled upward as though my analysis amused her.

Then my eyes flicked to my mother, who sat as still as stone next to Maddie on the couch. Her rod-straight back had me raising a brow.

"She has a stake," my mother explained. "Told me not to move or speak."

Fury ignited my blood. "Did she now?"

"Oh, don't worry," Maddie said, giving a nonplussed shrug.

She nudged my mother, who quickly darted across the room to the armchair.

"A girl can't be too careful these days," Maddie continued. "And rumor has it, you live with multiple vampires, including the renowned Dracula himself. I needed to take precautions. Couldn't have anyone ripping out my throat before we had a chance to speak. And not that anyone asked, but yes, this is a hawthorn stake that's been treated with holy water and monksblood. I take my business seriously."

"Your *business*?"

"Vampire slayer."

I froze. So did Sam. Did she just say... slayer?

"Now, before anyone gets their panties all twisted, I'm not here for any of your vampires. I only kill the bad ones."

I blinked. I'd never heard of a vampire slayer

"It's a new, lucrative business," she continued. "When a vamp breaks the law, what happens to them?"

"The queen usually—"

"Ah," Maddie taunted. "Except the queen's dead. And while her son is doing his best to maintain control, things are a tad chaotic across the pond. So, ta-da!" She flourished her arms. "Vampire Slayer, *a la moi*. When a vampire is naughty, the police put out a bounty on them, myself and others take care of that nasty little bit of business, and presto, my bank account gets a happy donation."

"Okay... and what exactly does that have to do with any of us? As you pointed out, no one has broken the law here."

"Oh, I'm not here for mommy dearest." Maddie lifted her stake and pointed it in my direction. "I'm here for you."

Sam's fingers gripped my upper arms.

Maddie rolled her eyes. "Any way we can have this conversation without your bodyguard?"

"No."

She blew out an exasperated breath. "He's just going to annoy me."

"Deal with it," I shot back.

"Fine!" She tossed up her arms, then reached behind her and hid the stake. When her hands returned to sight, she didn't have it anymore. "Like I said, I'm not here for her. I don't bother with law-abiding vamps. I deal with the sort who like to murder people or commit other nasty crimes."

I made a mental note to pass this along to Vlad. He'd likely want to look into this recent development.

"Look, I really didn't come here to start any trouble. I promise."

"Well, Maddie, that's a little hard to believe. You broke into my house and threatened my mother with a stake that we all know does a very good job of putting vampires down."

She flashed me a grin. "I'm just good at my job. And I didn't *threaten* her, per se."

"She told me if I so much as twitched, she'd plug me so full of wood, I wouldn't be able to walk straight for a week."

"Colorful," I said wryly.

Maddie's grin only grew. "I like my job."

"Clearly."

"Oh, come on. Don't be like that. Don't be like *her*."

Okay, now we were getting somewhere. My eyes slitted. "Like *who* exactly?"

"Olivia," she grumbled, her face twisting like she'd ingested something sour.

And just like that, my defenses slammed into place. My wolf took control, my fingers extending into claws.

"Okay." Maddie held up her hands. "I know you two have some beef. But that's between you guys, 'kay."

"No, not *'kay*," I repeated. Must be a favorite phrase of hers.

Maddie blew her bangs out of her face, then slumped against the wall. "Just let me explain."

"Make it quick," I snapped.

Maddie met my gaze, then right in front of me, she reached for her eyes and peeled away a set of contacts.

The second they slid aside, I realized her eyes weren't bright blue, but rather a piercing green. A very *familiar* piercing green.

"Allow me to introduce myself properly this time. My name is Madison Smith. You might know my father? One Reginald Hayes? That makes you my sister."

She waited eagerly for my response, her newly brandished green eyes watching me from across the room. I had no idea what she expected. Happy tears, excited screams, typical girly stuff?

Instead, what came out of my mouth was, "Oh, not again."

11

"WHAT?" MADDIE DEMANDED.

"What?" I echoed, heat flaming my cheeks. That probably hadn't been the response she'd been hoping for.

"You said—" Maddie's gaze snapped between Sam and me, confusion mottling her pale skin. "Never mind. I guess I shouldn't have expected a happy response considering our *other* sister."

This was turning into some sort of nightmarish fairy tale. Three sisters. One on the side of good, one evil, and one... well, I didn't know the first thing about Maddie, other than the fact that she was an alleged vampire slayer.

I made a mental note to check into *all* of this,

then slowly stepped into the living room. The weight at my back reminded me of Sam's presence, and I took extra care not to move too quickly. I couldn't afford to set his wolf off.

When I stood a few feet from Maddie, I inhaled deeply. The instant her scent hit my nose, I knew. "You're a werewolf."

She beamed at me. "Definitely gives me an advantage, don'tcha think?" Her chest puffed out and she shot me a wink. "I've killed seven vampires so far."

I wasn't sure how to gauge that number. Knowing how many vampires were in the world, it was pathetically small. But she was merely one person, and vampires had only been public knowledge for two years or so.

"I have other questions," I said before casually strolling to the couch and sitting next to my mother. Every inch of me had tensed with anticipation, watching Maddie's every move. She claimed to have come on friendly terms, but as already noted, I didn't know the first thing about her. Could be she was a liar. After all, she certainly was a killer.

"I'd be surprised if you didn't," she said, laughing. "I have some of my own."

"I'd be surprised if you didn't," I parroted.

"No one would doubt you two are sisters," my mother added. "Look, it's been an exhausting night, and if you two aren't planning to kill each other, can I go?"

I shot my mother a wry glance. "Really, Mom?"

"Oh, yeah, you can leave. I have no beef with you," Maddie said.

That caught my attention. "But you do with me?"

"Maybe. Maybe not."

"Anyone ever tell you that you can be a bit exasperating?"

"Oh, sweetie, all the time," Maddie said, her mouth splitting into a wide grin. "But don't worry, you'll come to love that about me. It's my best quality."

Somehow, I truly doubted that.

"How about this? Let's play twenty questions," she suggested. "You get one, then I get one. But no lying. If anyone lies, the game ends."

"And then what?" I asked, my stomach twisting with nerves.

"And then we see what we see."

Well, that was the vaguest answer I'd ever heard. "Fine. I agree to your little game."

Maddie strutted across the room and took a seat

in the nearby recliner, popping open the footrest and kicking back.

"Make yourself comfortable," I deadpanned.

"Thanks, I did. And I'm also ready." She waved her hawthorn stake at me like it was a wand. "Proceed, madam."

I raised my brows. Madam? Just how old did she think I was?

"Alright. You're a werewolf, and you claim to be a child of Reggie's."

"That's not a question," she said.

This time, I rolled my eyes. "I'm getting to it. Who turned you?"

"What makes you think I'm not wolf-born?"

I huffed out a quiet laugh. "Because I spent a year with Reggie. And I know for a fact that he had no wolf-born children. Let's just say he was a tad sore about that."

Her head dipped as she considered my answer. "Well, that explains a lot."

"Explains what, exactly?"

Maddie crossed her legs, her appearance that of someone who was completely relaxed. She even started using her stake to play with her cuticles, her attention wholly fixed on giving herself a manicure, right here in my living room.

"Because I never met our dear father."

"Sperm donor," I corrected. "And if you never met him, then who turned you?"

She paused in her ministrations and lifted her gaze to mine, her silence telling me everything I needed to know.

"Olivia," I said.

Maddie tipped her stake in my direction. "One point for big sister."

"Big sister?"

"Oh yeah," she said with another grin. "Definitely the big sister."

I stashed that information away for later. Asking her age didn't seem relevant to this conversation. Besides, it wasn't my turn to ask a question.

Maddie spun her stake back around and resumed picking at her nails. "Did you really murder Olivia's mate, Corbin?"

Whoa. I honestly hadn't expected that to be her question. But I didn't hesitate in answering, "Yes."

Maddie's eyes flew wide. "That's cold."

"Cold?" I sat forward on the couch. "No. Cold is how that bastard brutalized me. Did Olivia tell you how he stalked me through a dark house? How he tore into me with his teeth and claws? How he bled me dry in my friend's bedroom? He'd come to kill me. Not turn me. It was only because of Reggie's bloodline that I survived."

"Uh, no, she didn't—"

"Or did she mention how he literally came to America to try and kill me *again*? How he stabbed me with a silver knife? How he and his men nearly killed my parents? Don't sit there and pretend like I'm the problem here. Corbin *deserved* to die."

Maddie swallowed. Her steely façade weakened for a moment before she returned to her task at hand. "Guess he had it coming then, didn't he?"

Now, *that* surprised me. "Aren't you Olivia's ally?"

Her dark lashes fluttered as her gaze lifted to mine. "Is that your next question?"

I nodded. Yeah, that was definitely a question I needed answered.

Maddie's lips pursed as she considered me. Then she dropped the stake into her lap and folded her hands together. "Guess that depends on the outcome of this interview."

I snorted out a laugh. "Interview? Am I hiring you?"

"Maybe," she said with a shrug.

That seemed to be her favorite word. And I had a feeling it was going to drive me insane.

"It's your turn to ask a question," I said.

"I know. Just thinking of which one to ask next."

She steepled her fingers under her chin and studied me and Sam with a nonchalance that didn't quite ring true. Whatever question she was mulling over, it meant something to her, and I sensed it would make or break this sisterly meeting.

"Do either of you"—her focus darted from me to Sam, my silent sentinel, then back to me again—"have any ambitions to take over the world, enslave humanity, unleash genocide on unsuspecting innocents, anything like that?"

I gave a long and slow sigh. Was that what Olivia was telling people now? That we were homicidal lunatics hellbent on destroying the world?

"No," I bit out, my tone slightly exasperated

"A simple answer. I like it."

I leaned back on the couch, my gaze sharpening on her. My turn. "How did you meet Olivia?"

"Would you believe through an ancestry site?" Maddie said, shaking her head bemusedly.

"Wait, what?"

My harsh tone had Maddie's head snapping up. "What's wrong?"

"Shit," I breathed out. "She handed her DNA over to one of those sites?"

Maddie shrugged. "I guess. What's the big deal? I sent mine in too."

Sam's responding growl drew my attention. Our gazes clashed and I could only imagine he saw the same concern in mine that I saw in his.

"Werewolf DNA is never to be given out," Sam snarled.

I nodded. "The public doesn't know about us. We need to keep it that way. By sending in samples of our blood or saliva, who knows what the government could do with it."

Maddie frowned. "That's not good. If it helps, I sent mine in years ago, before Olivia turned me. Before I even knew about all this. If I wasn't a werewolf then, would my DNA reflect that?"

I had no idea. I wasn't a geneticist. Hell, I'd failed Biology twice in high school. But I had to imagine our DNA would be different from normal humans, being that our father was a werewolf. Surely that would reflect somewhere in our chromosomes.

"Do you know when Olivia submitted her sample?" Sam asked.

Maddie shrugged. "Recently. That's all I can say. The site notified me of her about a year ago, but it took me some time to work up the courage to reach out to her."

I thought back to Olivia's and my first conversation. At the time, she'd claimed Reggie had turned her into a werewolf eight months prior. Provided we could believe anything she said, of course.

"She might have been a human when she did the ancestry site," I said. "But if she wasn't, it won't be long before the government figures out she isn't human."

"If they haven't already figured it out." Sam sighed. "I should run this new development by my father, just in case. I'm sure he'd like to know."

"I'm sure all the alphas would like to know. This affects everyone." I ran my hands through my hair and blew out a heavy breath. "We need to spread word of this. Just in case."

Sam retrieved his cell phone and started to walk away. A few steps in, he stopped, turned, and faced Maddie. He lifted his hand and pointed his phone at her. "If you so much as breathe wrong in my mate's direction, I'll rip you to shreds." Then he threw her a sharp smile that made me shiver.

Damn. Protective Sam was scary.

And freaking sexy.

Yup, it was official. Something was definitely wrong with me.

Maddie's eyes widened for a fraction of a second, then narrowed. "Bring it, Wolfman."

Sam stormed closer, rage rippling beneath his skin.

I leapt to my feet and placed my hands on his chest. "Hey, hey... It's okay. I got this." I snuck a glance over my shoulder and glared at Maddie. "Don't goad him. Not if you want to make it home tonight."

Maddie pouted—*literally*—then nodded. "Fine. Sorry."

"We good?" I asked them both, my hands sweeping upward until my thumbs could caress Sam's jaw. "No ripping each other apart. And no stabbing." I directed that last bit at Maddie.

"Aww, you do get me," Maddie replied, adopting Anna-level snark. "We're gonna be good friends, I think."

I rolled my eyes. "Not looking for more friends."

She waved an empty hand in the air, her stake forgotten in her lap. "Sisters, then. Who wouldn't want another sister?"

Well, considering my track record so far, I wasn't sure how I felt about adding another to the roster.

Sam eyed the two of us once more, then turned and stalked down the hall, phone in hand. Not that he went far. A purposely calculated move to ensure he was nearby in case I had any trouble with Maddie.

"Now that your brute is gone, let's get back to our little game, shall we?" Maddie said. "I only have one more question to ask. After that, we're all done."

She made it sound simple enough, but I had a feeling we were far from over.

Maddie leaned forward, elbows braced against her knees. "Are you pregnant?"

And just like that, my world came crashing down.

My heart and pulse slammed into overdrive, and my breath quickened. My fingers lengthened into claws, and I felt pressure in my gums, as though my fangs wanted out. She'd asked a simple question, yet my wolf immediately came snarling to life, ready to rip Maddie to shreds if necessary.

"Whoa now," she whispered, her hands raised peaceably. "Guess that answers that question. Calm down. I'm not going to hurt you. Nor do I have any intentions of telling anyone."

"How did you find out?" I demanded and damn, my voice was *deep*. My wolf was definitely pissed.

The beast thrashed in my mind, and it took every ounce of strength I possessed to keep her from snatching control away from me.

"I'm a professional hunter," she said. "When I'm tracking someone, I learn everything I can about them. And I mean *everything*."

"How!" I shouted.

Sam stepped back into sight, and I waved a hand. I didn't want him here for this conversation.

"Okay, okay, geez!" She dropped her booted feet to the ground, as though preparing herself in case I did attack. Then she pointed at my purse.

I glanced down, only to see the corner of my sonogram picture poking out of the top. I started cursing like a sailor.

Sam came storming back into the room, his phone gripped in his hand and his eyes aglow with his wolf.

"Oh boy," Maddie whispered. "Everyone needs to take a breath and calm down."

My gaze swung back to hers, and I tracked her like a predator would its prey.

"Listen up, girls and boys, because I'm only going to say this once." Maddie didn't rise to her feet, likely knowing it'd be her death if she did. "I don't mean you or your baby *any* harm. You're safe with me." She held my gaze, probably waiting to see if her words registered in my mama wolf brain. "Okay?"

My head inched up.

"How about I tell a story?" Her wide gaze flicked between me and Sam. "Maybe that'll help?"

"Doubtful," Sam snarled.

"Well, let's give it the ole college try anyway. Just remember, I'm not here to harm anyone." She kept her hands folded in her lap. "Once upon a time, there was a young girl."

My responding snarl had her gaze snapping to me.

"No? Don't like fairytales?" She chuckled. "You'll have to get used to them eventually. Anyway. This young girl grew up in the foster system and was passed around more than a blunt on four-twenty." She lifted a brow. "Really? Nothing? Huh. I thought it was funny."

"Enough, Maddie," I snapped. Sam's growl echoed my words. "Cut the crap, stop telling jokes, and give me the whole story. Everything. Now."

Her eyes flashed to mine, but she must have sensed my frustration because she nodded and dropped the façade. "Fine. Long story short, I was never adopted. And when the time came for me to start my own life, I jumped on the opportunity. I didn't want to be tied to government programs anymore. I wanted my own life. But more than that, I wanted to find my family."

Maddie twisted her hands and she stared at the floor. "Sadly, the system had no records of my parents. All they knew was that I'd been left at a church. I had nothing to go on. So I moved forward. I got a job, found the smallest shithole to call home, and started putting my life together. About a year ago, once I'd saved up enough money, I purchased one of those ancestry kits. They take a few months to tabulate, but eventually, the results came back. Unfortunately, they told me nothing about my parents, but they did show that I had a half-sister. I searched for her on social media, and when I finally found her, I reached out. Thankfully, she was just as eager to meet me."

Listening to Maddie lowered my blood pressure, and I could breathe again. Grabbing Sam's hand, I led him to the loveseat across the room and together we sat, facing Maddie. Without all the humor and snark, I found myself empathizing with her. This could have been my life, after all.

"We met a few times before Olivia revealed the big secret to me," Maddie said. She gave a wry chuckle. "Never told me I had another sister, but she told me she was a werewolf. Go figure. Then about eight months ago, she offered to turn me, I admit, the thought excited me. Not only would I have a sister, but a pack. A family. Finally."

"She offered?" I murmured. "She didn't force it on you?"

"No, she gave me the option. I think she understood how important family was for me. Perhaps she took advantage of that. Except, she never told me that I..." Maddie fell quiet.

But I knew what she'd meant to say. "She didn't tell you that you had to die to become a werewolf."

Maddie wrung her hands together. "I don't hold that against her. I was just happy to be included. Until I actually met her pack. They were... insane. More like a pack of rabid wolves than anything else. And when I learned of Olivia's crusade..." Maddie shook her head. "I wanted nothing to do with that. I just wanted to find my family. I didn't want to join some murderous cause that endangered humanity. So I told her I didn't want to be involved, and I had no intentions of staying with her pack. The decision killed me. But I couldn't take part in that. I just couldn't."

Sam and I shared a glance before I turned back to Maddie, utterly stunned.

"And she let you?" Sam asked.

"She said she wouldn't force me to join. She wanted me to come to the same realizations as her and see that we needed each other. She wanted me to believe in her."

Maddie scrubbed a hand down her face. "Once again, I was alone. About a month after I left Olivia, I was out on a run when I heard a scream. I didn't even think, I just shifted and leapt into action. I came across a vampire feeding on a woman. It didn't look consensual. She was bleeding out, screaming, crying..."

I shuddered, thinking of the night Anna had been similarly attacked.

"The woman passed out when she saw me, so I killed the vampire," Maddie said matter-of-factly. "Tore his head clean off."

Shock widened my eyes. Yeah, that'd kill a vampire or two. And color me impressed that Maddie had been able to do such a thing. Many would have run away.

"I called 9-1-1, then disposed of the vampire corpse before anyone showed up. I'd torn his head off, I couldn't let the police see that. After the paramedics took the woman away, the police questioned me. I told them I fought and scared the vampire off. I didn't know what else to say. But once they had my statement, one of the officers suggested I join the new program they were building—the Vampire Slayer Academy. They said I clearly had what it took. They weren't wrong," she said with a shrug. "They just had no idea that I was a werewolf or that the vampire was actually dead."

"And suddenly you're a slayer?" I asked.

"It definitely wasn't sudden. I had to undergo the group's rigorous four-month training regime. During that time, I did nothing but eat, sleep, and breathe vampire hunter training. After I graduated, they sent me out on my first job. That night I made my first— well, second—kill. They just thought it was my first."

"Wait... you're telling me that in what... two months, you've killed six vampires?"

Pride shone in her eyes. "More like six weeks or so. About one a week. Crazy, right?"

Crazy didn't begin to describe it. Holy crap on a cracker. She had to be lethal then. Far more lethal than I'd originally guessed. Vampires weren't easy prey. And for my *little sister* to have killed seven in total... Wow.

"And the police don't suspect anything?" Sam asked. "Werewolves are faster, stronger than humans. We aren't allowed to partake in sports because it risks our exposure."

"No one has said anything," Maddie replied, her gaze sliding to Sam. "But I take precautions. When I'm around humans, I pull back. Drastically."

Sam gave a small nod, though I could tell this didn't sit well with him. I understood why it didn't. Maddie was playing a dangerous game.

"I'm careful," she assured him. "And I'm happy. I've made friends, started saving money, I was even able to buy some new furniture. It sounds pitiful, but for me, it's my dream. Then about two weeks ago, Olivia called." Maddie's mouth twisted. "She sounded desperate and a bit crazed, so I agreed to meet her, to make sure she was okay. That was when she told me about you. About how you massacred her pack and murdered her mate. She begged me to come back. Said she needed me now more than ever."

My breath caught at the image Maddie painted.

"I told her that I was sorry for all she'd been through, but I needed to think about her request. I'm building a life, and I can't just walk away from that. I asked for time to decide. She's my sister, and I want to be there for her, but her aspirations are dangerous. She got angry and stormed off, but she's called and texted a few times, asking if I've decided yet. I don't think I can put her off much longer."

"So that was when you decided to track me down?" I asked.

Maddie bit her bottom lip, then nodded. "Admittedly, I did some research first. Olivia only gave me your first name, so it took a bit to find you. When I learned of your living situation, I knew I needed to be smart about it."

"And you thought breaking into my house and holding my mother as a hostage was being smart about it?"

Embarrassment flooded Maddie's cheeks. "It worked, didn't it?"

I unleashed my big sister glare on her, the same one I'd perfected on Anna over the years. "No, it almost got you killed."

When Maddie puffed up, I held up a hand and silenced her. "Sam and I aren't some unsuspecting vampire who doesn't know they're being hunted. Granted, the stake at my mother's back did give me pause, but given the opportunity, we would have slaughtered you without breaking a sweat."

Maddie opened her mouth to argue, but I shook my head. "This isn't a game. We're at war with Olivia. And we'll perceive any threat as a dangerous one. Tonight might have worked in your favor, but it was risky. I'm just saying, this could have gone much differently. Promise me you'll be more careful next time."

Gentle laughter fell from Maddie's lips. She leaned back against the couch, then cupped her face and laughed even louder.

"What's so funny?" I demanded.

"You. This. Everything," she said, choking on her breath. "I wanted a big sister, right? Well, looks like I got one."

I thought of everything I'd just said to her and started laughing too. "Yeah, that did sound pretty protective and preachy, huh?"

"That's okay, I don't mind," she said.

We drifted into a comfortable silence, which was a far cry from a few minutes ago when I'd nearly torn out her throat. Which led me to my final question.

I sat forward on the chair, my hands loosely clasped in my lap. "You asked me your last question, but I still have one more."

Her mouth bent to the side. "Alright."

"What do you plan to do about Olivia?"

12

SOMETHING AKIN TO FEAR FLASHED ACROSS Maddie's face.

When she didn't answer, I pressed harder. "She's not going to give up. If she wants you in her pack, she'll keep pressing. So what's your plan? What answer do you intend to give her?"

"I... I don't know," Maddie stammered. "This whole thing is insane. I just want to be happy, you know? I've never had that before. I've been abused, starved, forgotten, ignored, you name it. But never content. I've never been with people who love and accept me. When I found Olivia, I thought this was my chance." She met my stare head on. "But I shouldn't have to kill anyone to get that."

My heart broke for her. "No, you shouldn't."

"And whoever I choose to be family with, I'd really prefer they aren't someone who's hellbent on murdering people."

A good choice.

"Then going back to my question, what's your plan? Do you want to side with me?"

"Do I have to choose a side?" she asked.

As much as I wanted to insist that *yes*, she absolutely had to choose a side, I suspected that wasn't the answer Maddie wanted to hear. She was an innocent in all this. Someone caught between two warring sisters. And it wasn't fair to push her to choose one of us. No matter how badly I wanted to.

"No," I finally said. "I won't force you to join me in the fight against her. I get that you're conflicted. Olivia is your sister. She's mine too. But there's too much bad blood between us for me to ever consider forgiving her. If I may suggest keeping your distance from her, though, that might be wise. Things are going to get worse before they get better. And I really don't want you anywhere near this when it implodes."

Maddie gave me a small but relieved smile. "I can do that. It might piss Olivia off, but I'll tell her I want no part in this, then I'll keep my distance."

"Thank you," I said, relieved. "Besides, you'll be too busy staking all those naughty vampires to get involved, right?"

"There really are so many that need a good staking," she teased. "What can I say, I like stabbing things."

Not words someone wanted to hear from their little sister, but so long as it kept her away from Olivia, I was happy. Funny how I found slaying vampires to be less dangerous than pack politics.

"Then go forth and stabby-stabby," I said.

Maddie burst out laughing. "I knew you'd be the cool older sister."

I groaned. "For crying out loud, how old do you think I am?"

She shrugged. "Dunno. But you're having a baby. So, old enough?"

"Gee, thanks."

"I'm twenty-two, in case you were curious." When I didn't immediately respond with my age, a small smile curled her lips. "And you're...?"

"Never mind," I grumbled. She didn't need to know I was quickly closing in on my thirties.

Her sly smile bloomed into a full grin. "Would you consider letting me join your pack?"

Sam tensed next to me. He'd been so quiet

throughout this, which I appreciated. But his body language spoke volumes.

I considered her question.

Truth be told, I considered *all* of her. Her story, her quirky personality that reminded me so much of Anna at that age, her hopes and dreams, and everything else I'd observed during our short conversation. As much as I wanted to welcome her with open arms and promise to forever be her big sister, I couldn't. At least, not right away. I had to be smart about this. I'd been down this road before with Olivia, and gotten burned.

"Let me be perfectly frank with you, Maddie."

"Please do."

"When I first met Olivia, she was a member of this pack. And she, too, fed me a heartwarming story about a mother who'd died from cancer, and a fiancé who had no idea what she was. But it'd all been a lie. She'd used her connection to me and Reggie to spy on the pack and learn how we operated. Then she betrayed us. Betrayed me. Because of her, Sam and my father nearly died. My mother *did* die. And we're missing three pack members. Two of them switched to her side. But we don't know anything about Scotia. We have no idea if she—"

"She's dead," Maddie whispered.

My gut plummeted. "She is?"

Sorrow darkened Maddie's eyes. "She didn't survive the change."

Well. Fuck. Just... *fuck*. I. gripped Sam's hand. This whole time we'd been hoping for *something*. Some sort of hint Scotia had survived. We'd known there was a possibility she hadn't, but we'd still held out hope.

"Damn," I whispered. "Thank you for telling us. At least her family will be able to move on."

Sam wrapped a comforting arm around my shoulders, my silent sentinel.

"Scotia..." Maddie bit her lip. It was the first nervous tic I'd witnessed from her. "Scotia didn't choose to become a werewolf. But Laini and Lincoln did."

My heart broke just a little more. "You see why I need to be cautious, right? Look at all the damage Olivia has wrought. I want to trust you. But I'm also the alpha of this pack. And I need to approach the situation from every angle. Olivia used her familial connection to infiltrate us. How do I know you're not doing the same thing? How do I know Olivia didn't send you?" My hand fell to my stomach. "And how do I know you aren't planning to feed her sensitive information about us?"

Maddie's face blanched and horror settled over her features. "You think I'm here to betray you?"

"I have to consider the possibility. What am I supposed to think, Maddie? You show up out of nowhere. You've admitted to me you have a connection to Olivia. That she turned you, for goodness' sake. That you're desperate for a family. So desperate to betray us to win Olivia's favor?" I lifted my hands in the air. "What else am I supposed to think?"

Her head bobbed as she listened, but I saw tears shimmering in her eyes, saw the quiver in her bottom lip. The scent of her anguish swept through the room. But her pulse didn't increase, nor did her eyes shift from side to side. She didn't look nervous. She appeared... sad.

Truthfully, I was inclined to believe her story. Either that, or she was a really good actress.

"Okay," she whispered, her voice weak. "I can see why you'd suspect those things, given your history with Olivia. But I'm not ready to give up on you. And I don't want you to give up on me."

Cripes, that was like a kick to the gut. This poor girl truly was desperate for someone to love her. Someone to accept her as she was. Eventually, the truth would out itself. It always did. Secrets were insidious little things that refused to remain hidden for long. But in the meantime, allowing Maddie to join my pack would put everyone at risk. Including my unborn child. That was not a risk I was willing to take.

"Look, we don't know each other," Maddie said. "I could very easily walk out that door and we both forget the other exists. Now that I've met you, I don't want to do that. I feel a connection between us—and maybe that sounds creepy—but I want to be upfront with you. I don't want to lose whatever this could be. I want a chance to have a sister."

God, I wanted nothing more than to wrap my arms around her and promise her she had a home with us. But I couldn't do that. I *couldn't.* At least, not yet.

"*You* were what I was looking for when I sought out Olivia," Maddie continued. "Someone to bond with. Someone to go shopping with, do our nails, gossip about boys..."

Things Anna and I had done. Something Maddie had never had.

"Maddie, just because I can't let you join my pack yet doesn't mean I'm turning you away."

Maddie frowned. "I don't understand."

"I can't in good conscience let you join my pack.

Not when there's sensitive information being passed out. I have quite a few lives to worry about and protect. Some are human. They have no stake in this fight. But I must protect them regardless. And I refuse to put you in the middle of me and Olivia. If she found out you'd joined my pack, she'd kill you. I'm already number one on her hit list. Let's not give her a number two."

Unspoken emotions filled Maddie's eyes as I spoke. I could sense her growing desperation, so I held up a hand. "But I very much would like to get to know you as my sister. And perhaps, one day, when the dust has settled, you can join my pack if you want. I wouldn't force that on you either."

"But you want to get to know me?" she asked, her voice brightening.

"Of course. We're blood, after all."

"Half-blood," she teased.

"Good enough for me."

"Me too," she murmured. "I really would like to get to know you. And Sam. You seem... I want to say nice, but that would be a lie."

I tucked closer to Sam's side and laughed. "He *is* nice. He's perfect, in fact. But it's been a very long day for the both of us." I shot the clock a glance and winced at the late hour. At this rate, the vampires would return home before we made it to bed.

"Hell, it's been a long couple of months," Sam said, breaking his silence.

"A long couple of years," I added.

"It's been that bad?" she asked. "With Olivia?"

"Corbin first, then Olivia—though we recently learned she'd been behind it all for a while now." I glanced up at Sam and smiled. "But Sam and I have our past too, and we've had a few rough spots."

His smile warmed my heart as he leaned down and kissed the tip of my nose. "Worth it, if you ask me," he said. "I'm going to give you two some space to finish your chat. I'll be nearby if you need me."

He kissed me again, then strode into the kitchen and out onto the back deck. The soft click of the sliding door surprised me. Guess he'd decided Maddie was trustworthy.

"I'd like to hear all about you two," she said. "How you met, how you figured out you were mates. Everything."

"Just like I'd like to hear all about your vampire slaying life."

She shrugged. "Not much to tell. Like I said, I only hunt vampires who have bounties on their heads."

"And who places their bounties?"

"The police," she said. "It's a fairly new system. They needed a way to handle criminal vampires. They couldn't exactly lock them away in a standard prison, and the vamp sheriffs are a bit useless."

My thoughts strayed to the one I'd met in New Orleans. For a vamp sheriff, I'd found him utterly useless. When a crazed ancient vampire abducted Anna, the sheriff had *petitioned* the queen for permission to stake the bastard. And when she'd rejected that petition, he'd claimed his hands were tied. So, Sam and I had taken matters into our own hands and rescued Anna. A werewolf and a human.

"And the vamps know about this new system?"

"I assume. The new king met with the president about half a year ago. They probably hashed this out together."

"Is that why you wear colored contacts?" I asked, referring to the set of blues she'd been wearing earlier.

"Yeah, just a little security. If someone comes after me, they can say they're looking for a woman with blue eyes when I have green. Sometimes I wear a wig too. Other times, I shift. Keeps them on their toes."

Clever. "So you only wear those things when hunting?"

She nodded.

"Then why were you wearing them tonight?"

Her mouth quirked. "My seventh kill was tonight, right before I came here."

"I have to admit, you're impressive," I said. "When I was twenty-two, Anna and I had no idea what we were doing with our lives."

"Yeah, well, you grow up fast in the foster system. Or you don't grow up at all."

I winced.

"How did you and Anna end up here?" Maddie asked. "You, an alpha werewolf with a mate and a baby on the way, and her, a vampire married to Dracula."

"Anna had always wanted to make it big as a journalist. And one day, we caught wind of a story we thought would make us rich. Instead, it'd killed her. And me too, technically. If not for her exposé on vampires and illegal blood slavery, neither of us would be where we are today. I tried to dissuade Anna. Told her a vampire club was not the place for us to be. But she refused to listen." I caught Maddie's eye. "Anna *never* listens. Best to know that going forward."

"It paid off in the end," Maddie said. "Don't you think? You and Anna are a pretty big deal, from what I've gathered. She's like a vampire princess or something, famous on social media, disgustingly rich. And you're her social media manager with an impressive salary yourself."

"Wow, you really did research us."

Maddie's cheeks flamed. "Can you blame me?"

No, considering I would have done the same. Twenty bucks said the instant she'd learned about me, she'd googled me. While there wouldn't be anything on the web about me being a werewolf, there were dozens of photos, if not more, of me with Anna. The paparazzi loved tailing her, even though she never showed up in their photos. Unfortunately, I did. Which meant the gossip sites tended to have me up there alongside my invisible friend. Lucky me.

What she said resonated with me. She'd researched us as best she could. She'd done the work, even if it'd been hard and painful. I could do no less.

"I know I said I wouldn't put you in the middle...." Damn it. I was going to hell for this. "But do you know Olivia's current location? We've been looking for her without any luck. I'm sorry to ask this, but..." I lifted my hands.

"But you have an entire pack depending on you."

I nodded. "The sooner we find her, the sooner..."

My words ended on a strangle when I caught the flash of shock on Maddie's face. "The sooner you can kill her?"

Ah, damn. "I'm sorry. Forget I asked. That wasn't fair of me. I said I wouldn't put you in the middle, and I truly meant it."

Maddie sucked her bottom lip between her teeth. I couldn't tell what was going on in that head of hers, but I had to imagine it wasn't good.

"Seriously, forget I asked." I bowed my head, hiding my reddening cheeks. "I shouldn't have."

"It's okay," she said.

No, it wasn't.

"I don't know her current location. When we last met, it was at a coffee shop. But I can find out for you."

My head snapped up. "What?"

Maddie leaned forward, a serious dent in her brows. "Listen. I appreciate you saying you wouldn't force me to pick a side. But we both know that isn't realistic. I don't see this going any other way. Olivia is going to lose her shit when she finds out we've met. And being that I'm not a homicidal lunatic—well, not entirely—I know whose side I'm going to choose."

"Maddie, no. We'll find some other way without pulling you into this."

A grim smile tugged at her lips. "Let me look into it." She glanced at the clock, then pushed to her feet. "It's getting late, and I still have a long night of paperwork ahead of me. Let's exchange numbers so I can call you in a day or two."

"And if you decide not to, that's okay too. I'll understand."

She gave me a grateful smile, one that softened her face until she looked younger than her twenty-two years. "Thank you, Lucy."

"For what?"

"For just being here. For understanding." She tucked her stake into the back of her pants, then strode toward me. Before I could utter a word, she snatched me into a hug. I hadn't noticed until then that she was taller than me. The older, *shorter* sister, apparently. What else was new? It sucked always being the shortest one, but I'd adjusted to that a long time ago.

"We'll see each other again soon?" she asked as she strolled toward the door.

I followed and opened the door for her, letting in the cool night air. "Absolutely. Don't be a stranger."

"Wouldn't dream of it."

"Glad to hear it."

She stepped across the threshold, then bolted down the sidewalk and to her car without a second glance back.

I closed the door with a soft click and leaned against it. Somehow, in the past two days, my family had grown by an equal number of people. And I honestly had no idea how to handle either of them. The only thing I knew for sure was I needed some sleep.

I'd already stripped off half my clothes by the time I entered our bedroom. I tossed them in the hamper, then crawled under our plush comforter. Every muscle in my body sighed with relief as I sank into the mattress. Sweet, sweet bliss.

I just prayed I'd find a way to sleep tonight. Though I'd managed some sleep after Sam's and my sexual escapades last night, I still felt like I hadn't gotten enough rest. Add in today's myriad of events, and I was bagged.

My head had just touched my pillow when Sam entered the room. I rolled onto my side and watched as he stripped off his own clothes. Moonlight poured through our windows, illuminating all his delicious planes in pale light. The man was a walking work of art, and I took great pleasure in enjoying the view.

Sam caught me staring and chuckled, the quiet sound rousing my own responding smile.

"How'd the conversation go with Adrien?" I asked. I hadn't had a chance to ask earlier.

"About as well as could be expected. He doesn't know much about wolf-born and human-born genetics either, but he thinks there's reason enough to worry."

Yay, more things to worry about. Olivia certainly enjoyed making life difficult.

Plumping the pillow under my head, I ogled Sam's delightfully defined abs as he stalked toward the bed.

"Let's keep this info to ourselves for now," I suggested. "It might not matter. No point upsetting everyone just yet."

"Exactly." He climbed into bed next to me, his arms like heat-seeking missiles as he pulled me into him. "We have enough to worry about without borrowing more problems."

I snuggled deep against Sam, my ass brushing against his groin. His breath caught in my ear, and I grinned.

"What a wicked little wolf you are," he murmured, his rumbly tone warming my blood.

I contemplated using my ass to tease him further,

but another yawn came over me, reminding me that I needed sleep.

"What about you? How'd the rest of your talk with Maddie go?"

"Interesting," I said. "I couldn't sense any lies from her. How about you?"

"I didn't pick up on anything. But she could just be an exceptional liar. Olivia fooled us all too."

I gave a somber nod.

"Do you trust her?" I asked.

"Not at all," Sam replied. "But maybe she'll prove me wrong. I hope she does."

"Me, too," I whispered. "I truly believe she just wants a family. And I would love to be that for her. But I can't welcome another estranged sister into the pack without at least first running it by them first. And that isn't going to happen until we put this entire Olivia matter to rest. My first priority has to be our protection. Yours, mine, our baby's, and the pack's. While Maddie seems like a wonderful person, I thought the same of Olivia at first too."

"I get it," Sam said, his lips brushing the back of my neck. "You're nervous about getting burned again. Which is completely understandable."

"But does it make me a bad person?"

"You don't have a bad bone in your body, love."

"Oh yeah?" I wiggled my ass again, giggling when he groaned, his dick firming up against me.

"Hey now, play fair."

I didn't wanna play fair, but I also wasn't sure I had the energy to stoke this ember into a raging inferno.

Sam tucked his head behind mine and ran his mouth along my bare shoulders. "You're one of the sweetest, kindest people I've ever met. Maddie has to see that too. I bet she understands your misgivings."

"I told her we could still be sisters." His lips brushed the base of my neck, and I shivered. "And that she could join the pack after we handled Olivia. She seemed happy with that answer. I gave her my number and told her to stay in contact. Her life until now sounded pretty miserable."

Sam's breath pebbled my skin. "I don't know much about foster care, but the things I do know aren't encouraging."

Yeah, that was my impression of it too. It killed me that she'd had to grow up like that.

"Did you know about these vampire slayers?" I asked.

Sam shook his head, the tips of his hair tickling my flesh. "This was my first time hearing about them, but it makes sense. The entire vampire system needed an overhaul. The queen was living in the Middle Ages. Gabriel seems far more modern and intelligent."

"I think so," I said, recalling the man I'd only met once, and briefly, after Corbin had changed me.

"It worries me she's out there hunting these monsters—and I don't mean all vampires are monsters, obviously. But if they have a bounty on their head, there must be a reason."

Sam's arms tightened around me. "She said she'd been trained. Hopefully that means by capable people."

"Maybe we should ask Vlad and Anna to spar with her. Make sure she's up to snuff. Vlad is over five hundred, and Anna trained me to fight, so it could help her."

"It could," Sam agreed. "She's bagged seven vampires already. So I don't think you need to worry about her." He brushed another kiss, this time against the side of my throat. "But I love that you are. Shows that she means something to you already."

I pondered his words and realized he was right. I'd already connected with Maddie, and on a much deeper level than I had with Olivia too—before she'd betrayed me, of course. I had to wonder if that meant something. If, deep down, I believed Maddie was trustworthy.

"These are all thoughts for tomorrow," Sam said. "We should sleep."

"We should," I agreed, then wriggled my ass once more. "But we don't have to, not yet anyway."

A light knock came on the wall adjacent to us seconds before my mother's shrill voice carried into our room. "Need I remind you two that I'm home?"

I pressed my lips together to keep from laughing. Right. I actually *had* forgotten about my mother's presence. She'd been so quiet since returning to her room. And to think, I'd almost hopped on Sam's dick with her only twenty feet away. Talk about awkward.

"Sorry, Mom," I called back.

I caught wind of her exasperated sigh, and I burst out laughing. Good to know I could still scandalize my mother after all these years.

THE NEXT MORNING, I SAT ON THE EDGE OF THE tub and turned on the taps. Warm water came rushing out, and I watched as it started slowly rising. I grabbed the thermometer Anna had left on the counter for me—a late night drug store purchase care of the Draculas last night—and stuck it under the faucet. It felt a little silly and was likely a bit more paranoid than I was willing to admit, but I had no idea what normal consisted of for pregnant women. So I was winging it. And what did it hurt to use the thermometer friends had gone out of their way to acquire for me.

After a few seconds, it beeped and flashed ninety-six at me. The websites recommended not exceeding a hundred. Sounded like a good temperature to me.

Stripping out of my robe, I sank into the almost hot water and tipped my head back against the headrest. A bath had been the only thing on my mind this morning after I'd woken. I wanted nothing more than to close my eyes and relax in the warm water.

After, I had to get to work. I'd told Cole, Paul, and Dominic that I'd look into Reggie's documents, and I wanted to have some information for them when they came to the meeting tonight. Perhaps I should have saved the bath for *after* I finished sleuthing in a dusty garage, but oh well. Sometimes, a girl needed to pamper herself *first*.

Unfortunately, it didn't take long for the water to grow cool. I quickly washed up, then climbed out. After toweling myself off and blow-drying my hair, I returned to the bedroom to find Sam still tucked in as snug as a bug in a rug, his head cushioned against *my* pillow, and his body cocooned in our comforter. For a moment, I debated crawling back in with him, but that would rob me of a few precious hours of research.

Procrastination was a dear friend of mine, and I recognized its ugly face whenever it came knocking.

Finding Olivia had always been a priority, but now we had a deadline. Which meant I needed to start combing through Reggie's old things.

I quietly dressed myself, then snuck out. I'd never been a huge fan of breakfast, and even now, my stomach didn't seem interested in food, so I slipped on a pair of old, faded Crocs and strode into the garage.

Once upon a time, this place had housed a vehicle. But after cleaning out all of Reggie's things, we'd needed somewhere to store them. The garage had seemed the smartest bet. So we'd evicted the car, and started stacking boxes upon boxes.

I didn't even know where to begin. Mountains of various-sized boxes stood before me. When I'd first suggested this, the idea had seemed logical. Now it seemed insurmountable. Like climbing Mount Everest.

Sighing, I stomped down two wooden stairs and across the concrete floor. I came to a stop in front of the first pile of boxes. It towered above me. Of course, most things did. So, I grabbed the nearby step ladder and got to work, shuffling things around. I ended up with four boxes labeled "Office Things." If memory served me right, I'd also labeled a few with things like "Personal Information" and "Family

Records." Those were definitely on my radar. Only challenge was locating them somewhere in this hoard. Had I been smart, I would have set them aside from the rest of the clutter. But, at the time, my only thought had been clearing out Reggie's things.

One by one, I carried the office boxes into the living room and deposited them next to the couch. Then I trudged back into the garage and resumed my search for the rest. By the time I'd located the family records, my skin was slick with sweat and my back ached.

"Need some help?"

Sam's teasing tone startled me, and with a gasp, I whirled around, my hand clutched to my chest. "God, Sam! Make some noise when you sneak up on me."

A smile brightened his face. He leaned against the doorframe, his ankles and arms crossed. "Now, where would the fun be in that?"

I waved a hand at him, then turned and pointed up to the tallest tower of boxes. "Can you reach that one at the top?" In retrospect, this was so very dangerous. Why on earth had we stacked them like this? Sure, they had a wall to lean against, and someone had roped a few of them to keep them from falling, but it didn't seem like a very safe system.

I glanced over my shoulder in time to watch Sam push off the doorframe. His tousled hair told me he'd only just woken up, but I didn't mind one bit. Rumpled hair was my favorite look on him, especially if he was naked.

Heat flushed through me, and I blinked, startled by my body's reaction.

Sam chuckled, likely aware of what was going on with me. "Don't worry, I think you look pretty damn cute right now too."

"Huh?" Oh, very eloquent, Luce.

He reached up and swiped my nose, then showed me his fingers. Dust covered his skin.

I held my hands out and grimaced at all the dust coating me. Yikes. Guess I would be taking a shower after all this.

"You look like a lost research student," he said, lowering his head to nuzzle my throat. "Especially with your hair tied up like this. Did you do that purposely?"

My dusty hands flew to the nape of my neck. I hadn't even realized I'd twisted it up into a bun, but it made sense. My hair fell to the small of my back, and it was *always* in my way. More often than not, I had it tied up in some fashion to keep it out of my face.

"Now we just need to find you some thick-rimmed glasses."

"Oh, Sam," I said, laughing.

After stealing an impassioned kiss, Sam reached for the top box and removed it without any sign of strain. Ah, so he'd been the one to stack them then. The towering height didn't seem quite as dangerous to him as it did to me.

"Want this in the living room with the others?"

"Please." I turned away and started searching the rest of the boxes.

For every three I moved, I found one that seemed relevant. And by the time I was done, I had nine boxes sitting in the living room. This task seemed more daunting than ever, considering we'd filled every box to the brim.

Hands on my hips, I surveyed the mess, my lips twisted. "This is gonna take a while."

"Definitely. How about I order in a pizza?"

A quick glance at the clock told me it was well past lunch, and my stomach was finally showing signs of life. "Yeah, that sounds great."

I honestly couldn't see us combing through all nine boxes before the meeting tonight. Nor did I love the idea of piling them back into the garage to make space for my pack members. But no point in backing out of this now. The sooner we started, the sooner we'd finish.

I sat cross-legged in front of the first box labeled "Personal Information" and popped the seal. Sam ordered pizza, then sat next to me and grabbed a matching box.

"You doing okay?" he asked.

I waffled on my answer. Reggie was a sore spot for me, considering the bastard had literally knocked up my mom, then abandoned her after she'd given birth to me when he'd realized I was human-born. What a piece of work, huh? I hadn't learned about any of this until a few years ago. It hadn't changed anything for me. My dad was the man who'd spent his life raising me, not this piece of shit.

I'd spent a year with Reggie after Corbin changed me, only to realize that he and I were too similar to ever get along. Our conversations had mostly revolved around us insulting each other. And him forcing me to be his heir. Which was how I'd ended up here.

We hadn't liked each other. Surprise, surprise. But it still pained me to go through his things like this. To learn more about his life and who he was. I hated that it bothered me, but there was a part of me, that lingering bit of a little girl desperate to meet her "real daddy." My brain made no sense, even to me.

"Let's just get this done," I said.

Two hours, and a belly full of delicious pizza, later, we hadn't found much. But we'd also only sorted through two boxes. Since we hadn't gone through anything before packing it up, we were coming across stacks of receipts and other financial documents that were older than me. Reggie had been a bit of a compulsive hoarder, it seemed, especially when it came to his financial records.

"What exactly are you looking for?" Sam asked when he reached for the next box.

Truth be told, I wasn't entirely sure. It was one of those things where I'd know it when I found it. But that didn't help Sam any. I couldn't expect him to keep going through all this crap without some direction.

"I guess... anything that might be pertinent to Olivia? Or me? Or Maddie even? Any sort of personal family details. Ideally, we'd find a family tree. Wouldn't that be nice? To see how many women he'd knocked up before jumping ship. To learn how many siblings I have out there."

"That's a tall order," Sam commented. "He seemed almost compulsive about saving his receipts and ledgers, but I haven't found the first mention of family."

Unsurprising, considering the man's history.

I plunged my hand into the bottom of my current box, then paused when my fingers hit something hard and solid, which was far different from all the papers we'd piled up. I grasped whatever it was and pulled it out, my mouth parting at the sight of what looked like a dusty leather journal.

"Sam," I murmured, turning the book over in my hand.

It looked worn and well-loved. And when I lifted the cover, the book fell open as though it wanted to be read. Reggie had certainly made good use of this journal. The only question was, for what purpose? Knowing him, it was likely just another log of financial transactions.

I flipped through a few pages, then stopped when my fingers grazed a torn edge. My eyes started scouring the page. "Oh wow, it's his personal journal."

Sam scooted closer and peered at the book.

We fell into silence as we read, and after a few pages, I shook my head, scoffing, "The man was so determined to produce a legacy. He was obsessed."

Sam grunted, then pointed at the margins of the most recent page. "What do you think these mean?"

I studied the markings Sam had brought our attention to. Down the entire margin, each line had two letters. JA, SV, DR, BW, and so on. Next to some were checkmarks, and more *X*'s. Next to the ones with checkmarks were dates. And beside those dates was another column of *X*'s. All the way down.

It wasn't until I saw a familiar date that my breath caught. "That's my birthday."

"Hmm?"

I pressed my fingers to the date, then dragged them back to the initials BW. Just like that, it clicked. "Holy hell. Sam, this is his list."

"Of?"

"Of all the women he slept with. Look at the initials. BW, as in Barbara Williams. My mom. The checkmark next to her name must mean he slept with her? Or, no. Why would he log initials for women he didn't sleep with...?" I considered his little chart, then nodded. "The dates. That's my date of birth. And only those with a checkmark have dates. So the first column must be for whether she got pregnant. If yes, a check. If no, an X. Then the next column is his child's date of birth. And the last column, all those *X*'s? I'd bet you anything that references the fact that we were human-born. Not a single checkmark in that column."

I skimmed the page, my finger trailing all the different initials. "My god. The man was fanatical about this. Look at all the women he impregnated. Some must have overlapped based on the children's dates of birth."

Disgusted, I pushed the book off my lap and stood, stretching out my sore limbs.

This just confirmed it. Reggie was a sick asshole. One might even think he was addicted to knocking up women. He had his "reasons," but that didn't justify his actions.

"Eleven," Sam said.

So lost in my thoughts, I almost didn't hear him at first. I had to repeat what he said. "Eleven?"

"Eleven children."

Wait. What? Did he just say eleven *children*? I whirled around and faced Sam. I had to pick my jaw up before I could speak again. "He had *eleven* children? Is that including me?"

Sam nodded.

Holy crap. So, I had ten half-siblings out there, including Maddie and Olivia. I'd gone from being an only child to suddenly becoming a member of the Partridge Family.

"Are there any names?" Had Reggie even cared to log that information? Or were we little more than X's next to a series of dates.

"None that I can see," Sam said. He lifted his head and met my gaze, his face soft with sympathy. "Maybe he kept your names out purposely? To protect you? He didn't name the mothers either."

That didn't help anyone. I still wanted to reach into his grave and throttle him by his bony neck. What the hell was wrong with him? And why was I so mad? He was dead. It wasn't like he was still out there, impregnating women left, right, and center. It wasn't like I could slap him around, no matter how badly I wanted to. Yet seeing his disgusting little ledger enraged me. That he cared so little to even jot down our names told me everything I'd needed to know about him.

Sam stood and pulled me into his arms, running his hands up and down my back. "Just remember, that man wasn't your father. You have a wonderful dad."

I nodded.

"And a wonderful future father-in-law too."

Okay, that made me smile. Adrien was amazing. I had no problem admitting that.

"I just can't believe I came from him," I said.

222

"Sperm means nothing. Reggie didn't raise you. So you're nothing like him."

Except there were a few similarities between me and Reggie. I remembered comparing us when we'd first met, noting how we were both stubborn as a mule and quick to anger. Sperm didn't mean nothing exactly because it carried the genetic components that made us who we were. But Sam was right. My *real* dad meant more to me than Reggie ever had.

Or ever would.

14

WHEN ONLY A COUPLE OF HOURS REMAINED before tonight's pack meeting, Sam and I decided to call it quits. We were both tired of scouring financial records, and my back ached from all the bending over. We'd each cleared one more box, but five remained. The thought of going through them exhausted me, but it had to be done.

Anna had offered to help when she'd woken for the day, but I'd seen her eyes glaze over when she reached for the first box, and I'd told her it wasn't necessary. She'd stuck around long enough for me to fill her in about Maddie, then she'd ventured off on her own to post on her social media accounts. An equally important task, considering all our household income hinged on her success.

So far, the only things besides the journal that Sam and I found in the boxes were a few random photos. I'd recognized Reggie in a few, but other than that, nothing. I had to imagine they were my paternal family—cousins, aunts, uncles, grandparents. But since I'd never met any of them, nor had any desire to do so, I merely tucked the pictures back into the box.

Flustered, I ran my hands through my hair, then reached for one of the sealed boxes. We needed to move them out of the way to make space for tonight's meeting. Dismayed by our failure to find anything remotely important, I might have lifted one box too quickly and without proper support. The tape split open, and all the box's contents came spilling out at my feet.

"Ah, crap!" I shouted, peering down at the mess.

Sam glanced over, his face pinched. "Oof. That's quite a mess."

I threw the box aside and dropped my arms, my hands slapping my thighs. "Help me clean this up, please?"

Sam quickly shoved all the boxes to the side of the room, then came to help me. He grabbed the box and turned it over, inspecting the damage. "We can still use it. We'll just need to tape it up really well. Keep it from splitting again."

"Okay. Why don't you grab the tape, and I'll start making piles."

Sam jogged into the kitchen, and I sat with a huff. I didn't bother reading the documents. We didn't have time to sort through it all. Instead, I just grabbed whatever I could and started stacking, readying it to be placed back in the box.

When Sam returned with the packing tape in hand, I'd built four small stacks. Only a few things remained at my feet. I'd just begun scooping the rest up when my fingers brushed against something rigid. I paused, then cleared away a bunch of loose-leaf papers to find yet another journal.

"Oh, for crying out loud," I muttered. "I swear, this man had a *problem*."

I could only imagine what this journal held. More names? More children? Would my ten siblings become fifteen? Or, god forbid, twenty? Just how many people was I related to out there? This felt like the world's worst joke.

"We have a little time left," Sam said. "Let's see what it is."

I groaned, but lifted the journal and flipped open the cover. Inside was a photo of... me as a baby... in

Reggie's arms. A very young Reggie with a Backstreet Boys wannabe hairstyle, leather jacket, and ripped jeans.

"What the hell," I breathed. "What is this?" I mean, I knew what it was. A picture told a thousand words. But I'd *never* seen this photo before.

"How old are you in that picture?" Sam asked. "A couple months?"

I barely nodded, still startled into silence. It wasn't just the photo itself that stunned me, but the look on Reggie's face. The way he held me. As though he cherished me. Anyone who hadn't known him might have thought he'd actually loved me based on this photo.

That didn't even remotely line up with what I knew about the man.

Yet, there he was. Smiling down at me. His arms wrapped around me so protectively.

With a trembling hand, I removed the photo from the front of the journal and turned it over. He'd only written my name and birthdate on it. I returned the photo, then glanced at the cover page.

Lucy Adaline Williams.

Was this journal... about me?

I flipped the page and started reading. By the third paragraph, I was near tears. Reggie had documented everything. How he'd met and fallen for my mother; how excited he'd been when he learned she was pregnant; how she was different from the other women he'd been seeing; how she made him feel something other than duty.

Then the passages switched from focusing on my mother to me. I scoured the pages, word for word, drinking it in as though I couldn't stop. The entries talked nonstop about how much he loved me, even before I was born. Once I was born, the love he showed for me in his writing only grew. To the point where I almost didn't believe his own words.

But then the tone changed. The love devolved into depression, desperation, and so much sadness, it made my chest tight. He'd stayed for six months. That was it. Just long enough for him to realize I'd been born wholly human. His earlier passages suspected, but when he finally came to the conclusion that I would never shift, his tone grew so dark. He wrote of how it was his duty to produce a werewolf child. How that child would inherit his pack. How he needed to build a legacy.

Then came the next passage. Compared to the others, it was short and simple, but enraging. He announced that he'd packed his stuff and left. Just abandoned me and my mother without looking back.

Rage broiled under my skin.

How could a man who claimed to have loved us just take off like that? I'd read his words, felt his emotions and feelings. He'd loved my mother. Then discarded her as though she were nothing because their daughter had been born human.

I ground my teeth and focused on my breathing.

I hated him.

I'd hated him before. But this made me hate him all the more. To see what he'd done to my mother. What he'd put both of us through. Based on the dates, my mother met my father soon afterward. And the rest, as they say, was history. My mother *loved* my father. Of that, I had no doubt. She'd been deliriously happy with him. So I knew I shouldn't hate Reggie too much. His leaving had opened my mother up to finding her one true love.

But it changed nothing for me.

"Are you okay?" Sam asked.

I leaned back against his chest and sighed. "No. I'm not."

His arms closed around me, and he slowly rocked me. "I'm sorry you had to see that."

"I'm not. It wasn't anything I didn't already know. The man was a dick." I shoved the book off my lap, then sat up, slowly pulling away from Sam.

"What scares me the most is how someone can claim to love someone and just leave like that. Just abandon their child and the woman they love."

"Hey." Sam's fingers touched my hand. He pulled me back toward him, then turned my head until our gazes met. "Nothing in this world could take me from you. You know that right? I would never leave you. Or our baby."

The tears I'd been fighting squeaked out. "My mother probably thought the same thing."

Sam's eyes fluttered shut, and his jaw tensed.

I knew better than to compare him to Reggie. They were nothing alike. But it was hard *not* to wonder about these things. Reality was a bitch. Families broke up. People left. I knew that. Nothing was guaranteed.

"Ignore me," I murmured, leaning in to press a kiss against his stubbled cheek. "It's just hard to see these things he wrote, all while knowing he broke my mother's heart. And mine."

Sam dragged me into another hug. "I swear to you, Lucy, this will never be our fate."

I nodded into his shoulder. "You'd never leave."

"I would *never* leave," he vowed. "I can't even begin to explain how much I love you. And if our child is born human, I'll love them the same.

Because none of that matters to me. Our baby is what matters to me, regardless of who they turn out to be."

A small smile tugged at my lips.

When we pulled apart, I glanced down at the journal. The passage about him leaving had been in the middle of the book. So curiosity had me opening it and flipping to the back.

My eyes widened as I took it all in. "He kept track of me."

"What?"

I practically shoved the book into Sam's face. "Look at this! He kept track of me." I lowered the book and skimmed it, my index finger pressed to the aged pages. "What schools I went to, neighborhoods I grew up in, when I graduated, my GPA, my SAT scores... He even has Anna in here, listed as a vampire and who she married. Sweet lord, he has her net worth jotted down, and *mine* too. He must have written this in right before he died. How on earth did he get this information?"

"From me..." came a quiet voice.

My head snapped up to find my mother standing nearby. I'd been so engrossed I hadn't heard her approach. Hadn't even known she and Vlad were awake.

"From you?" I repeated. "You gave him this information?"

She nodded, guilt darkening her features. "Your father—"

"Reggie," I corrected with a growl.

"Right. Sorry. Reggie *did* love you. When we first met, the man was open and honest with me. He flat out told me he was a werewolf. I didn't believe him until he shifted right in front of me. He also told me that any children he had needed to be werewolves too. I didn't think anything of it. I didn't understand what he was telling me. A few years after he left, he reached out and asked me to keep him informed about your life. I got scared. I thought he planned to come back into your life, which I absolutely would not allow. So when he told me he didn't want that, he just wanted to know about your life, I agreed. Every year, I sent him a manilla folder with whatever I kept on hand. Grades, clubs you were in, the friends you'd made, kid stuff."

"That's all about me though. What about the stuff in here about Anna?"

She shook her head. "I never gave him that."

"But that information is easily searchable," Sam offered.

My gaze bounced between him and my mother.

Neither looked too impressed by the book I held in my hands. "Why would he need to know her net worth?"

No one offered any suggestions. This man... I would never understand the things he did. Perpetual disappointment—that was the only thing my sperm donor offered me.

"Alright," I commented. "Well, if he kept this information on me, maybe he did the same for his other kids."

I flicked a glance at the clock and winced at the time. Seven-thirty. Meaning we only had thirty minutes before pack members started showing up in droves. But with everyone awake, there were five of us and only four boxes remained, thanks to me breaking this one.

"We have a half an hour," I said. "And four boxes. If we each take one, maybe we can quickly check to see if there are any more journals. Anna? Vlad?" I didn't need to call too loudly, thanks to their vampy hearing.

Both appeared in the living room.

"Care to help? It'll go faster if we all chip in." I waved Reggie's journal in the air. "We're looking for similar books. If they're like mine, they'll have a photo on the inside cover and a bunch of information about the child. From what Sam and I discovered, there should be ten more books like this."

"Ten," my mother whispered.

"How old was he when you two met?" I asked.

"Same age as me, or so he said. I was thirty-one."

If that was true, then it was possible I may not have been the first child. And I certainly hadn't been the last.

"Okay. Those four boxes there are the last ones to go through."

"Why don't you go shower?" Sam suggested. "Let us take care of this. You need to get cleaned up before the pack starts arriving."

I glanced down at myself and grimaced. The dust from the garage still clung to my clothes, and my hair had long since fallen out of its bun. I looked like a bedraggled mess, especially in my T-shirt and leggings. Pack meetings didn't require a dress code, but I tried to at least look the part of an alpha. Especially for tonight's meeting. I still wasn't sure how to handle everything. Not only were we announcing I was pregnant, but I also had to inform everyone that Scotia was dead—according to Maddie. The thought of breaking that news, then announcing ours, shredded my insides.

"Thanks," I said to Sam, brushing a light kiss

against his mouth before standing and stretching out my back.

"You okay?" my mom asked.

"Yeah, just a bit cramped."

She ran a comforting hand up and down my back before stepping away to grab one of the remaining boxes.

I headed for the bathroom, my thoughts still circling Reggie's journal. Had he been that meticulous with all his children? We could only hope. After all this, maybe he'd be the one to help us find Olivia.

15

I'D JUST STEPPED OUT OF THE SHOWER AND WAS rifling through my drawers for something to wear when Sam entered the bedroom. I glanced over my shoulder and gasped at the sight of his hands, stock full of leather journals.

"Are those them?"

"Every single one," Sam said. "All eleven children, including yours."

"My god," I whispered. I abandoned my search for clothes, clutched the towel tighter to my body, then approached Sam. "Did you find anything useful in them?"

Sam shook his head as he lowered the journals

onto the bed. "No. We all agreed you should be the one to go through them. Not us."

I wasn't sure how I felt about that. While I appreciated the thought they'd put into the decision, it would have been easier for them to go through these books than me. How would it feel to read about all these siblings I'd never met? Would I feel compelled to find them? My whole life I'd wanted a brother or sister, but Anna had always filled that role. Then to learn about Olivia, only for her to betray me —it'd cured me of the desire for more family.

Until Maddie.

Granted, I knew very little about her, but she reminded me *so much* of Anna at a younger age. Strong, willful, sarcastic. I could see myself as a big sister to her.

But what about the others? What if they were like Maddie? Abandoned to the system and forgotten. And if Reggie had followed all of us, then why the hell hadn't he taken Maddie in? Why would he let her suffer as she had? I just wanted to strangle his corpse—not that it would accomplish anything.

"Has anyone from the pack arrived yet?" I asked.

"Cole and Dominic are here. Darla just arrived too. She's setting up the refreshments."

So I had a little time then.

I eased down onto the edge of the mattress and stroked the nearest leather journal. After taking a deep breath, I flipped it open. Just like mine, there was a baby picture tucked into the front. Except, this time, Reggie wasn't in it. It was just the baby, wrapped in a blue blanket, with a little hat perched on his head.

"A brother," I murmured. "Kristopher Grey Harrison." I turned the first page and read his birthdate, my breath catching. "He didn't live more than a few hours."

Sam leaned close and studied the page.

"Is that normal?" I asked breathlessly.

"No less so than any other baby, I assume. Maybe he was sick."

I touched my fingers to the picture, a weight pressing down on my shoulders. I gently closed the journal and placed it aside. He might not have survived, but he'd still been my brother.

I reached for the next journal and startled when I spotted the name Madison Anne Smith. "This must be Maddie's."

Again, her baby photo didn't include Reggie, but it did include her mother, who stared down at Maddie with such affection in her eyes. Except,

Maddie had ended up in foster care, so her mother must have abandoned her as well.

Something didn't feel right about that assumption. How could someone who gazed upon her baby with such love leave her?

As much as I wanted to read her journal, I couldn't. Not right now anyway. I needed to find Olivia's and hopefully find something I could pass along to the pack.

"Help me find Olivia's," I said to Sam.

But Maddie's, I slid behind me. I wanted to go through it, but now that she was in my life, it seemed invasive to go through it without her—even though that was exactly what I intended to do with Olivia's.

I picked up a third and flipped it open. Just like the others, there was a baby photo taped to the inside cover and on the first page, Reggie had printed the name Westley David Black. Another brother. One that still lived. I set his journal aside and blew out a heavy breath. Each name echoed in my head. I had brothers out there. Family.

"Here it is," Sam said.

My heart leapt into my throat as I stared at the journal. It was just as worn as mine, the cover faded and creased. I took it from Sam with trembling hands and flipped it open. Again, another baby photo. But in this one, her mother and another man crowded around her, smiling so happily. No Reggie.

Was I the only one Reggie had taken an interest in?

"Sam, do me a favor and check the birth dates of all the other children."

"Okay. What am I looking for?"

"I want to know if I'm the oldest."

Returning my focus to the journal, I turned to the first page and started reading about Olivia's childhood. From what I could gather, the man in the photo was her stepfather. Much like me, her mother had found someone else. Except, according to Reggie's notes, Olivia had been conceived via an affair. One that Olivia's mother had never openly admitted to. So Olivia hadn't known that her father wasn't her biological father until later in life, just like me.

I turned to the next page, but there wasn't much left for Olivia. No notes about school grades or friends. No personal notes whatsoever about how much Reggie had loved her. Her journal was nothing like mine. It was so cold and calculated.

Frowning, I flipped to the back, and sure enough, just like mine, Reggie had kept a tally of her net worth. And her parent's.

"Check this out," I murmured to Sam. "Olivia's *parents* own some properties here in the city."

Sam sat beside me, the mattress dipping to conform to his weight. "Okay. So what does that mean?"

"Well, when we researched Olivia, did we look for any properties under her parents' names? Maybe she's using one of them, and we never noticed?"

"That's a possibility," Sam said. "We could get Paul to check these out."

"And maybe I could speak to Olivia's parents? See if they know what their precious daughter is up to."

Sam tensed next to me, claws suddenly sprouting from his fingers. They gouged the papers clutched in his hands, but thankfully, didn't shred them.

"No," he growled, his rumbly voice vibrating in his chest. "You aren't going anywhere near that family. What if they call Olivia and tell her you were there? Hell, what if Olivia is *there* when you show up? They're her parents, for crying out loud. They would never side with a stranger over their own child."

"Sam...."

"Lucy, no. Please. Let us look into these properties first. The thought of you going

244

anywhere near Olivia or her family right now, I can't—"

"Shh." I placed my hand on his thigh and gave a comforting squeeze.

He shook beneath my touch, his wolf clearly trying to take control.

"I'm her half-sister," I said. "Her mother knows she conceived Olivia by another man. She may even know about werewolves. I could ask questions, find out where Olivia is staying, maybe even—"

"It's *dangerous*," Sam snapped.

"I know. I wouldn't go alone."

"You aren't going at all," he announced.

My eyes widened. "Excuse me?"

"Lucy, you're pregnant—"

"I am well aware of that," I argued, "but that doesn't make me an invalid, Sam. I can take care of myself, remember? What are two humans compared to werewolves? I could handle them in my sleep."

"That kind of overconfidence can get you killed. If they know about werewolves, like you suggested, then they'll know what can hurt us. All it takes is one silver bullet and you're dead. Along with our baby."

I cringed away, his words hitting their mark.

Sam faced me, his expression shifting into horror as he realized what he'd just said. "I'm sorry," he said.

"I shouldn't have said that." He blew out a heavy breath. "It's my wolf. He won't stop pushing, and it's getting hard to control the bugger."

My mouth twisted, but I nodded.

Sam wrapped his arms around me and pulled me tight, his cheek resting against my head. "Just promise me you won't contact her parents," he begged. "Please? I'm not sure I could handle that right now. At least not yet. If we don't find anything at these properties, then we'll talk about it. Okay?"

"Okay," I agreed.

Sam gave me a squeeze, then released me and rose from the bed. As he strode out of the room, he turned and said, "Oh, you're the oldest of all the children, by the way."

My focus dropped to the journal cradled in my hands. So many siblings. But it was clear Reggie had put more care into my journal than the others. His firstborn. And possibly, the child of the only woman he'd ever loved. It didn't change my opinion of the man, but it made me wonder what my life would have looked like had he stuck around. I didn't regret his choice to leave, because my mother had met a wonderful man who I considered my true father. Nevertheless, it raised questions.

The sound of the doorbell pulled my attention

back to the matter at hand. Time to get dressed and face my pack.

I KNEW FROM PAST MEETINGS THAT MOST OF THE pack members carpooled, which meant the majority had already arrived by the time I'd finished dressing.

I headed to the living room, a smile tugging the corners of my lips as I listened to the sound of their animated chatter and laughter.

When I neared the corner of the hall, I paused and rested a hand against the wall. From here, I could see them all. My living room was practically bursting at the seams. People sat on the couches and chairs, leaned against walls, crowded into the attached dining area, and hovered in the kitchen. Seemed most of the inner circle had made an appearance tonight.

But that wasn't the sight that stole my breath.

Oh, no, no, no.

It was the sight of someone shoving little bites of something that resembled *chocolate* into their mouth. I knew it wasn't actual chocolate, but my stomach didn't care. It looked and smelled like chocolate and that was all I cared about.

I must have made a noise because Sam turned toward me and held out a hand, his other clutching a plate of those delectable-looking goodies. I immediately pushed off the wall and headed toward him, almost as eager to feel his skin against mine as I was to snarf every last snack in the room.

Without saying a word, he leaned in and pressed a kiss against the side of my throat.

"Glad to see the festivities are already underway," I said, my gaze snagging on the plate. Even Dominic held a small tray full of them.

Cole belted out a laugh, then turned to take in the room. "Yeah, people tend to go a little crazy for Darla's homemade brownies."

Brownies? Sweet lord, did he just say *brownies?* It'd been so long since I'd had anything remotely baked. Was I drooling? It certainly felt like it. I wiped my mouth, then asked, "But I thought we couldn't eat chocolate?"

"We can't," he said. "Darla didn't let that stop her though. These are her infamous carob brownies."

I had no idea what carob was, and I didn't care. I snatched one off Dominic's plate and tossed it into my mouth with absolutely no hesitation.

"Damn," Dominic whispered, his eyebrows shooting upward. "Did you even taste that?"

I swallowed and shook my head. "I haven't had chocolate in years..."

"You still haven't had chocolate," Cole said, laughing. "Carob isn't chocolate."

I shrugged. "Don't care."

"So I see."

"Would you like another?" Sam asked.

"Or a dozen?" Dominic teased.

"I'll definitely take a dozen. And a glass of milk, I think. Please."

All three men laughed, and embarrassment flooded my cheeks. The pack didn't know I was pregnant but to be perfectly honest, this had nothing to do with that and everything to do with how long I'd gone without anything remotely chocolate in my diet. I didn't care if they had to take white sugar and color it brown to resemble chocolate. I wanted it.

Sam ventured off to complete the quest given to him, and I gestured to Cole. "A moment?"

He nodded and excused himself from Dominic.

I led him into the last remaining spare bedroom in the house. I didn't want anyone to overhear us, and hopefully with all the chatter, I'd be able to keep this from getting out yet.

Cole leaned against the wall and crossed his arms. "What's up?"

"Last night, after the community center, Sam and I came home and found a visitor in the house."

He immediately pushed away from the wall, concern etched into his face. "Olivia?"

"No. But she was another sister of mine."

"Wait, what?"

Pitching my voice as low as I could so not to be overheard, I regaled Cole with everything that happened last night. When I reached the part about Scotia's death, he swiped a hand through his hair and cursed under his breath.

"Shit. I'd hoped..."

"I know, me too," I said. "So tonight, I have to break all this to the pack."

Cole turned and considered me, his eyes narrowed in concentration. "I think we should keep Maddie's name out of this, just for a little while. We can tell them we have a source, but we don't need to divulge who exactly she is. After Olivia, I'm not sure they'll be too welcoming of another sister."

"Agreed. I also told Maddie she couldn't join our pack. At least not yet, and she accepted that without any issue. So I don't think she's here to suss out information for Olivia."

"But can she give us anything? Help us find Olivia? She's in direct contact with her."

"I asked, and she said to give her a few days, but Cole, we may not need her to help us now."

He blinked, a severe frown darkening his features. "What do you mean?"

"We went through Reggie's boxes today, and I found a bunch of journals he'd written. Guess he kept one for each of his children. And in Olivia's, he has a list of properties owned by her parents."

I wanted for the understanding to sink in. It didn't take long at all. Hope brightened his face.

"We need to scout those addresses," he said.

"That's the plan. As for the rest, here's how tonight's gonna go down. I'm going to talk to Scotia's family—"

"Let me do that," Cole interrupted. "I've known them longer. I think this news might be better coming from me."

After considering his request, I nodded. "Okay. After you've told them the news, send them home. I don't want them here for the rest. They don't need to learn their child is dead the same night I tell the pack I'm pregnant."

Even Cole winced. "Yeah, that'd be rough."

"Once they've left, I'll address the pack and give an update. Then we can divide and conquer these addresses."

"I want to lead the scouting parties."

"Sounds good to me."

Excitement had me bouncing on the tips of my toes. Finally—*finally!*—after weeks of running in circles, we had a lead. There wasn't anything concrete yet, but this still felt like progress. We needed this. All of us. To know that this whole mess would soon come to an end.

"All right! Let's go talk to the pack then," I said.

16

A FEW HOURS LATER, I STOOD NEXT TO THE DOOR, thanking everyone for coming, and wishing them safe travels home. Though the mood was somber— thanks to the news of Scotia's death—most stopped to wish me and Sam well before leaving. Their encouraging smiles reassured me that we'd done the right thing in telling them. At least now they knew and were prepared for whatever else might come their way.

Marcus was the last to take my hand and wish me congratulations. With his Scottish brogue still echoing in my ears, I leaned over the porch railing and spotted Sam standing in the yard with Cole and Dominic. In the dim streetlight, I could see their faces etched with determination and concentration. Some extreme scheming was going on over there. Scheming I likely should have been involved in, but instead, it reassured me to see Sam becoming invested in my pack.

I was about to shut the door and leave them to it when I spotted our three resident vampires strolling up the walk. Huh. Being that it was barely eleven p.m., I was surprised to see them. Usually they stayed out until an hour before sunrise. But I guess they were eager to hear about the meeting. Although they weren't permitted to attend, I kept them apprised of everything that went down at the meetings. They lived in the same house as me, and they were deeply involved in this battle with Olivia. I refused to keep them in the dark simply because they were vampires.

Anna wished Marcus a good night, then breezed through the door and stepped past me, a hint of a skip to her step. Her nose wrinkled as she flopped on the couch. "Stinks like wolf in here."

"Gee, thanks," I teased.

Anna waved a dismissive hand, but the corners of her mouth tugged. She enjoyed yanking on my tail —metaphorically.

"You guys are home early," I commented.

Vlad claimed the seat next to Anna, and my mother dropped into the rocking chair, her eyes closing as she leaned her head back.

Anna shrugged, but there was a tightness to her eyes. "Seemed best to stick close to home for the next few nights, ya'know?"

Yeah, I did know. Guess I wasn't the only one suffering a little anxiety.

"So, how'd the meeting go?" Anna asked.

"Well enough." I headed into the kitchen and grabbed myself a cold drink from the fridge. "Better than expected. Scotia's death hit them hard, but many had been expecting it, since we hadn't been able to find her. They handled it pretty well."

"And the other stuff?" Anna called from the living room. "You know, Maddie and whatnot."

The whatnot being the pregnancy. "We decided to keep Maddie's paternity to ourselves. At least for now. Until we're completely sure about her. Considering my other sister is guilty of stealing three pack members—and killing one—I didn't think they'd be that open to me introducing another one. Not yet anyway."

"And the baby?" Anna pushed.

A small smile pulled at my lips. I cracked open my bottled water, then headed back into the living room and flopped down on Anna's other side. "They're excited about the pregnancy. It was a tad unnerving telling them. Imagine a bunch of wolfy eyes all staring at your stomach."

Anna snorted out a laugh—a sound I'd never heard her make before—then clapped a hand over her mouth in embarrassment. I burst out laughing, then choked when water came shooting out of my nose. What a pair we made, rolling around on the couch, choking on our own laughter.

I waved a hand in the air while tears pricked at my eyes. Oh god, I hadn't laughed like this in what felt like ages. And all because of a snort.

"My goodness, you two," my mother said. But I caught a smile peeking out from behind her cool veneer.

When I could finally suck in a steady breath, I said, "Thank you for helping me find those journals today."

Anna wiped her own blood tears away. "Did you find anything in them?"

"I've only looked at Olivia's in depth, but yes. We learned her parents own four properties. Ones we hadn't found when digging into Olivia's background."

"Four properties. Wow. Her parents must be loaded."

"Guess so. Either way, it's a lead. Cole and I discussed it, and he's going to divide the pack into four scouting teams. Each team will take one address. Fingers crossed we find something."

"I hope these are people you trust," my mother chimed in.

I shot her a confused glance. "What?"

"These scouting teams you're sending out. Are they people you know you can trust? Who haven't or won't side with Olivia. She was part of this pack for how long? She probably made connections. You need to take that into consideration."

I shook my head. "No one in the pack would side with Olivia. Not after everything she's done."

"Are you sure about that?" my mother asked, a hard glint to her eyes. "How do you know she doesn't have spies in the pack right this second? They might have been here tonight. Maybe they're going to report back to her not only that you have these addresses, but also that you're pregnant."

My breath suddenly clogged my throat and fear scrambled my thoughts.

I hadn't thought of that.

Why hadn't I thought of that?

Could Olivia have spies?

"You said Laini and Lincoln willingly joined her pack, didn't you?" my mother continued. "So why wouldn't you assume there are others?"

Why hadn't she voiced this thought *before* the meeting? Before I'd told everyone I was pregnant! And *why, oh why,* hadn't I thought of this myself?

"Mom...," I rasped, terror stealing my voice.

"Barbara," Vlad chided, his voice truly startling me. "Stop scaring her."

Anna laid a hand on my thigh and squeezed. "Lucy, try not to worry about things you can't control. *If* someone in your pack betrays you, we'll handle it. Just like we've been handling everything else."

I threw my head back against the couch cushion and sighed. I truly hated all this. I just wanted it over and done with. Wanted to be free so I could do *normal* things, like enjoy being pregnant and plan a wedding. I didn't want to sit here thinking about traitors and spies and betrayals.

"In the meantime, let's all just remain calm," Anna continued.

Easy for her to say.

"For all we know, your pack will find Olivia tomorrow, and this will all be over."

A girl could dream, right?

Needing some space—and some serious alone time—I slapped my hands down on my thighs and shoved to my feet. "On that note, I'm going to bed."

"Oh," Anna said, as though disappointed.

"I'll see you guys tomorrow. Goodnight."

The three sent back their own well wishes as I headed toward my bedroom. To my right sat the master bathroom, and for a moment, I debated a bath. The warm water would undoubtedly lull me into a false sense of security. Instead, my eyes shunted to the left, where my bed—and the journals —sat.

Nothing like a little light reading before bed. Not that reading those journals would relax me. But they did contain a lot of information I was dying to know.

I caught the sound of the front door opening and knew Sam had returned. But his deep voice mingled with Vlad's, telling me they were discussing something. Doubtful that conversation would last long. They preferred to avoid one another whenever possible. But it gave me some time.

I crawled atop the bed, then reached for the nearest journal.

Maddie's.

No, I couldn't read that without her.

Instead, I fished my phone out of my back pocket, snapped a picture, then fired it off to her in a quick text that explained what it was. I asked if she had any interest in reading it. After I hit "send," I berated myself. It was after eleven. I should have waited until tomorrow to message her. But then I remembered she was a twenty-two-year-old vampire slayer. Odds were she was still awake.

When my phone pinged two minutes later, I almost laughed.

Ah, to be young again.

> M: I'm so glad you texted first.
> Didn't wanna seem needy.

I chuckled, then froze, staring at the screen. Wait, did that make me the needy one?

> M: Wow. I don't even know what to say. He knew about me this whole time?

My heart broke for her. I couldn't imagine how this felt, learning your biological father had known about you for your whole life and done nothing to help you when you so desperately needed it. Hell, it made everything he'd done to me pale in comparison.

L: We can do whatever you'd like. If you want me to burn it, that's fine. It's technically your journal. Not mine.

It took a few minutes for her to respond, and I pictured her pensive green eyes screwed up in concentration as she considered her options.

M: Please don't burn it.

More time passed. This had to be so hard for her. She was so desperate for answers, and here they were.

M: You can look, if you want.

L: What if it mentions your mother? Would you like to know anything about her?

Silence again. I just wanted to reach through the phone and give her a hug.

M: Okay.

That was it. One word. Okay, clearly time to change the topic.

> L: Speaking of journals, I found Olivia's too. We may have a lead. I'll let you know. For now, don't do anything that might attract attention to yourself.

> M: Sounds good, sis.

My mouth slid to the left as I read that last word.

> M: Sorry, just wanted to try that out. It felt awkward even typing it.

I quietly chuckled. Awkward, yeah, that was one word for it. Anna and I had known each other all our lives, and we'd never once referred to each other like that. *Bish*, sure. But never sis. It just sounded so cringeworthy and forced.

> L: You hunting tonight?

> M: You know it. Wish me luck! Time to stabby-stabby.

I burst out laughing, then typed out my next message.

> L: Please be careful and don't die.

M: Aw, there you go being all big sisterly again. Don't worry, I know what I'm doing.

Of that, I had no doubt.

Maddie sent one more text that was a series of emojis. I stared at it blankly. It read like a whole other language. Oh god, was I really that old already? I wasn't quite thirty, so technically, I should be able to keep up with my little sister. But this text proved otherwise. She'd sent what looked like a door, a runner, and... was that... a fart cloud? Based on the puffy cloud behind her butt, had the runner farted?

I had no idea. And I was too embarrassed to ask what it meant. Maybe I could ask Anna tomorrow. Surely, she kept more up to date on this stuff than I did.

Hoping to help my image and self-confidence, I sent back a thumbs-up. I mean, that worked for all situations, right? If she was telling me she had to poop or she was going for a poop, the mighty thumbs-up would give her all the boost she needed.

Clearly, it'd worked, because she hadn't messaged me back.

Or did that mean I'd failed?

Holy hell, texting was stressful. And didn't that make me sound old. Ugh.

Time to move on to something else. Putting the weird emoji language out of my mind, I picked up Maddie's journal and flipped it open. She'd said she didn't mind if I read it, and this would give me some insight into my little sister. She'd already given me a fair deal during our impromptu meet up last night, but it couldn't hurt to dig a little deeper.

I stared at her baby photo, unable to tear my eyes off her mother. She gazed at Maddie with pure unadulterated love. So where was she now? How had Maddie ended up in foster care?

I kept reading in search of that answer.

Based on Reggie's entries, he'd met Rachel—Maddie's mother—at a bar. He didn't have much on her other than the fact that she'd been a college student studying philosophy. According to his notes, her scent had assured him she'd carried the potential to give him a wolf-born. So they dated. He knocked her up. She gave birth. End of story for Rachel. There wasn't much else in his notes about her... I skimmed the pages, searching for anything, then froze when I caught sight of a small, scribbled note at the bottom of the page.

Mother died a few days after birth. Postpartum complications.

Holy shit. He hadn't even used her name. Just

"mother." It was like everything I read about Reggie only further proved how wretched of a person he was.

Another thought wiggled into my brain, and I cocked my head as I turned the page.

If Rachel had died shortly after childbirth, then Reggie must have been the one to give Maddie up. I kept reading and groaned when I found it. He'd taken Maddie home and raised her until she was six months old. But when she showed no sign of being wolf-born, he'd dumped her at the nearest church.

I fell back against my pillows and stared blindly across the room.

He'd given her up, as though she'd meant nothing.

All because she hadn't been wolf-born, and because Rachel hadn't had any family for him to give Maddie to. I wondered if Maddie even knew her mother had passed. Unlikely from what she'd said last night, that she'd joined the ancestry site in search for her parents. Plural.

Cursing Reggie's name, I read the next few pages. He'd kept track of Maddie throughout the years and jotted down all her foster families. When she'd said they passed her around more than a blunt on four-twenty, she hadn't been exaggerating. The numbers astounded me. Her journal talked about behavior issues, what counseling she'd undergone, which group homes she'd stayed at. It even detailed the few run-ins with the law she'd had. Trivial things like stealing *food*.

I couldn't handle any more.

I closed the journal and tossed it aside.

It was official. Reggie was a piece of shit. I'd already known that. But the way he'd handled Maddie proved it tenfold.

Would the other journals read just as badly? Were there others Reggie had surrendered to the system? It horrified me to believe there likely were. Clearly, he'd never stuck around long enough to actually raise one of his children.

A sudden thought had me stacking all the journals in front of me.

What if there were others trapped in the system? Reggie had only died a few months ago. I doubt he'd stopped procreating before his death. Sam had confirmed I was the eldest, and yes, Maddie and Olivia were adults. But that didn't mean the rest were.

I quickly combed through the remaining journals, noting all the birth dates.

The youngest was a boy named Stephen Adrian

Black. And he was five years old, living in Colorado. According to his journal, his mother had packed Stephen up and left Reggie when Stephen was an infant.

I wanted to high-five this woman. She'd clearly caught on to Reggie's dickishness and ran for the hills. Literally. But the idea that I had a five-year-old brother out there baffled me.

A quick skim told me I didn't have any other siblings in foster care. They were all alive and well and living their best lives with their mothers.

Thank goodness.

And thank goodness Reggie wasn't around anymore to knock anyone else up.

The sound of the bedroom door easing open had me lifting my gaze from the most recent journal to find Sam.

"You okay?" he asked.

I nodded. "Just doing some nighttime reading."

His mouth twisted at the sight of the journals. "Fun."

"Ever so much. Remind me to find a necromancer tomorrow, okay?"

Sam's eyebrows shot up.

"I want to resurrect Reggie and kill him all over again."

"Ah." Sam coughed out a laugh. "I'll get right on that. Anna and your mother went back to the community center. Guess your mom wants to check out one of the hobby classes. Vlad said he'll stick around tonight for added protection, but he went for a walk to patrol the neighborhood. So, it's just you and me tonight, love."

With an eyebrow wiggle, I patted the spot next to me. "Coming to bed then?"

"Absolutely," Sam responded, a teasing twinkle in his eye.

I knew that look. And with a mischievous grin, I squealed and buried myself beneath the covers. Had to make the man work for it, after all.

17

Yet again, I woke to the sound of muffled voices in my house. Thankfully, they were familiar, so instead of leaping out of bed, I snuggled deeper and buried my head beneath the pillow. Over the past few months, my house had understandably become *werewolf central*, but that didn't mean I had to like it.

It wasn't until I wriggled my hips that I realized the spot next to me was empty.

No Sam.

Sighing, I reappeared from beneath my pillow and reached out, touching the cool sheets. He'd been up for a while then. A quick glance at the clock revealed it was almost noon.

Holy crap!

I'd slept till *noon?*

Why had no one woken me?

I jumped out of bed and scrambled into my closet, throwing on the closest clothing I could find. A quick sniff told me they were clean enough—laundry wasn't my strong suit. Then I dove into the bathroom and quickly took care of business.

Bladder relieved and mouth minty-fresh, I hurried into the kitchen to find the usual suspects. Cole, Dominic, and Paul sat on one side of the table, Sam on the other.

"Morning," came Sam's gruff voice. "Or should I say afternoon?"

I rolled my eyes. "Oh, ha-ha. Perfecting your dad jokes already?"

Cole snickered into his own coffee mug.

"Why didn't anyone wake me?" I demanded as I reached for a glass and filled it with water.

"Isn't there a rule about never waking a pregnant woman?" Sam teased.

"I think that only applies to babies."

"No, it definitely applies to pregnant women," Dominic chimed in.

I shot him a curious stare, my eyebrow quirked. "And how would you know about that?"

"I have the internet," he said, laughing. "People talk."

Huffing under my breath, I cooked myself a quick breakfast of bacon and eggs—yum, bacon—then took the open seat next to Sam. When he reached for a bacon strip, I immediately lashed out, swatting his hand away. Death to those who dared touch my bacon.

"Dude!" Paul burst out laughing. "You're taking your life in your hands, stealing your pregnant mate's breakfast."

Sam chuckled and rubbed the back of his hand. "Vicious."

"And don't you forget it." I shot him a pleasant smile.

"I remember you being nicer a few weeks ago," he said, though love shone in his eyes.

"Not when it came to bacon."

Sam cocked his head, the corners of his mouth tugging upward. "True."

The men continued to chat amongst themselves while I wolfed down my meal. A few days ago, the thought of food had nauseated me. Now I couldn't get enough. This baby had better be cute, was all I was saying.

When I finally lowered my fork, I realized the

room had gone silent and all four men stared at me with what looked like humor and pride shining in their eyes.

"Well, that was something to watch," Cole commented.

I quietly scoffed. Like they'd never seen a woman eat before. In all fairness, I couldn't recall a time they'd watched me pound back four eggs and eight strips of bacon. But still!

Grabbing my water, I took a long drink, rinsing out my mouth. Once I placed the glass down, I glanced at each of them. "Care to tell me what this impromptu meeting is about?"

"Right." Paul reached for his laptop and fired it up. I swear, I never saw him without his techy toys. "I reached out to whichever alphas I could find who have missing members to let everyone know what Olivia is up to, like you asked. The response has been quite intense."

"Intense?" I leaned back in the chair. "Intense, how?"

"Well, word started spreading, and more packs came forward regarding their missing members. But beyond that, the alphas have been discussing the situation."

"Which alphas?"

Paul lifted his gaze and met mine above his laptop. "All of them."

I blanched. "*All* the alphas?"

"As many who have been involved in this, yes. And they've requested a meeting with you."

My gut twisted and suddenly my bacon and eggs threatened to come back up. I pushed my fist against my mouth and focused on breathing. When my stomach finally settled, I swallowed and straightened. "How in the blazes do they suggest we do that?"

Cole rolled his eyes and gave a quiet laugh. "You know, for someone who manages a famous vampire's social media accounts, you are woefully lacking in technological knowledge. They want to meet via video conferencing. It's a way to—"

"I know what video conferencing is, Cole," I snapped, steaming at his "woefully lacking" comment.

He raised his hands peaceably. "Okay. They scheduled a meeting for this afternoon at two p.m. our time."

Which gave me an hour and a half to prepare, both physically and mentally. The thought of meeting with all these alphas... Was I ready to face that? I barely felt like an alpha myself. What if someone called into question my lack of experience? Talk about imposter syndrome.

At least I could shower beforehand.

Sam's hand twined with mine and he gave my fingers a supportive squeeze. "Don't worry. We'll be there with you."

"Have you ever done anything like this before?"

He shook his head. "This is a unique situation. Usually the packs operate separately from one another. Each alpha is responsible for their own territory, so the other alphas don't involve themselves in anyone else's business. But Olivia is crossing boundaries. She's stealing people from all over. Rumor has it some have even flown here from Asia."

My jaw fell slack.

"She's broken all the rules. So we need to adapt," Dominic added. "But I will say, prepare for an intense meeting. They're all alphas, which means tempers and egos will flare. Expect some fights to break out and prepare for the worst. Alphas can be... testy when they're forced into positions like these."

Great. Because that was just what we needed. Temperamental werewolves with god complexes.

"Both my parents will be on the call," Sam said. "And Aimee too."

So we'd have some support from our neighboring pack slash family.

"What about the scouting teams?" I asked. "Any update from them?"

Cole shook his head. "I put the teams together last night and contacted them all this morning. The first two teams set out about an hour ago. The last two teams just left. Hopefully we hear from them soon."

Hopefully. How I hated that word. It meant we had no control over any of this. And that was a thought that nearly sent me spiraling toward a panic attack. The thought that one of the teams may find Olivia today gave me hope that this whole fiasco was coming to an end. But then came the niggling fear. What if Olivia and her pack discovered them first? What would happen to them?

No, I couldn't think like that. I had to remain positive. Today, this all ended. I could feel it deep in my gut.

"Don't worry," Cole said, obviously picking up on my anxieties. "They know what they're doing."

I had to take his word on that.

Nodding, I rose from my chair and stretched my back. "I'm going to grab a shower and make myself presentable for the meeting. Is there anything else I need to know beforehand?"

"Not that I can think of," Cole said. "Paul?"

The wolf in question shook his head. "The post is still garnering a lot of attention, which is a good thing. We need everyone to know about Olivia, and we can address their questions during the meeting. Otherwise, it's just a matter of tracking her down and putting an end to this."

"Which we *will* do," Sam assured me.

I forced a smile. "I know. Thanks, guys."

A cacophony of thoughts deafened me as I headed for the shower. But those weren't what concerned me. No, it was the feeling of dread and fear that had settled deep into my gut. That one terrified me the most.

Two p.m. on the button, I sat on the couch in the living room, my hands purposefully clasped in my lap to keep me from fidgeting.

To my left sat Cole, his phone in his hand. For the past half hour, he'd been in communication with two of the scouting teams. Sadly, both had been unsuccessful in locating Olivia. That left us with teams two and four, who hadn't yet reported in. Cole's body language told me he was more than concerned about their whereabouts.

Sam sat on my right, his arm draped behind my back in a silent show of support. Every now and then I felt his fingers ghost across my waist, but instead of finding his touch arousing, it grounded me. It told me I wasn't alone in this.

Paul and Dominic stood across the room from us, next to the television and out of view of the camera. Paul had rigged everything up so that the camera, mounted to the top of the television and hooked up to the laptop with a series of cables, would broadcast us. Kudos to him for knowing what the heck he was doing.

"Ready?" Paul asked.

I sucked in a deep breath in an attempt to settle my nerves, then glanced at Cole. "Any news from the scouting teams?"

"Not yet," he said, grim faced. "I'll keep you apprised during the meeting."

"Thanks."

I faced Paul and nodded for him to begin. I could do this. I could. I just needed to remain calm and levelheaded. No matter what the alphas said, at the end of the day, their approval didn't matter. This was my pack and my territory.

Paul leaned toward the laptop and clicked a button. A screen popped up on the television, reflecting me, Cole, and Sam. Then it connected to the meeting, and suddenly what had to be at least a dozen other werewolves joined in. If not more.

"Holy shit," I breathed out, my voice barely above a whisper.

"You got this," Sam said.

Right. I got this.

"We're still muted," Paul said. "Before I unmute you, know that you're the host of this call. So all the power resides with you. I've muted everyone else, and they'll have to raise a hand to speak. If you need me to mute a speaker, just tell me. I can also boot anyone out."

Oh, I bet the alphas loved that. But it made sense. We couldn't have people talking—more like yelling—over each other.

"Thanks, Paul," I said.

I stared at the television and met the gazes of so many alphas. All hard and steely-eyed. My focus strayed from one face to another. Everyone looked so different and yet so alike. The strong jaws, the stern features, the weathered faces, regardless of skin color or gender. Even without speaking, these people screamed *alpha*. Approximately one-quarter of the attendees were female. It bolstered my strength to see that, to know I wasn't the only female alpha in attendance.

Then my gaze snagged on Adrien and Elena, and I couldn't help but smile. Seeing their friendly faces calmed me. Elena grinned back and gave me a small wave, but I couldn't hear anything she was saying. Based on Adrien's nod, they were conversing privately.

Paul waited for my nod, then clicked the button to unmute me.

"Welcome," I said, hoping I spoke loudly enough for them to hear.

Based on the many alphas snapping to attention, I had.

"For those who don't know me, my name is Lucy Williams, and I am the Alpha of the Mississippi Pack."

Heads bobbed in acknowledgement.

"I want to thank you all for being here today. I also want to honor your time, knowing that you likely have other important things to do, so I'll make this as brief as possible. Once I've conveyed the information, I'll open the floor up to questions." I took another breath and squared my shoulders. "I know this matter is unprecedented, but circumstances such as these require extraordinary attention. From all of us. My pack isn't the only one that's been affected by all this. So, on that note, let's begin."

I quickly walked the alphas through the timeline of events, starting with my attack in England. Eyes sharpened at that. When I'd first returned to New Orleans, Sam had warned me that rumors of my change had spread. Now, I'd confirmed them, and the method in which I was turned. I only hoped the other alphas handled this information responsibly, but I predicted a sudden spike in the werewolf population in the coming weeks.

When I reached the part about Reggie turning Olivia, a few alpha's lips curled upward in distaste. I continued my briefing, explaining how Corbin and Olivia had been recruiting from all over, using the dark web as their source. How they had wanted to rule over humans. Heads bobbed again as though they'd seen the posts. Next came Corbin's death, and Olivia's subsequent disappearance.

"My pack is currently out scouting a few locations we managed to dig up," I continued. "Two of our teams have checked in—"

"Three," Cole commented, pointing at his phone.

I dipped my head. "Thank you. Three teams have checked in, but there's been no sign of Olivia yet. We have a fourth team still due to check in. When we hear something, I will let you know. In the meantime, let's open the floor up to questions."

Hands immediately shot in the air.

Oh, doggy.

"Paul, if you wouldn't mind, let's go in order. Left to right, top to bottom."

"Yes, Alpha," Paul responded. He unmuted the first alpha.

"Thank you for your report," the alpha said. "My name is Darren Legrand, and I'm the alpha of the Colorado Pack. I think what many of us here want to know is why have you allowed this to happen."

Shock rippled through me quickly followed by a flare of anger. "Excuse me?"

"You're the alpha. It's your duty to keep issues like this under control. Olivia was your responsibility to shut down."

"In case you missed *everything* I said, I've only been the alpha for a few months."

"Yes, and in that time, you should have tracked your sister down and removed her"—and by removing her, he likely meant kill her—"the second you learned she was involved."

"I didn't *learn* she was involved until after I killed Corbin," I reminded him. "Nor have I seen my sister since."

"And what have you done in that time to find her?"

I ground my teeth. My pack had tirelessly combed the city in search of her, but I didn't feel the need to defend myself further. "Next question, Paul."

Darren's mouth parted as though he intended to argue, but Paul quickly muted him and moved to the next alpha.

"Julie Taylor." Her voice rang through the television. "Alpha of the Arizona Pack."

I acknowledged her with a nod.

"You intend to kill your sister, right?" Julie asked.

"Yes," I bit out. There'd be no avoiding that.

If I wasn't mistaken, I caught a flash of sympathy on Julie's face, but she didn't say another word.

"Next."

Paul unmuted the next, who didn't bother to introduce himself before he asked, "You mentioned earlier that Reginald turned Olivia after learning about this process. I've heard rumors about Reginald.

Do you know if you have other siblings he's changed?"

Somehow, I managed to maintain my poker face. This was not a question I wanted to address. I refused to put Maddie or anyone else at risk.

"As far as I'm aware, Olivia was the only one he changed." And that wasn't a lie. Olivia had changed Maddie, and Corbin had changed me.

The questions persisted. Digging deeper into Olivia's motivations, diving into the motivations of those who abandoned their packs. On and on it went until their voices droned into one long noise.

After muting the current alpha and before Paul unmuted the next in line, I saw Cole gesture to him. "Excuse me for just one minute," I said before quickly muting us.

"The fourth team still hasn't checked in," Cole said. He gripped his phone so tight, his knuckles bled white. For a moment, I worried he might snap it in two. "It's been too long. Their location was only thirty minutes outside of town, and they set out at noon."

Considering it was well after three p.m., they should have been home by now, let alone contacted Cole.

"Try calling them," I suggested.

"I've been texting and getting no responses. I didn't want to call just in case they were somewhere they didn't want to be overheard."

"I think we're beyond that now," I said. "Call them."

"Lucy, the other alphas are trying to get your attention," Sam said.

I shot the television a quick glance to find them watching this scene unfold. Instead of acknowledging them, I listened to the sound of the phone ringing. With each ring, my heart dropped further into my gut. That feeling of dread had returned.

"No answer," Cole said, cursing.

"Which location were they scouting?" I demanded.

"The farm."

I knew the one. Of the four, it'd been the only farm. "That has to be it then. If they aren't responding, we have to assume they found Olivia's pack."

"We don't know that for sure," Cole argued.

"What other explanation could there be?"

His jaw tightened, and he nodded. If they hadn't found anything at the location, they would have contacted us. I turned back to the call, about to signal for Paul to unmute us when my phone suddenly came to life, blasting out my ringtone.

At the sight of Maddie's name, I considered sending her to voicemail. Now wasn't the time for a sisterly chat. But something urged me to answer the phone. Call it intuition, call it fear, I wasn't sure. But with our missing team, something pushed me to see what Maddie wanted.

I snatched up my phone and connected the call.

"Lucy!" Maddie shouted. "You there?"

My pulse immediately shot into the atmosphere. "Yeah, it's me."

"I'm on my way to your place right now. You need to get the fuck out, you hear me?"

Adrenaline surged through my veins, and I shot to my feet. Sam followed suit, his hands immediately gripping my sides.

"What's going on?" I demanded.

"Did you send a team to scout Olivia's location today?" Maddie asked.

"Yes."

She unleashed a stream of curses that turned my ears pink. "Get out of the house now. Go. Olivia knows you found her. She's coming."

I wanted to demand how Maddie knew that, but I couldn't waste time asking questions. "I can't just leave. Vlad, Anna, and my mother are asleep—"

"Olivia doesn't want them!" Maddie shouted. "She's coming for *you*, and she's bringing the whole pack. She plans to kill you. Get the fuck out. *Now*."

18

"Did you hear me?" Maddie demanded. "Tell me you're leaving, right this second."

I didn't respond. Not when I caught movement out on the street. Sam and I hurried to the living room window and peered through the slatted blinds as four vehicles came to a screeching halt outside the house. Each with at least five silhouettes inside, that I could see.

"Fuck," Sam growled, his wolf taking possession of his voice.

Fuck, indeed.

Twenty werewolves had just pulled up outside my house. There were only five of us. I was no mathematician, but even I knew those odds were not in our favor.

"Lucy!" Maddie shouted through the phone. "Get out of the house right now. Lucy—"

The call suddenly disconnected.

I lowered my phone and frowned at the screen. No service. What the hell? That'd never happened before. I always had reception unless I was out in the country somewhere.

"Sam," I muttered. "My phone..."

He shot me a glance, then dug through his pockets for his own, lifting it into view. "Yeah, mine too."

Okay, this was *really* bad.

"Paul, Cole, Dominic, are your phones—"

"All dead," Cole said.

"The video call disconnected too," Paul informed me with a sharp curse. His gaze narrowed and he stalked to the window, peering out through the blinds. "They've done something to disrupt our connections. Phone and internet." He fell silent for a moment, then cursed again. "Jammers. They must have brought jammers."

I'd never heard of a jammer, but I could figure it out from context. They'd crippled us technologically.

Paul faced me, his grim expression tying my

stomach in knots. "If it's a professional grade one, it can affect all connections within a mile radius."

I dragged a hand through my hair. "So we can't call for help."

"Not unless you have a landline."

Of course I didn't. No one had a landline anymore.

I tossed my phone onto the couch like the useless brick it now was and turned to Sam. My crazed, wild-eyed Sam. His luminous gaze burned into mine, his jaw clenched tight. He was struggling with his wolf, who likely wanted to rip out some throats. A feeling I sympathized with.

"Lucy," he growled, his hands clutching mine. "You need to run."

Surely, I'd misheard him. "What?"

"You *need* to run," he repeated, his upper lip curling back to reveal sharpened canines. Clearly, he was losing the struggle.

I shook my head without even thinking. Run? I'd *never* run. Never abandon him or the others. I couldn't.

"Lucy!" he snapped, his voice shattering my chaotic thoughts. "*I* need you to run."

My breath quickened and tears pricked at my eyes. I couldn't imagine doing what he asked of me.

The thought of leaving him to this mess, of *losing* him to this mess, shredded my insides. "You can't ask that of me."

Sam swore and spun around, flicking open the blinds to peer outside. Olivia's pack moved toward the house, their steps slow and purposeful as though they were enjoying dragging this out, enjoying taunting us. They knew we were helpless and isolated in here.

"Do you see that?" Sam jabbed a finger toward the window. "Twenty werewolves are about to break in here. There's only four of us. It's a fight we won't win."

"Five," I whispered. "There's five of us."

He faced me again and clutched at my arms, yanking me into his chest. "No, there isn't. There's four of us. Because you're going to run. You *need* to run." He dropped his forehead against mine, his panicked breath brushing my face. "I need you to run, Lucy. Do you understand?"

"No!" I shouted. "I won't leave you."

"Lucy, Sam's right," Cole chimed in. "If you stay, you'll be a distraction. You're vulnerable right now. And we can't let Olivia get her hands on you. If you leave, we can focus and hopefully take some of them out with us."

What? My wide eyes darted between my mate and my second in command. The way they spoke... they believed they would die here today. And they expected me to just *leave* them and let that happen?

I gripped Sam's arms. "We can all run. Together."

"And then what?" Sam demanded. "They'll just follow us. And they'll catch us. Then we're back to square one. No, we need to stay and fight."

This was insane. What he was saying was *insane!* I refused to abandon them. Not when I could stay and help. I wasn't useless. Hell, Cole had trained me for this. I'd killed Bryn, Corbin, and quite a few of his lackeys. I wasn't some pathetic little girl incapable of defending herself.

"Lucy." Sam closed his eyes, severing me from his wolf. "You have to go. If you're here, I'm just going to get hurt trying to protect you."

The sound of jeering and laughter grew louder. Olivia's pack was spreading out, surrounding the house.

"Sam, I can protect myself—"

"And our baby?" He opened his eyes and placed his hands on my stomach.

I froze, my heart stuttering to a dead stop in my chest. In all the chaos, I'd forgotten about the baby.

Forgotten I was pregnant. And just like that, all my anxieties reared their ugly little heads.

Sam nodded, as though understanding my thoughts. "You can't stay. If they hurt you..." He bit off his words, clearly too frightened to speak the rest aloud. "I can't lose you. Either of you. You must do what's right for the baby, and that's running."

"Sam..."

"Go, Lucy!" he shouted, gold burning in his eyes. "There's no more time to argue. Don't go out the back door, they'll be expecting that. Use Anna and Vlad's window."

This didn't feel right. They needed me here to help them. But even as that thought came to me, my hands dropped to my stomach.

Sam's hands cupped my face as he leaned in and kissed me. It was so soft, so tender. As though he knew this would be the last time he'd ever kiss me. My heart broke into a million pieces and my tears came faster, wetting his palms.

When we parted, he gave me a gentle push. "Go."

My eyes never left his face as I took one step backward. I memorized him in this moment, even though I wanted nothing more than to stand by his side.

I took a second step back. Then a third. The distance between us grew, as did the void in my chest. I'd never felt pain like this before, this visceral agony that threatened to destroy me.

"I love you," he said, his voice cracking. "I'll always love you."

"I love you," I whispered back in an anguished tone.

"Don't look back," was the last thing he said to me before I turned and fled.

I tore through the house at top speed and flung myself into Anna and Vlad's bedroom. Pitch blackness welcomed me thanks to their UV resistant windows and blackout curtains. Not a shred of light existed in their grave-like room. But thanks to my heightened senses, I could still see. I raced toward the window and gripped the curtain, about to pull it back, when a terrifying sound came from the living room.

Glass shattering.

Followed by a chorus of vicious snarls.

They were inside the house.

Fear sluiced up my throat and nearly paralyzed me. No, I couldn't stop. Sam had begged me to run. To escape. With my hand on the window, I froze.

He'd begged me to leave. And I would. But that didn't mean I couldn't send help.

I spun toward the bed.

Anna.

I glanced at the clock and noted it was now almost four o'clock. Which was when she often woke for the day. Soon, she'd wake. And *she* could help.

Abandoning the window, I hurried to Anna's side of the bed, my hands hovering above her. I'd never touched Anna when she was dead before, but now wasn't the time for such squeamishness. Sam's life could depend on me waking her.

So I gripped her cold shoulders and shook her with all my strength.

If she'd been awake, I might have worried about knocking her head clear off her shoulders. Instead, I simply shook her harder.

"Anna," I whisper-hissed. "Anna, wake up. Wake up, wake up, wake up, *wake up!*"

Christ, I didn't even know if she could be woken. I'd never asked how this whole thing worked. She'd told me they were truly dead during the day. Did that mean they *couldn't* be woken? Was I wasting time here?

I shook her again, so hard I thought we might

bounce off the bed. Neither she nor Vlad so much as twitched.

"Anna!" I screamed, then pinched my eyes closed in regret.

When I opened them, Anna was staring back at me, her blue eyes aglow in the darkness. "Lucy?"

Ferocious growling filtered into the bedroom. Anna's head snapped to the side, her eyes narrowing as she took everything in. She scrambled off the bed and pushed me behind her.

"Olivia's pack."

"Shit." Anna darted to the door, cracked it open, and peeked out. With a startled cry, she slammed it shut seconds before a heavy body crashed against the wall.

"Sam wants me to run," I mumbled.

"Good."

Anna ran with impressive speed to the window. She shot Vlad a quick glance, then ripped the curtains free of the rod. Sunlight exploded into the room, but thanks to the UV resistant glass, Anna and Vlad were safe.

Curtains in hand, Anna blurred to Vlad's side and wrapped him head to toe. Then she rushed back to the window. So long as she kept away from direct sunlight, she'd be fine.

"Go," she said, pointing at the window.

I flicked the lock open. "Stand aside."

Anna nodded, then pressed herself flat against the adjacent wall right before I threw open the window. Sunlight entered the room, but it hit neither Anna nor Vlad. Momentary relief loosened my muscles, but they tightened again when I thought of my mother.

I was abandoning *all* of them. My whole family.

Anna snapped her fingers at me and gestured to the window. "Stop overthinking and go. I'll help Sam and the others, I swear." Then a terrifying grin twisted her lips. "Good thing I'm hungry."

With a sharp curse, I scrambled outside.

The instant my feet touched the plush grass, I turned to close the window, my back to the yard. Stupid, in retrospect. Especially when a pair of muscular arms snaked around my throat and dragged me backward.

I gurgled out something incomprehensible, then snapped my head back. My skull connected with my attacker's nose, and a satisfying crunch rang through my ears. This wolf was strong though. Their grip didn't loosen.

I threw back my elbow and drove it deep into their gut, then stomped on the top of their foot. The sound of their raspy breath and pained groan spurred me into motion. Together, we stumbled forward, toward the house. My chest ached for air and my head throbbed. But I could do this. I could break their hold and get the hell out of here.

I spun around, ready to drive them back against the wall.

Instead, the weight behind me vanished.

With a stuttered gasp, I sucked in a lungful of air, my chest and throat burning with relief.

I pivoted toward the window, stunned to find Anna standing in the sunlight, her arms locked around the werewolf's throat. The sun blazed a path over her undead skin, igniting it in flame. Both she and the werewolf screamed, a sound I'd never forget, as she dragged the wolf into the house and into the darkness.

"Anna!" I shouted.

I gripped the edge of the window and leaned inside. The tension drained from my body when I spotted her crumpled in the middle of the floor, mouth latched onto the werewolf's neck. With every pull of blood she took, the flames died, and the blisters healed.

Christ, she could have died, stepping into the sunlight like that.

Anna's incensed gaze flashed to mine seconds before she unlatched her mouth and dropped the wolf's dead body.

"Why are you still here?" she demanded, her voice almost demonic.

"Are you okay?"

"I'm fine, Lucy. Go!"

"Anna—"

"Lucy, for the love of god, get the fuck out of here!"

Biting my lip, I nodded to Anna, then turned and ran, like the coward I was.

19

I TORE OUT OF THE BACKYARD LIKE A BAT OUT OF hell, all the while fighting back tears.

But I didn't make it far.

Once I reached the neighbor's yard, a good half mile away, a pang of regret stopped me. My mother had always told me to listen to my instincts, and right now, my instincts were *screaming* at me to go back. To stay with Sam. To protect them. To fight with them.

After all, that was what a true alpha would do, right?

I understood Sam's fears. Hell, I could barely think straight. I was so afraid. But Sam was my mate, my one true love. I couldn't begin to describe how important he was to me. Or consider life without him. He *was* my life. Without him, I was nothing.

And Anna. She was my sister. A sister who had risked her own life, time and time again, to save me. A sister who'd once been trapped in a crypt and nearly burned alive, but hadn't let that phobia stop her from protecting me. She'd walked into sunlight for *me*. To save me.

How could I leave them like this?

I *couldn't*. No matter what they said. No matter how much they begged me to.

Cursing under my breath, I turned back the way I came and considered my options. I'd left my damn phone in the house, so I couldn't call for help. Even if I had it, who knew if I'd have reception even here. I had no idea how far those *jammers* could reach. The only option I had was going back. Fighting for them. Maybe I could take a few out before anyone even realized. By now, they had to know I wasn't in the house.

My inner wolf came forward, encouraged by my thoughts. She didn't want to run either. She wanted me to shift and give her free rein. Let her rip out some throats. I was inclined to let her.

My trembling fingers touched the hem of my shirt. I hadn't shifted since learning I was pregnant.

Meredith had assured me there was no risk for the baby. But what did she know? Yes, she was a doctor, but all her patients had been wolf-born. I was a human-born who'd been changed into a werewolf. She'd never dealt with one of my kind before. What if my body couldn't actually handle the stress of the change?

No, I needed to trust the doctor, and my instincts, and my wolf. Every bone in my body told me to shift, to run, to kill. I had to trust that my wolf would keep us safe, that she knew what to do. She would never endanger me or the baby. I couldn't let fear make my decisions for me.

Sam. Anna. Vlad. My mother. Cole. Dominic. Paul. Everyone I loved was in that house right now, trapped because of the sun or fighting for their lives. How could I not go back and help them?

Closing my eyes, I let go of my fears, stripped, and initiated the change. Thanks to my months of practice, I'd reduced my shifting time to forty-five seconds. But even that felt like an eternity, knowing my entire family was in danger.

Finally, I stood on four legs and shook out my fur. I'd never shifted in the middle of the day before, but I hadn't heard any screams, so it seemed safe to assume no one had spotted me. Trusting in that assumption, I threw myself into a sprint and raced back to the house.

The closer I came, the more I heard. The fight continued indoors, the sound of breaking glass and shuddering walls making me wince. As much as I wanted to dive inside, I had to be smart about this. I needed to clear the outer perimeter and reduce their numbers if possible. Take them on one at a time.

I bolted to the side wall and crouched low, my ears quirked. The sound of movement in the backyard caught my attention. Someone was on the deck, their steps quiet, but not quiet enough. I toed through the grass, silent as the grave, and peeked around the corner.

A wolf stood in the middle of the deck with his back to me. Alone, from the looks of it.

I inched forward. Once my paws hit the deck, he'd hear my nails against the wooden planks. I'd need to be quick about it then. I crept forward until I couldn't get any closer. Then, without so much as a single breath, leapt into the air. My paws connected with the werewolf's back just as I bit into his neck. I gave it a hard twist as we fell.

He was dead before he even hit the ground.

Once upon a time, killing a person would have

destroyed me. Now, I hardly batted an eye, and instead, rose to my feet and pressed onward.

Hurried footsteps approached.

Guess my kill hadn't gone unnoticed. Someone must have heard his body hitting the ground. I rushed forward, preparing to meet this new wolf head-on. They must not have expected that, because when they came rushing around the corner, they jumped at the sight of me.

I reacted on instinct and leapt into the air, my jaws closing around his throat. This time, I felt my teeth puncture his flesh. And as we fell, I ripped his throat out. Perhaps the sound of him gargling in his own blood should have upset me—and maybe it would later, when I would inevitably replay these moments in my head—but my focus was on one thing and one thing alone.

Sam.

Tucking around the side of the house, I hurried to the front. It seemed a safe bet to assume I'd find more wolves there. Question was, how many? I could handle one, maybe two at once. But any more than that put me and the baby at risk. I could fight, but I had to be smart about it.

The sudden sound of shattering glass had me jumping back a step. Then came the distinct sound of a body hitting the ground. It'd come from the front of the house, so I couldn't see it. Not yet. But if I had to wager a guess, I'd say they had thrown someone through the living room window. I only hoped it wasn't one of my boys.

I increased my pace, then paused when I reached the final corner. Once I took this turn, I would be in full view of whatever the hell was going on in the front yard.

Fighting resumed. Grunts, cries, shouts, snarls. There'd be no hiding this fight from my neighbors. Not anymore. Which meant I had to assume the cops would be dispatched soon. Normally, that thought would terrify me. We couldn't involve humans in our matters. But suddenly, I didn't give a shit anymore. My mate was in trouble. And if that meant involving the police, so be it. We'd deal with the fallout after.

I ducked low, about to come tearing out of the grass, when I heard a hard *crack*, a grunt, a soft exhalation. Then silence.

A silence that sent my heart into overdrive.

Did that mean the fight was over?

Oh god, was Sam dead?

I leaned around the corner and caught a quick glimpse of the scene unfolding on my front yard. At the sight of Olivia's goons dragging Sam toward the nearest car, I nearly fell flat on my face. He didn't move. Didn't struggle. Didn't so much as look my way. Because he couldn't. His head lolled back against the chest of the man carrying him, eyes closed.

My inner wolf gave a plaintive cry, one only I could hear, and nudged me forward, demanding I leap into action. Shred these assholes. Rip them apart for daring to harm my mate. But I couldn't. Because half of Olivia's men stood on my front lawn.

Sam wasn't dead. I had to believe that. If he were, they wouldn't be stuffing him into a car. If they'd killed him, they would have left him where he fell.

But the sight of him unconscious—because he *had* to be unconscious, I wouldn't accept anything else—gripped my heart.

While a few of Olivia's men shoved Sam into the backseat, others circled our cars and slashed the tires. My lip curled and I unleashed a snarl no one seemed to hear. The bastards!

They slammed the backdoor shut with Sam inside and started laughing about how easily they'd taken Sam out.

Easy, my ass. There were twenty of them against the six of us—including me and Anna.

A deep growl escaped my throat as I memorized each of their faces, committing them to the darkest recesses of my mind. I would kill them all. And I wouldn't stop to wonder whether I should care about their deaths.

Two men circled to the front of the car, then hopped into the driver's and passenger seats. A third ventured toward one of the other vehicles, finding a space among the remaining men. I only counted ten in total. Pride overwhelmed me that my boys had inflicted that much damage, even while outnumbered. I didn't have time to think about that though, not when the car holding Sam took off down the street.

Silently cursing, I turned to stare at the house. I had no idea what'd happened in there or what awaited me inside. Nor could I stay to find out. Not when they had Sam. And considering our cars were now useless—thanks to the slashed tires—I only had one option.

I started running.

I chased after them in wolf form, uncaring if any human eyes spotted me. Let them see me. They could call and report a wolf for all I cared.

Let them finally realize werewolves lived among them.

The only thing that mattered was getting Sam back.

The miles dragged on. Whenever I could, I used a backyard to save time and reclaim any lost distance. People cried out from their windows, but I didn't stop. I couldn't. I raced through swampland, trees, and open fields, all in pursuit of the SUV.

When I lost sight of them, I didn't panic. I was ninety-nine percent sure I knew where they were taking him. The farm just outside Jackson. It had to be there. That was where the fourth scouting team had gone missing, which had triggered Olivia's attack. It was too coincidental not to be that location.

It didn't matter that every step ripped open my paws, or that my legs and joints screamed in agony. It didn't matter that my chest grew heavier and heavier or that my heart was racing so fast, I thought it might explode. I couldn't give up.

My inner wolf pushed me onward, and my instincts told me where to go.

I had to trust them. I refused to lose Sam.

I'd just passed a highway sign when one of my legs gave out. I crashed into the ditch with a quiet whimper, but I couldn't lie here panting for breath.

I had to keep going.

Forcing myself back to my feet, I took a jarring step forward, about to push myself onward, when a car came squealing to a stop in front of me.

Shit. Someone was stopping to help the injured wolf. I'd seen videos like this on social media. Good Samaritans stopping to help injured animals. They must have seen me fall.

The last thing I wanted was to deal with some human playing out their savior complex. I pivoted away from the car and limped into a nearby field when I heard my name shouted.

I froze, then whirled around, stunned to find Maddie standing on the side of the road.

"Lucy, get your ass in the car!" she shouted.

Maddie... how the hell? Then I remembered her phone call before all this started. Somehow she'd known about Olivia's plan. She'd told me to get out. She'd *known*. Had she betrayed us? Was she actually working with Olivia?

A low growl rose from my chest as I contemplated that.

Maddie's eyebrows rose, as though shocked I'd growl at her.

But she had to know. Had to suspect I'd be pissed.

And if she'd betrayed us, oh, we'd be having words. More than words. I'd rip her throat out. Especially if Olivia harmed Sam.

"Well, now, hold on there," she said, planting her hands on her hips. "You keep those growls to yourself, alright?"

My lip curled up to expose my fangs.

Maddie blanched. "Lucy, what the hell is wrong with you? You need to get the fuck in my car, right now!"

I slitted my eyes. I wasn't getting in that car with her. Not until I knew her intentions.

Sighing, Maddie ran a hand through her hair, then shielded her eyes against the setting sun. "I don't know what this is about, but fuck, we don't have time for this."

I hobbled forward with another snarl.

"Lucy Williams!" she shouted at me. "Get your furry ass in my car right now!"

When I didn't move, she threw her arms up in the air. "Look, I don't know what's going on in that head of yours. And surprise, surprise, I *won't* know until you shift back and talk to me. What the hell are you even doing all the way out here anyway? I told you to get out of the house, not to go for a run!"

Like she didn't know. If she was involved, she

had to know Olivia had taken Sam. And if Maddie had been in on that, well, I'd have one less sister in a few minutes.

"I know where Olivia is staying," she continued. "So we really need to rally the troops. You get me, girl?"

Yeah, I got her. I just wasn't sure I trusted her. The timing of everything raised my hackles.

Clearly frustrated with me, Maddie leaned against the trunk of her car and crossed her arms. She looked ever so much like a petulant teenager angry with her mom.

"Fine," she bit out. "Just fine. We'll keep standing here, I guess. Until the police show up, wondering why I'm arguing with a *belligerent wolf!*" She yelled the last part. Then she fell into silence, content to wait me out.

I considered my options. Getting into Maddie's car didn't appeal to me. But driving was certainly faster than running. And hopefully, I'd get some answers along the way. I was done with this game. Done playing by Olivia's rules. Time to play by mine.

So, Maddie's car it was then.

The only question that remained was whether my sister lived to join me.

20

"YOU'LL FIND SOME CLOTHES IN THE BACKSEAT," Maddie told me as she wrenched open the back door.

I hopped in, wincing when pain flared through my leg, then paused. There was an entire wardrobe back here. Made sense, I guess, from a slayer perspective. Maddie wouldn't have any way of predicting when she needed to shift, and keeping clothes in the back would prevent any nudity issues. Issues similar to what I was facing right now.

Shutting the door behind me, Maddie hurried to the driver's side and hopped in. She shot me a quick glance in the rearview mirror, then put the car in drive and executed a sloppy U-turn. One that immediately threw me to the car floor.

Limbs sprawled in the air, I clawed my way back up onto the seat, and growled.

"Oh, stuff your growls," Maddie barked at me.

With a haughty glare, I crouched low and let the change come over me. The snapping of my bones echoed in the small confines of the car, but the sound didn't faze either of us, considering this was our life now.

Once back in human form, I stretched out my sore arm with a grimace, then grabbed the closest clothes I could find—a pair of dark purple yoga pants and a light-yellow T-shirt with a smiley face and the words "I'm dead inside" scrawled over the head. My first thought was how much Anna would love this shirt, then I froze.

Anna.

In all the chaos, I'd forgotten about her. I hadn't checked in on her before bolting after Sam. Had she survived the fight? Oh god, please let her be alive. Her death would destroy me. *And* Vlad. I hated the thought of what he might wake to tonight.

But I couldn't focus on that right now.

Instead, I leaned down and cuffed the extra-long yoga pants, then crawled to the front seat and belted myself in.

"You're going the wrong way," I snapped at

Maddie, glancing over my shoulder in the direction I'd been running. "Sam's that way."

"Sam?" Maddie shot a quick glance behind her. "Where's Sam?"

"Olivia has him!" I shouted.

"What?" She gripped the steering wheel tighter, as though afraid I'd yank it from her hands. "Is that why you're all the way out here?"

"I was tracking them," I said. "Turn around."

"And do what? Take down Olivia and her pack? Just you and me? No, ma'am. That's how people die, and I like living."

"Maddie—"

"No, Lucy!" Maddie shouted back, her cheeks flaming with color. "We can't take Olivia on with just the two of us. That's a suicide mission that I want no part of. So, let me get you home. You can call the pack in, and together, we can storm the castle."

"We?" I repeated. "You want to be a part of this? Is that why you called me earlier? How did you know Olivia was coming for me? Did you betray me? Rat us out to her?"

"Holy shit, that was a lot of questions."

And I had more.

The color faded from Maddie's cheeks, and she

shot me a wary glance. "Is that what was bugging you back there? You think I betrayed you? Need I remind you that Olivia already knew where you live? You're lucky it took her this long to come after you. The only reason she did was because—"

"Because I found her location," I finished. *Fuck.*

"Bingo. Well, that, and she's finally replenished her pack numbers. Believe me, I had nothing to do with Olivia's attack today, or her abduction of Sam. I would never agree with that."

Shame heated my face. I shouldn't have assumed Maddie betrayed us, but after everything with Olivia, maybe I'd developed some trust issues. "Sorry. It's just you called right before they showed up, and you still haven't told me how you knew they were coming."

A strained breath rushed past her lips. "You asked me to look into her location, right? Remember that?"

"I also remember asking you to hold off so you didn't get caught in the middle," I grumped.

"Yeah, you did. But I didn't."

"Maddie—"

"What?" She shot me a sullen glance, one that reminded me she was only twenty-two years old. "Look, you asked me to look into her location. So I did. I reached out to Olivia. I told her I wanted to meet with her, but I didn't say why. We met this morning at the same coffee shop as last time. I did my best to sniff out some answers without making her too suspicious. Eventually, she started talking. She didn't give too much away, but she did mention that she didn't need me anymore."

Oh, that didn't sound good at all.

"She told me I would be proud of her. That soon I would see that she was right about everything. And that after today, Mississippi would belong to her." Maddie bit her lip and glanced my way before focusing back on the road. "I didn't know what she meant, so I followed her back to her location."

I sat straighter in the seat. "Her parents' farm? Is that where she's staying?"

"Yeah. I hid on top of the barn and watched as she rallied her people and ordered them to take you out. I wanted to call you right away, but I couldn't. I had to wait until it was safe for me to move again."

"A little heads-up would have been nice," I griped. "*Before* you followed her back to her place."

Maddie shot me an apologetic glance. "I know. I'm sorry. I wasn't thinking."

Frustration heated my blood, but I accepted

Maddie's apology. "Fine. Tell me more. How many people does she have?"

"Forty. Maybe fifty."

My jaw dropped. "What?"

"I know. I couldn't believe my eyes. They didn't look too organized yet. I saw groups forming within. Cliques type thing. But that doesn't matter. She has the numbers." Maddie freed one hand from the steering wheel and rubbed her brow. "I hate to say this, but I don't see this ending until one of you is dead. Just... promise me it won't be you."

The weight on my chest lessened. "So, you didn't betray us."

"No!" she shouted. "Damn, that you would even think I would... No." She blew out a breath. "I understand why you would. You and Olivia have a complicated past, and I'm caught in the middle. It's hard to know who's on your side." She said the last part to herself more than me.

"Okay." I patted her thigh. "I trust you."

Her face softened. "Good. Because I'm in this all the way. I've chosen my side." She turned and met my gaze. "And it's yours."

Well, didn't that make me feel all warm and squishy inside. Maddie and I hadn't known each other long. Only spoken once really. But after learning all about her in Reggie's journal, I wanted her in my life. I was glad to see she wanted the same.

"How'd you find me?" I asked.

"After our call disconnected, I gunned it for your place. I was speeding down the highway when I caught your scent on the wind, heading in the opposite direction, so I tracked you."

I blinked in stunned surprise. "I'm not sure which I'm more shocked by. That you drive the highway with your windows open, or that you could smell me on the wind. I'm not sure my sense of smell is that sensitive."

Maddie shrugged. "We all have our strengths. Now tell me about Sam."

A lump formed in my throat. "He told me to run, and I stupidly did. I didn't get far before I turned back. I took out two of her men, but it didn't help any. She sent twenty people to my house. We were drastically outnumbered. They knocked Sam out and took him. I came in at the end, when they were loading him into the car."

"Damn." Maddie blew out a breath. "She didn't mention that plan to me at all. Why take him?" She drummed her fingers against the steering wheel. "To control you?"

"That or revenge. Don't forget, I did kill her

mate." Her plan would work too. Because Olivia held my heart in the palm of her hands. I would do anything to save Sam.

"What about the others?"

"I don't know," I said quietly. "I took chase after Sam. I didn't see what happened to Cole, Dominic, or Paul. And Anna, Vlad, and my mother can't leave the house."

Maddie briefly removed her hand from the wheel to give my arm a squeeze. "I'm sure they're fine."

Yeah, hopefully.

"I guess there's only one thing we can do," I said, deciding on my plan of action. "We head back to my place, and as you said, call in the pack and storm the castle."

Maddie's mouth twisted. "You sure that's a good idea?"

"Why wouldn't it be? Weren't you the one suggesting that a few minutes ago?"

"That was before I knew she had Sam. Lucy, she could kill him. If you rush onto her farm with your whole pack, she'll likely do just that."

A chill shivered down my back. "I can't just leave him there with her."

"And we won't. But we could be smarter about this. Take precautions. Make plans."

"Like what?"

"Like, an extraction."

I rotated in my seat to stare at my little sister. "An extraction?"

"You know, like covert dark-ops operations. An extraction. Put together a team, they sneak in all quiet like, undercover, and *bam* rescue the damsel in distress. Or in this case... the duke in distress? What phrase would they use for a man?"

That didn't sound right at all, but that wasn't the important part. "Where did you hear about extractions?"

She rolled her eyes. "Duh. I watch movies."

Right. Movies. Because everything in the movies always worked out.

"Look, if you charge in all willy-nilly like a Viking on a battlefield, Olivia isn't gonna like that. And she's gonna do something rash. Like ixnay your boy."

"Yeah, I'd like to avoid that if possible."

"Good. Because I know how to be sneaky. And I can help."

I just... struggled to picture Maddie as sneaky. My little sister with a smiley face T-shirt and brazen attitude. In my head, the two didn't go hand in hand. Then again, I'd only met Maddie recently. She'd taken out a total of seven vampires in her short time as a slayer. That had to count for something.

"Alright. We can discuss this option with the pack," I said, even though it made my skin crawl to think about waiting. I wanted Sam back *now*. Not two days from now after a successful extraction. And honestly, I wanted Olivia dead. I didn't care if that made me a bad person. Much like I'd promised the alphas, she needed to die. And much like Maddie had pointed out, that was the only thing that would put an end to this.

Maddie exited the highway and whipped through the local streets, clearly in a rush to return to my place. I hated the thought of slowing down when we were in such a rush, but speeding meant cops. And they were the last thing we needed to deal with right now.

"Maybe you should slow down a little," I said, watching the traffic behind us in my side-view mirror.

Sure enough, as soon as I suggested it, police lights came to life a few cars back.

"Shit," Maddie whispered, her attention briefly flicking to the rear-view mirror.

"They might not be coming for us," I said. "Just slow down, see what happens."

"If they pull us over and ask us to get out of the car, don't argue. I'll take care of everything."

My eyes flew wide, and I tore my gaze off the side mirror to stare at Maddie. "What?"

She sucked her bottom lip into her mouth, then released it with a soft pop. "Okay. So you know the show *Supernatural*?"

Who didn't?

"I, uh, may have taken a page out of their book. My trunk is riddled with weaponry." At my gasp, Maddie cringed. "For hunting vampires!"

Oh fuck. "How does this vampire slayer business work? Do you have a license? Are you permitted to carry?"

The police car came up behind us, sirens wailing.

"Yes," she replied before she pulled over to the side of the road and slammed the gear into park. "But some of the things I'm carrying aren't quite legal."

I didn't ask her to elaborate. Instead, I glanced out the back window in time to watch the cop car zoom around us and fly toward the next intersection. He zipped quickly around the corner—the same one we needed to take—and vanished from sight.

Both Maddie and I released a relieved breath.

Until a nagging thought crept into my head. That cop had been flying. And he'd taken the same turn we needed, which would lead him right to my place.

"Shit, Maddie. Do you think...?"

"That they're going to your place?" she finished. "It's possible. Someone might have called the cops."

Someone probably *had* called the cops. It would be stupid to assume no one had noticed the broken windows and brawling werewolves on the front yard. My neighbors didn't live close by in the traditional sense, but someone could have driven by, spotted the fight, and called the authorities.

"Let's go," I said. If the cops were now involved in werewolf business, I needed to know.

Maddie placed her hand on the gearshift, but paused, her nostrils flaring. "Do you smell that?"

I sniffed the air and shook my head. "I don't smell anything out of the ordinary." Not above the scent of exhaust and oil and gasoline.

Eyes narrowed, Maddie shifted into drive and slammed her foot down on the gas pedal.

I gasped as we jerked into motion, tearing across the pavement. She wrenched the steering wheel and tore through the intersection, turning on a dime.

"Holy shit!" I cried out, clutching the chicken grip above my door. "Are you trying to get us killed?"

She didn't respond, too focused on the road and whatever she was sensing to respond.

Maddie accelerated down the street, but the second my house came into view, my heart stopped dead in my chest.

No, no, no, no, no.

This wasn't possible.

Surely, I was seeing things. Surely, someone was playing a trick on me! This couldn't be happening. It just couldn't be.

"Oh my god," Maddie whispered, leaning forward for a better view.

"Stop the fucking car!" I screamed.

Maddie jumped at the sound of my voice, then slammed on the brakes. I wrenched on my seatbelt, practically ripping it apart, then dove out of the car and burst into a run.

Toward the police.

Toward the firefighters.

Toward the smoke and flames.

Toward my smoldering house.

21

"No!" I shrieked, my legs and arms pumping as I raced toward the inferno.

Flames engulfed the entire house, the crackling echoing in my ears as smoke wafted up into the sky. Firefighters surrounded my house, hoses in hand, blasting the flames with water. But the fire didn't seem remotely fazed by it. As though something fed them from inside, something more powerful than water.

My feet hit the walkway and I sprinted toward the front door.

I had to get inside. I *had* to.

Shouting rose from everywhere and footsteps pounded behind me.

"Lucy, no!" Maddie shouted.

"Stop her!"

"Ma'am!"

"Stop!"

Heat blasted my cheeks as I reached the porch steps, but before I could grab the doorknob, someone took me out at the knees. Together, we toppled into the singed and ashy grass.

"Get off me!" I screamed, throwing elbows and punches whenever I could.

I heard Maddie's soft curse behind me. But being the trained slayer she was, she adeptly evaded my clumsy hits. Instead, she wrapped her arms around me and rolled us across the yard, away from the encroaching flames.

"Lucy, listen to me," her calm voice murmured in my ear. "You *cannot* run in there. You'll die."

I screamed wordlessly and tore free of Maddie's hold. Fingers gripping handfuls of grass, I lunged back to my feet and staggered toward the steps. I had to get inside. She couldn't hold me back. Couldn't keep me away from them.

"Lucy, no," Maddie repeated, hands pulling at my arms. "I got her! Back off, I said I got her!"

I whirled around and shoved Maddie in the chest. She staggered back, tripped over what looked like a firefighter's boot, and fell to the ground, her face pinched as though I'd hurt her. It didn't keep her down for long. She leapt back to her feet and wrapped me in an unforgiving bearhug before dragging me away from my fiery home.

"You can't go in there!" she shouted. "The fire will kill you."

"I don't care," I muttered. "I don't care! Don't you understand?"

I squirmed against her hold, straining with every ounce of strength I possessed to free myself. When her hold didn't break, a fresh panic ignited within me.

"Let me go, Maddie," I pleaded. "Let me go! They're trapped in there. Oh my god, they're in there. All of them. Maddie, please let me go."

"I can't," she said. "Shh. It's okay. You're okay."

My pleas slowly turned into cries, and the fight drained from me. I broke at the waist and slumped in her arms, sobbing.

"They're in there," I repeated, my words slurring together. "All of them."

"I know," Maddie whispered. "But you can't go in there. You'll die. And they're..." Maddie's voice cracked. "They're already gone."

Everything in me broke when her words registered.

They're already gone.

Anna. Vlad. My mother. Cole. Dominic. Paul.

I hadn't stopped to check on them before running after Sam. My only thoughts had centered on him, on freeing the man I loved from my evil half-sister. For all I knew, Olivia's people had already started the fire before I'd left, and I'd just left them here to burn. Cole, Dominic, and Paul... if they'd been alive or conscious, they would have fought to save Sam. Which told me they'd been incapacitated. And Anna? Vlad? My mother? They wouldn't have been able to leave the house. Hell, Vlad and my mother wouldn't have even been awake yet.

Oh god, the fire would have trapped Anna inside, awake and seeing the flames come for her.

Anna. My sister. My best friend who had a phobia of flames thanks to her past. Burned to death.

Hysteria swept over me, and I crumpled to the ground, my face buried in my hands.

How could Olivia have done this? How could *anyone* do this?

Olivia knew I lived with vampires. She knew they'd be asleep this time of day. She would have known they'd be at their weakest. The woman was truly demonic.

And I was just as complicit. If I'd thought of someone other than Sam, if I'd gone inside to check on them, I might have been able to stop this. *Or been caught in the flames with them,* a voice rose in my head. A voice I so didn't want to hear right now.

This was all my fault.

"I'm so sorry," Maddie whispered.

She held me close, her head pressed against mine and her arms wrapped around my middle as she rocked me. I couldn't hear my cries over the sound of the crackling inferno devouring my home, but I could feel them, could feel my heart shattering into a million pieces.

"This isn't happening," I whispered.

"Ma'am?" a voice called to us.

I lifted my head and gasped. The sight of approaching police officers broke the spell on me, and everything came rushing in. The deafening sound of the roaring flames. The thunderous water spewing out of hoses. The blazing heat and light. The flashing sirens. The nosy bystanders clustering on the street.

Chaos reigned, and I could barely stand it.

Two police officers came to a stop in front of us. "Ma'am, do either of you live here?"

I slowly nodded, tears streaking my cheeks.

"I'm Officer Black, and this is my partner, Officer Taylor," the one on the left said.

I stared into his face, noting the aged wrinkles lining his features. A seasoned officer. Paired off with a rookie.

"We received a call to this address," Officer Black continued. "The caller reported a fight and a fire. When we arrived on scene, the house was engulfed in flames. Do you know who could have done this?"

Of course I did, but I refused to give them Olivia's name. That would simply rob me of the pleasure of ripping her apart with my own bare hands. So, instead, I shook my head, staring at them mutely.

"Do you know anything about the reported disturbance?"

I shook my head again. When I opened my mouth to speak, my mouth felt as dry as the fire raging behind me. "I wasn't home."

The officers nodded, having clearly seen us pull up in Maddie's car.

"Where were you?" Officer Blake asked.

"Lucy's a runner," Maddie told them. "She was out training for an upcoming marathon. I picked her up on Route 49, a couple miles outside Pocahontas."

Sticking as close to the truth as possible.

Officer Taylor raked me over with a glance. "You aren't wearing running gear."

I gestured toward Maddie's car. "I changed in the backseat. Hate sweaty clothes."

They nodded, their hands resting on their belts. But Officer Black's gaze never left mine. As though he knew I was lying. "Can anyone confirm your whereabouts?"

"No," I admitted. "I run alone. I've only been with Maddie."

"Are you suggesting we did this?" Maddie demanded. "Why would anyone burn down their own home?"

The officers ignored her question and kept their focus trained on me. "Can you tell us if anyone was inside the house?"

"I—" Another sob escaped my throat. "My family."

"Your family?" the officer asked. "We need specifics, ma'am."

I cleared my throat. "I live with vampires. And there were others visiting. Friends."

"Their names?"

"Vlad Vasek, Anna Perish, Barbara Williams"—
my voice broke, and I dropped my head into my
hands—"and my friends Cole, Dominic, and Paul."

"The three males," Officer Taylor said.

My head snapped up. "What?"

"Firefighters pulled three men from the flames.
One was conscious enough to give us their names."

Hope blossomed in my chest, and I struggled to
my feet. "They're all right? They're okay? They're
alive?"

Maddie's hand grabbed mine, and she squeezed.

"They've been taken to the hospital to be treated
for smoke inhalation and other injuries."

My pulse drummed in my ears. We weren't
supposed to go to the hospital, but I honestly didn't
care anymore. All I cared about was their health.
And if that meant doctors, so be it.

"What other injuries?" Maddie asked, drawing
the attention away from me.

"Broken bones, lacerations, injuries consistent
with a fight."

"And... and the others? Vlad, Anna, my mother?
They're vampires. They'd be asleep. My mother
sleeps in a coffin still. But Vlad has a bed. And

Anna... she'd be awake. She can be awake this time of day," I rambled.

Something akin to sympathy chased across Officer Blake's face. "Ma'am, I'm sorry. The firefighters haven't come across anyone else, and they haven't been able to access the back half of the house."

I sucked in a rough gasp and closed my eyes. "That's where they sleep."

"Is there any chance they might have escaped?" Officer Black asked. "I realize the sun hasn't set yet. But—"

"No." The word scraped my throat raw. "Sunlight is lethal to them. Vlad and my mother wouldn't even be awake yet. The sun doesn't set for like..."

"Another hour," Officer Taylor finished.

Meaning they were still in there. Trapped. Burning.

I spun around and retched into the bushes.

Maddie smoothed her hands down my back, and she whispered comforting words. Words I couldn't even focus on right now. Not while knowing what was happening in my house right this second. To think Anna would have been awake for this. The fear she must have felt. The horror. At least my mother wouldn't know any pain. But Anna...

I threw up again. The thought of her torment squeezing my stomach tight.

"Maybe we should discuss this down at the station," Officer Taylor suggested. "Away from all this."

"Why? Are we under arrest?" Maddie demanded, her hands pausing on my back.

"No, but your friend is clearly upset."

"She's my sister," Maddie bit out. "And we aren't going to the police station with you. Can't you see she's been through enough?"

"Maddie," I croaked. "It's okay."

"It's not okay. You didn't do anything wrong."

"They aren't arresting us, they already said that." I straightened and wiped my mouth.

Strangely, the first thought that entered my head was I had no toothbrush with which to brush my teeth. Everything I owned, every single item down to underwear, was gone.

"We should go to the hospital to check on the others," I said. And to get them the hell out before the doctors discovered something they weren't supposed to. "You said they were okay?"

Officer Black's face smoothed, as though seeing

my concern for Cole, Dominic, and Paul assured him of my innocence. Maybe guilty people didn't go to hospitals? I had no idea.

"The paramedics said they'd be fine, but the doctors will know for sure."

I only wished I could say the same for the rest of my family. Anna, Vlad, and my mother were gone. Then there was Sam. I couldn't even bear to think about what he might be undergoing right now. The few moments I'd spent with Olivia, I hadn't gotten the feeling that she was evil. But clearly, I was wrong. This was the woman who'd tried to kill me a month ago. The same woman whose mate I'd killed. Guess I was now seeing the extremes she'd go to for revenge.

My head turned of its own volition, and I stared at the house, my heart heavy in my chest. I lost myself to the flames, watching as the firefighters struggled to contain the blaze.

"We suspect accelerant was used," Officer Taylor announced behind me. "It could be why they couldn't access the bedrooms in the back. We won't know for sure until they conclude their investigation. But in the meantime, is there anyone you can think of who might have a grudge against you? Anyone who might want to do you or anyone in your house harm?"

I clenched my jaw and forced myself to shake my head. To lie. "We haven't lived in Jackson long. A couple months at most. Our lives are pretty quiet and uneventful."

"Okay. Well, if you think of anyone who could be responsible, please don't hesitate to reach out to us. Do you have somewhere to stay in the meantime?"

"She can stay with me," Maddie proclaimed.

"Good." Officer Black reached into his pocket and extracted a business card. "We'll also need a way to contact you in case we have more questions."

I opened my mouth to rattle off my phone number, then gave a jarring laugh.

"Something funny?" Officer Black asked.

"No, not funny. Horrifying, really. I just realized I don't have any way for you to contact me. Everything I own is in that house. Including my phone."

Officer Taylor perked up, his brows lifting. "Wait, you went for a run without a phone? How did your sister know where and when to pick you up then?"

Maddie scoffed under her breath. "We have an

arranged pickup spot. Ever gone running before, Officer? Other than for your training, I mean."

His brows climbed higher. "Can't say I have."

"It's annoying dragging electronics around with you. Ladies' workout pants don't always have pockets. Smooth lines and all that." She rolled her eyes, spouting off these lies as though they were the simplest thing in the world. "Unless you carry a fanny pack, which is even more annoying because it slides around everywhere, where are you going to stash your things?"

"Huh," Officer Black murmured.

"Lucy and I keep a schedule. Same time and spot every day so that I know where to find her." She gripped my hand and tugged me behind her. "You can have my number. You'll be able to reach her through me."

I listened as Maddie rattled off her number, all the while staring at the flames, mesmerized. I couldn't believe this. Couldn't believe Olivia would stoop so low. First Sam. Now Anna, Vlad, and my mother. She'd destroyed my whole life. All gone in the blink of an eye.

"Come on, Luce," Maddie said, unknowingly adopting Sam and Anna's nickname for me. "We need to get you away from all this smoke. It isn't good for you."

When Officer Black looked as though he intended to explore her statement a little deeper, Maddie clucked her tongue and sighed. "She's pregnant, okay?"

His eyes widened. "You're training for a marathon while pregnant?"

"My god, tons of women run when pregnant," Maddie sniped. "We aren't invalids."

"Uh, sorry." Officer Taylor cleared his throat. "Maybe take a second to get checked out by a doctor then. Since you'll be at the hospital looking in on your friends anyway."

My head bobbed noncommittally as I followed Maddie to her car. Unfortunately, without my phone, I had no way of contacting my doctor, or anyone else in the pack for that matter. Without my phone, I was effectively cut off from everyone. Just how Olivia wanted me.

Maddie opened the passenger side door and guided me in, taking care to place her hand on top of my head so I didn't hit it on the frame. Damn, I must have looked as bad as I felt if she was taking these extra precautions.

I plopped into the seat and stared out the windshield, the flames reflecting in the glass.

Hopefully, once the fire was out, I'd be able to come back. Anna had once told me that when vampires were set on fire, they burned away until nothing remained but ash. But I wouldn't let that stop me. At the very least, I'd find their remains and put them to rest.

But in the meantime, I had work to do and a mate to save. And I didn't care what it took to accomplish that.

For this, Olivia would die.

Then... Then I would grieve.

22

Maddie had barely hit the brakes before I leapt out of the car and dashed through the hospital's glass sliding doors. The receptionist glanced up as we rushed inside. At the sight of our soot covered faces and ashy hair, her eyes widened. I'd caught a quick glimpse of my reflection in the car, but here, under the blinding hospital lights, we must have made quite the sight.

I came to a stop in front of the counter and slapped my palms down. "We're looking for three men who were brought in by ambulance."

I listed their names, my entire body trembling from head to toe. From the feel of it, my adrenaline had faded, and shock was starting to set in. I couldn't stop myself from shivering, no matter how hard I tried.

The receptionist typed in their names while I drummed my nails against the counter, fighting the urge to shake her until she produced results.

"I'm sorry, ma'am, but I don't see anyone here under any of those names."

"What?" I demanded.

No, that couldn't be right. This was the closest hospital to my house. This was the *only* hospital the paramedics would have brought them to.

I pressed, "Check again."

The woman blinked at me, then repeated her search on the computer, her blunted nails clacking against the keys. When she shook her head a second time, frustration heated my blood.

"They *have* to be here," I growled, my voice dropping uncharacteristically low.

The receptionist blanched and rolled back in her chair, as though something within her sensed the predator in front of her.

I forced myself to suck in a deep breath. My wolf was on edge, riding the forefront of my mind. She'd been inconsolable since Sam's abduction. And though I'd shifted earlier, she was far from placated. Especially considering everything that'd happened since. She craved blood and death. She wanted to close her jaws around Olivia's neck until she heard a satisfying snap. In all fairness, I wanted those things too. But I couldn't—not until we found my packmates.

"I'm sorry, ma'am, but there's no one here by those names. Could they have been taken to a different hospital? The next closest one is—"

"No," I snapped. But before I could bite out more of a response, Maddie gripped my arm and hauled me backward, her fingers digging uncomfortably into my flesh.

"Take a breath, Cujo," she hissed. "Just because they loaded your guys into an ambulance doesn't mean they ever checked into the hospital. We aren't supposed to come to these places, remember?"

I jerked a nod.

"Great. So, they probably denied medical assistance and signed themselves out. Do you have a pack doctor?"

I forced another nod, still gritting my teeth.

"They're probably with her then. Can you contact her somehow?"

"I don't have my phone," I snapped. "And I never memorized anyone's number. Why bother when I always had my phone on me?" I choked out a bitter laugh. "Lesson learned, huh?"

"Look, there's no point in working yourself into a tizzy. So you don't have a phone or any phone numbers. It's not the end of the world. You know where Cole lives, right?"

"Yeah." I whipped a hand through my hair and pushed it back from my face, my fingers snaring in a series of knots, thanks to the ash. I needed a shower, but that was so low on my priority list, I didn't even know where to put it. The first thing I needed to do was calm down, but my pulse was hammering away in my ears. "I trained with him when I first became alpha. We sometimes used his place to hold meetings when we couldn't use mine."

"Okay. That's probably where they went. Hell, they might even be expecting you. They know your place was burned down. Cole has to figure that you have no means of contacting anyone. Let's go check out his place. If he isn't there, then we can start panicking."

At least it was a plan. Though it certainly made me feel useless.

We should be discussing how to rescue Sam. Making a plan. Implementing it. Not running around like chickens with our heads cut off trying to locate each other.

Maddie led me out into the dimming sunlight. When she reached her vehicle, I stopped and stared at the horizon. Strange how much my life had changed since Anna became a vampire. I was much more aware of sunset and sunrise. I'd researched her kind. I'd involved myself in the supernatural. She'd been my anchor to this world. And now... I felt adrift.

"Lucy?" Maddie called.

I blinked, breaking focus with the sunset, then hurried into her car.

I couldn't stop and think about Anna right now. If I did, I'd break down. And I couldn't break down. Not when Sam's life was at risk. After, I could lock myself in a room and cry for the next year.

Maddie started the engine and tore out of the parking lot. I directed her to Cole's place, my voice numb, but at least I wasn't hysterical or growling at people anymore.

Fifteen minutes later, Maddie pulled up in front of Cole's house.

I gave a shuttered cry at the sight of lights blazing out of the windows.

Then, before I knew it, his front door swung

open and countless pack members came streaming out of the house. Within seconds, I was in Cole's arms, then Dominic's, then Paul's. They passed me around like a hot potato, letting the entire pack touch me, as if to reassure themselves I was actually alive.

They handled me like glass, almost like they were afraid to break me, which made me cry.

Cole's hand pressed against the small of my back centered me. I lifted my head, our gazes meeting for the first time. Much like mine, soot darkened his face, but so did a litany of bruises and lacerations. My second in command looked like he'd been through hell.

The sound of a car door shutting drew my pack's attention, and one by one, they all turned. They fell silent at the sight of Maddie strolling casually up the sidewalk.

"Everyone, this is Maddie," I told them, my voice hoarse. "My sister."

A collective gasp rippled through the pack, their heads swinging toward me in search of answers.

"Let's go inside," I said. "We have a lot to discuss."

Cole squeezed my shoulder, then led me into his living room, along with the rest of the pack. Not everyone was present, but it was still enough to make it awfully uncomfortable—in a good way. A way that assured me I still had people in my life.

I took a seat on the couch and watched as my pack members copped a squat on the floor in front of me. Maddie kept her distance, and instead, leaned against the farthest wall, watching us with a keen eye.

Turning to Cole, I said, "Give me your phone."

Without question, he handed over his device. I scrolled through his contacts and gave a relieved sigh when I spotted the name I needed. I typed out a quick but succinct message, then dropped my hands to my lap, the phone resting between my palms.

Almost immediately, it lit up with a response. *Already en route. Will arrive within the hour.*

Relief nearly had me slumping back against the couch. Suddenly, we weren't alone anymore.

"Lucy?" Cole asked.

Right. The pack was waiting on me. But first, there were things I needed to know. "What happened back at the house? After I..." I couldn't finish that sentence. I hated admitting that I'd run away.

Compassion softened Cole's expression. "We held out as long as we could, but we lost the fight. They were well-trained, so either Olivia is working with them, or they came pre-trained from their original packs. Either way, it didn't take them long to overwhelm us."

"And what about... Anna?" I choked out her name.

"She came running in like a banshee after you left. She took out a few of Olivia's people and was still fighting when I got knocked out."

My mouth tugged into a small smile. Of course she was. That was my Anna.

"But when I woke up," Cole continued, "the house was on fire, and firefighters were dragging us out."

A shudder ripped through me. I couldn't imagine waking to such a scene. "Did you see her?"

"No, we were already outside." He went very still, his gaze locked on mine. "Did she... did she somehow make it out?"

My lower lip wobbled before I very slowly shook my head. "The, um..." I rubbed my eyes before new tears fell. "The police said they suspect accelerant was used. Which means they must have taken out Anna before setting the fire. She wouldn't have let them burn down the house."

"Jesus." Cole dropped his hands into his lap. "What about Vlad and your mother?"

I forced myself to swallow. "The firefighters couldn't access the back rooms. The flames were too out of control."

"Then they..."

I sniffled and nodded. "They're gone."

"Fuck," Cole cursed. "Lucy, I'm so sorry. When we woke up, we were disorientated. They loaded us up into two separate ambulances and drove the three of us to the nearest hospital. When we arrived, Dominic managed to distract them and we took off, but by then..."

"It was already too late," I reassured him. "Maddie and I arrived after they carted you guys off. Flames had already engulfed the house. Vampires..." I scrubbed my hands down my face and tipped my head back against the couch cushion. "Vampires and fire don't mix. It's one sure way to kill them. Not to mention, it was still daylight outside. So even if Vlad and my mother had been awake, which they weren't, it would have been like jumping from one inferno into another. I just hope they didn't wake up."

Unlike Anna, who'd been awake for all of it. Unbearable pain pressed on my chest.

"And Sam?" Cole asked, his voice a near whisper.

My heart cracked at the sound of his name. "Olivia has him."

Cole swore. "I'm so sorry, Lucy."

"Don't be sorry," I bit out. "Be angry. I am. I'm fucking pissed. And it's time to do something about it." I met the stares of my packmates and straightened. "We finally know where Olivia and her pack are located, thanks to our scouting teams. So, tonight we bring the fight to her. And when we're done, it'll be *her* home burning to the ground. I'm done playing nice. I'm done playing games. She started this war, but I'm sure as hell going to be the one who ends it. Who's with me?"

My pack let loose a singular cheer, hope blazing in their eyes.

After tonight, Olivia would never hurt any of us again. Tonight, I'd put her in the ground if it was the last thing I did.

"We have someone here tonight with direct insight into Olivia's pack." I gestured to Maddie, who pushed off the wall and strode toward me. Wariness haunted her eyes, something I hadn't seen in them before, but also completely understood. We were unfamiliar. Yes, I was her sister, and hopefully, she trusted me, but she didn't know my werewolves.

I gestured toward Maddie and waited for her to take a seat at my side.

"This is Maddie," I said. "She's another of Reggie's daughters. But believe me when I say we can trust her. This morning, she met with Olivia—"

Voices rose at once, all shouting their displeasure.

"Enough!" I called out, lifting my hands for silence. When they fell quiet, I resumed my little speech. "As most of you are aware, this morning, we sent out four scouting teams. Unfortunately, only three reported back. Meaning, one of our teams has gone missing. We assigned them to a farm just outside Jackson. This morning, Maddie trailed Olivia back to her location, which was the same farm we'd sent our scouting team to."

"Did you see our people?" someone shouted from somewhere in the middle of the room.

"No," Maddie replied. "But I wasn't able to inspect the grounds. Olivia could be holding them anywhere."

A whisper of despair swept through my pack. The thought of losing four more people weighed heavily on me. Tonight wasn't just about rescuing Sam. It was about rescuing everyone.

"Maddie also confirmed that Olivia's pack has

grown since we last dealt with them. She counted between forty and fifty people. Now, I estimate we were able to kill ten during their attack today. But that means Olivia could have anywhere from thirty to forty people at the farm right now, guarding Sam and the others."

If they're still alive...

No, I couldn't think like that. We were engaged and expecting a baby. I couldn't afford to picture any outcome other than our happily ever after. And for that to happen, Sam had to be alive.

"We're more than thirty," someone called out. "We can take them down!"

"We can, and we're going to. We have the numbers and the training. But more than that, we aren't going in alone tonight."

Questioning murmurs broke out amongst the pack.

I lifted Cole's phone and illuminated the screen. "In less than an hour, Adrien and the New Orleans Pack will arrive. As everyone knows, Adrien is Sam's father, so believe me when I say he has a vested interest in seeing his son returned home safely. With Adrien's pack at our side, we more than double Olivia's. They won't stand a chance. No more waiting. Tonight, we end this. Tonight, Olivia dies."

23

I WAS AS NERVOUS AS A TURKEY AT Thanksgiving, standing by the side of the road, awaiting Adrien's arrival. After the meeting, I'd messaged him to give him our current location, as opposed to him heading toward my non-existent house, and I expected his arrival any minute now.

Sweat dampened my palms. I rubbed them against my thighs, all the while anxiously fretting over our impending conversation. Would he hold me responsible? Forbid Sam from marrying me? Tell me I was a horrible alpha? Every possible outcome played on repeat in my head, like a broken record.

They didn't know Sam was missing, and I dreaded being the one to tell them. It hadn't seemed like something I should tell them over the phone. So that meant telling them in person, where I'd be privy to their every emotion and disapproving glare.

Sam's family had recently gone through a tragedy—thanks to Corbin, who'd murdered one of Adrien's daughters. And now Corbin's mate had his son.

God, what would I tell them? I couldn't even assure them Sam was alive because I had no idea. I doubted Olivia would have had abducted him just to kill him when her men could have done that for her back at the house. But I didn't pretend to understand my half-sister's brain. The things she did and the things she wanted were so foreign to me. So how could I promise them she hadn't killed Sam yet?

"Lucy?"

I spun around at the sound of my name to find Maddie stalking toward me, her long, blonde hair blowing in the breeze behind her. Anger twisted her features, her scent almost rage hot.

"What's wrong?" I demanded, suddenly afraid my pack had done something to offend her. Not everyone was happy about us finding another of Reggie's children. They'd demanded to know how many more were out there—information I'd kept to myself, for the children's protection.

Maddie stopped in front of me, her upper lip curling back in disgust. She shoved her phone at me and grumbled, "It's for you."

Huh? I frowned and stared at her phone like it carried a communicable disease.

Maddie sighed, then grabbed my wrist and slapped her phone into my open hand. "It's *her*."

Her could only mean one person. My eyes widened, and I stared at the screen, where Olivia's name stared back at me. This couldn't be good.

Knowing this wouldn't end until I took the call, I lifted Maddie's phone to my ear. "Yes?"

"Hello, Lucy." Olivia's voice rang across the line. "I see you've met our little sister. Been running all over town with her too, from what I've heard."

My jaw tightened. Had she put one of her men on us? Were they watching us right now too? Reporting everything back to Olivia?

Maddie seemed to have the same thought and lifted her hand with her middle finger extended. I almost laughed, then remembered it was Olivia on the other end of the line. Unlikely she'd take well to me laughing.

I covered the microphone with my hand and lowered the phone to my side, all to keep Olivia from overhearing the next bit. Then I leaned close to

Maddie and whispered, "Tell Cole to message you know who. Give him a different meeting place. We can't risk Olivia's people learning about his arrival."

Maddie's middle finger turned to a thumbs up, then she slowly strolled back inside, so as not to arouse suspicion.

I brought the phone back to my ear. "What do you want, Olivia?"

"You know what I want," she snapped. "I want everything. Your pack. Your people. Your territory. All of it."

Talk about middle sibling syndrome. She wanted what I had because she couldn't have it.

"You will announce me as the new alpha and tell your people they belong to my pack now."

"Yeah, that won't be happening," I said. "And you, of all people, know it doesn't work like that. You want my pack? Challenge me. Fight me fair and square. If you win, they're yours."

"Do you think I'm stupid?" she hissed.

A rhetorical question, obviously.

"If I challenged you, I'd lose. I was there the night you fought Bryn. I saw what you did to her. I know Cole and your vampires trained you to fight. If it came down to brute strength and skill, I'll lose."

Fair point. And one that made me smile.

"But I have the brains," she continued. "I wasn't expecting our sweet little sister to betray me, but that's fine. I'll deal with her after I take control of your pack. In the meantime, you *will* name me the new alpha, and you *will* relinquish your territory to me. Tonight. Or I'll kill *everyone* you love."

I froze, my heart screeching to a stop. "What?"

Her laughter echoed through the phone. I cringed and pulled it back from my ear for a brief second.

"I don't just have Sam, you know," she said, clearly enjoying her villainous monologue moment. "Say hello, darling."

I caught the sound of movement. Olivia possibly handing the phone to someone else?

Then came a weak voice, "Lucy?"

"Ohmygod, Anna..." rushed past my lips. My knees buckled, and I dropped to the ground, clutching the phone with both hands. "Anna, is that you?"

"Lucy! Oh thank god you're okay!"

"Me? What about you! I thought you were dead. But you're okay? You're alive?"

Her faint chuckle was like music to my ears. "Well, no less so than yesterday."

"What about my mom? And Vlad?"

"They're here too," she said. "Safe and sound."

My eyes blinked shut, and I tipped my head back to the sky, thanking every god in existence. Anna was alive. She was *alive.* It was like all my dark thoughts suddenly vanished from my mind. I had hope again. If she was alive, if she and Sam were together, I would do anything to save them.

"That's enough," Olivia barked, her voice now the one ringing in my ears. "There you have it, your precious best friend is fine. And so is her husband and your mother."

"How?" I croaked. "How did you remove them safely from the house?"

"They wrapped us in the curtains," Anna called out from what sounded like across the room.

The curtains! I hadn't even thought of them. Anna had wrapped Vlad in one like a mummy to protect him from the sunlight when we'd opened the window. Moving them outside, even wrapped, had been a dangerous gamble, but it'd clearly paid off.

Every inch of me trembled with relief. They were alive. They hadn't perished in the fire. They'd survived. No one was dead. God, I wanted to weep right here in the middle of Cole's front yard, but I refused to give Olivia or her people the satisfaction.

Instead, I forced myself back to my feet and drew a deep, steadying breath.

"What about the scouting team from earlier today?" I demanded.

"They're fine. They'll rejoin the pack once you hand them over to me. It'll be just like how you took over for Reggie. They'd had no choice then either. Plus, they know me. Deep down, they know I'll make a better alpha than you. Do this, and I'll let you and everyone you love go."

No, she wouldn't. The second I fulfilled her demands, she'd kill me. Sam too. She couldn't allow us to live. That was why alpha challenges were always to the death.

"Say I agree to your terms," I said. "My people would never accept you. They'll just challenge you at the first opportunity. As they did me. I had to earn my place with them. You haven't done that. They'll kill you."

Olivia laughed. "Who said I'm going to play by their rules? I have my own people, you know. They're all loyal to me. They won't let anyone threaten me. Your people will come around in time. They'll see the truth. That I'm better than you."

Boy did that sentence speak volumes. She really had lost her marbles.

"How do I know Sam is alright?" I asked.

Olivia scoffed. "Here. Tell her."

Someone fumbled with the phone. "Luce? It's me again."

I nearly rejoiced at the sound of Anna's voice. I wanted to assure her everything would be fine, but I couldn't risk Olivia overhearing. So, I stuck to the conversation at hand. "Is everyone okay? Sam? Vlad? My mother?"

"More or less," she answered. "Sam's a bit beat up from the fight. I'm fine. Vlad and your mother haven't woken yet, but they should soon."

"There," Olivia interrupted, having clearly stolen the phone back. "Everyone's fine, like I said. Now, are you going to do as I say? Or do I get to kill *your* mate like you did mine?" She snarled that last sentence, telling me she certainly hadn't forgiven or forgotten.

I considered my options. There weren't many. Olivia would kill Sam and me the second she took control of my pack—if I handed them over. She'd only taken him as leverage, and once she got what she wanted, there'd be no need to keep either of us alive.

Her plan was incredibly flawed though. Not only was she banking on her people keeping mine in line—which would be quite the task, considering I had an equal amount of people—she also didn't know that Adrien had come to help.

She was finished.

She just didn't realize it yet.

And I could work with that.

"You want my pack?" I said, hoping my acting skills weren't as terrible as I remembered them being. "Fine, they're yours. But I'm not telling them shit until you hand my family over. All of them. Sam, Anna, Vlad, and my mother."

Olivia fell quiet, clearly trying to figure out my angle. "Bring your pack to my farm in two hours. We'll make the exchange here."

Where she believed she had the upper hand.

"Obviously, I know you have some sort of plan unfolding in that little head of yours," Olivia continued. "So, let me assure you of something. If I even catch a whiff of betrayal from you, everyone you love dies, including our sister. And speaking of, tell her she has one night to get the hell out of *my* territory. If I so much as hear of her stepping foot on my land again, I'll give my people free rein to hunt her down. See how she likes having a bounty on her head. Two hours, Lucy. Don't be late."

The call disconnected.

I pocketed Maddie's phone, then turned to face the neighborhood, wondering where Olivia's people were hiding. As my gaze skipped across all the houses, my mind wandered to something my mother had said. *How do you know she doesn't have spies in the pack right this second?* I faced Cole's house and let the thought trickle through my mind. I hadn't given it any consideration before, but it couldn't be possible, right? If someone in our pack was a spy, surely they would have told her about Adrien's planned arrival. Unless they had, and Olivia had kept her knowledge of that from me.

I rubbed my chin as I considered this option. My gut said no, we didn't have a traitor. But it wouldn't be the first time someone had surprised me. And this time, I refused to go into the final battle without knowing the truth. My ignorance of Olivia's betrayal had nearly killed Sam last time. I wouldn't let that happen again.

I hurried into Cole's house, then waved him over and led him into the kitchen.

Keeping my voice low so not to be overheard by a house full of werewolves, I said, "Send a few people out to sweep the neighborhood. Olivia knew about Maddie being here with me. Which means either she has someone watching us..."

"Or someone in our pack is working for her."

"Or both," I said, hating that we had to even consider this.

Hoping to appear nonchalant, I opened the fridge and reached for a bottle of water. *Look calm and casual*, I told myself. Don't attract any wayward attention. Just in case.

"Olivia didn't mention anything about Adrien's impending arrival, so that makes me think she stationed her people in the neighborhood. But we need to be sure. We can't have any surprises. We also can't let her people follow us when we meet with Adrien. How soon can we do this?"

"I can send a few I trust. Marcus—"

I scoffed.

"We can trust Marcus, even with your history. I'll go, and I'll send Dominic out too. We should be able to clear the neighborhood within an hour."

Which would leave an hour to meet with Adrien and head to the farm. It was tight, but we could make it work.

"Olivia has our scouting team," I told Cole. "And Sam, and Anna, Vlad, and my mother. She has them all. So we can't afford to be sloppy. Last time, Olivia nearly killed Sam. That can't happen again. And last time, we walked blindly into the trap she set for us.

They were armed with guns. We weren't. We need to take better precautions this go-around. She thinks I'm handing the pack over to her, but she has to suspect I'll change my mind or have some trick up my sleeve. We need to be ready for the worst-case scenario."

Cole rubbed his jaw and took a swig of his own drink. "Unfortunately, guns aren't something we have on hand. And I can't see us arming an entire pack in just a few hours."

Though I'd guessed as much, the disappointment still stung.

"Hopefully, she has the same problem. We can scout the farm first though. Send our people in, use Adrien's people as a second wave. If she doesn't know about them, *they'll* be our secret weapon. Might even be best to send them in as wolves."

"Agreed," I said. "Back to the task at hand. We can't announce we're searching the neighborhood in case someone in the pack is working for Olivia. We can't risk them giving a heads-up. Take out whoever you find. This is life or death. As I said before, the time for games is over."

"Yes, Alpha," Cole said, bowing his head respectfully.

An incredibly unwelcome thought jumped into

my head. What if Cole was the spy? If there even *was* a spy. That would just about kill me. However, it also made the most tactical sense from Olivia's point of view. In my eyes, Cole was the perfect second. But that didn't mean Olivia hadn't sunk her claws into him at some point. I'd learn the truth soon enough. Until then, we had to move forward.

The clock was ticking, after all.

Only two more hours to go until this came to an end.

Cole, Dominic, and Marcus had returned swiftly from their neighborhood sweep, where they'd found—and *silenced*—three of Olivia's people. According to my second, they'd claimed to have been following us all day, after they'd spotted me running after Sam. Imagine their surprise when Olivia's little sister showed up in the middle of nowhere to pick me up. They'd reported that back to Olivia, then tailed us back to my house and to the hospital. Her eyes had been on me all day and I'd been oblivious to it all.

Not anymore.

After dealing with them, we'd assembled the pack and headed out to meet with Adrien. I told the pack to keep their eyes peeled for anyone else who might be following us, but that was a tough request, especially when so many of us traveled together. We were like a procession line, cruising through the streets.

Sixty-five minutes after Olivia's call, I sat in my parked car with Cole and Maddie, my fingers drumming against the steering wheel. We were only ten minutes away from Olivia's farm, but before we could continue onward, we first had to meet with Adrien and his pack.

The sound of approaching vehicles had me turning in my seat.

Adrien's vehicle pulled in behind mine, and the rest of his pack fanned out wherever they could find a spot. I killed the engine, shoved open my door, and stepped out. A faint spring breeze swept over me, cooling my flushed skin. Adrenaline, fear, and the pregnancy had me running a temp a smidgen higher than normal. Annoying, but manageable.

Adrien and Elena stepped out of their car and immediately started toward me with friendly smiles. That would soon change, and I hated it. I especially hated knowing I had to be the one to share the news with them.

"My dear Lucy," Elena said, sweeping forward with open arms.

I hugged her, then shook hands with Adrien.

"It's so good to see you. We were worried about you. We had no idea what was happening, and no one was answering their phones. Adrien and I agreed it was time for us to come help. We know there are rules about territories and whatnot, but we figured you wouldn't mind—"

"Not at all," I assured her, cutting off her soft ramblings. "But there is something I need to tell you."

I spared a glance at Adrien and noted that he wasn't looking at me. His gaze was scouring my pack, his eyes skipping from one person to the next.

"Where's Sam?" he asked.

I lifted my chin and delivered the news that Olivia had him.

As I spoke, Elena grew frightfully pale and Adrien's jaw clenched so hard, I thought he might crack a tooth. His hands curled into fists, and he turned away from me, facing his own pack.

"I'm so sorry. He told me to run, and by the time I came back, it was too late."

"Of course he told you to run," Elena said, gently. "That's my Sammy for you. Always thinking of the safety of others and never his own. Adrien would have done the same for me."

"I *will* get him back," I vowed. "Olivia thinks she has the upper hand. She has my whole family. But she doesn't know about you. And I'm hoping to use that to our advantage."

"What's your plan?" Adrien demanded, his voice terse.

Elena instinctively reached out, her gaze never leaving mine, even as she gripped her husband's hand. I couldn't *feel* their fear, but I could smell it. It rolled off them in waves. But I couldn't let their emotions affect me.

"Essentially, Olivia wants me to hand everything over to her. Her demands are simple enough. I give her the pack and my territory, and she releases everyone she took. But..."

"But you don't believe her," Adrien concluded.

"I don't. Her mate is dead because of me. I suspect she wants to return the favor."

Elena gasped and pressed her free hand to her mouth, tears shimmering in her eyes.

"We aren't going to let that happen," I assured her, trying damn hard to keep my voice from wavering. I had to appear strong, if not for my pack, but for Adrien's as well. Sam meant something to *everyone* here—whether he was a son, a mate, an heir, or their friend. These people would do whatever it took to guarantee his safe return.

"I'm going to do exactly as Olivia said. I'm going to walk right up to her doorstep and offer her my pack, but only under the condition that she returns everyone to me first."

"And your pack is aware of this?"

I nodded. "I briefed them before we left." I glanced over my shoulder to find my pack gathering behind me. I'd expected to find a look of dread on their faces, but thankfully, all I saw was determination and confidence. I had faith in my pack, as they did in me.

When I'd first moved to Jackson, that hadn't been the case. These people had barely known me. And those who knew of me hadn't been impressed. But things had changed since then. I finally felt like the alpha I claimed to be. And I absolutely refused to let them—or Sam's family—down. I wouldn't fail them. I refused to.

I turned back toward Adrien and Elena. "Thankfully, the sun has already set, which will put my vampires back into play. Vlad isn't going to appreciate waking up to find himself a captive. With luck, we may arrive to find a bloodbath already awaiting us."

Elena's mouth ticked upward. "A violent one, is he?"

"Only when Anna is in trouble."

Adrien stepped closer to his wife, then leaned down and placed a kiss against her cheek. "I can understand that."

"So can I," I murmured because I was feeling a little murderous myself. I held my hand out to Cole, who immediately slapped his phone into my palm. "So, here's my plan. I'm going to keep Cole's phone on me, and I'm going to use it to call your cell. We'll leave that line open between the two of us."

Adrien nodded.

"You and your pack will shift and head for Olivia's. I'll show you where to go on the map beforehand, but it'll be faster to cut through the fields. I brought something from home that I hope will help."

I gestured to Maddie who handed over a fanny pack.

"We can strap this around you so you can run in wolf form and hear what's happening," I said, glancing at the time on the phone lock screen. "We'll take the roads and arrive at Olivia's exactly ten minutes from now, right in time to make the exchange. Once you see her free Sam and the others, that's your signal to attack."

Determination hardened Adrien's gaze. "You mean to kill her?"

"And anyone who gets in our way," I told him. "With our two packs combined, Olivia's won't stand a chance."

"After the jammer disconnected you from the video call, a few of the alphas started bickering," Elena chimed in. "They want their people back."

I gritted my teeth and shook my head. "I won't make any promises. If they stand against us, they die."

"Understood," Adrien said. "We'll back you on that decision. These people are dissenters. They abandoned their pack and joined a rogue one. They shouldn't be allowed to return home where they can continue to spread discord."

Nor should they be allowed to take over for Olivia and continue building this new pack. No, they were like an anthill. One that needed to be fully exterminated. If we let any live, we risked them regrouping and starting all over again.

"Does my plan work for you?" I asked Adrien and Elena.

"Yes, of course. But, dear, what about you?" Elena reached out and snagged my hand. "I know you want to rush in and save Sam, but that endangers you and the baby."

I considered her stance. Hell, I'd even expected it. Sam was so much like his mother, after all. He had his father's strength, but his mother's compassion. They'd raised him well. So I had to choose my words wisely.

"The last time Sam asked me to run, my enemy abducted him. I understand you all want to protect me because I'm pregnant, and I appreciate that. But let me remind you that I'm not useless. And I need to be able to defend myself. I can't hide and cower until the baby is born. I will be there, alongside my pack, helping to free the people I love."

Elena's mouth tilted to the side. I could tell she disapproved of my position. Adrien, however, stared down at me with pride shining in his eyes. I'd won one over, but not the other. Fifty percent would have to do.

"Just be careful, Lucy," she said. "Sam wouldn't survive if something happened to you or the baby."

"I know. And I won't let anything happen, I promise."

"You can't promise that," Elena said. She leaned

in and hugged me, her arms tightening around my shoulders. "Sam isn't the only one who loves you here. Don't forget that."

"Thank you," I whispered.

"Now, go. We're running out of time."

I extracted myself from Elena's embrace and glanced at Adrien. "You ready?"

"You bet." He pulled out his cell, and I dialed his number from Cole's cell to connect them. I only hoped we didn't disconnect during all this. There were some spotty reception areas. We'd mapped our route out accordingly, but stranger things had happened.

"See you when this is all over," I said.

Adrien gave my shoulder a squeeze, then returned to his wife's side. He spoke to his pack, who all began stripping at once, preparing to shift. That was my cue to return to my pack.

"You all know the plan?"

Heads bobbed.

"Remember, Olivia won't be happy when she realizes we've double crossed her. Expect an immediate attack. Be on your guard. Shift if you feel the need to do so, but remember it will make you vulnerable for a short window of time. Don't get caught with your pants down, literally."

A light chuckle broke out within the group.

"When this is all done, we'll arrange a night of laser tag and paint ball. How's that sound?"

More laughter.

"Pizza and beer?" I added.

"Scotch!" someone shouted.

Laughter escaped my lips. "Yes, Marcus. We'll get some scotch too. We'll shoot each other first, then get drunk. Sound good?"

An uproarious cheer rose from my people. I'd truly never seen them so focused before, but considering their lives were at stake, it made sense.

Footsteps raced behind us, and I turned in time to watch as Adrien and his entire pack bolted into the nearby fields. I bit my lip and considered this plan of mine. There were so many ways things could go wrong. But the main one running through my mind was some innocent bystander catching sight of a pack of fifty wolves tearing through his lands and calling the authorities. Wolves weren't native to Mississippi anymore, so it would definitely cause a stir.

I couldn't let that distract me though.

We had a war to win.

So, with my own cheer, I pointed to our cars and shouted, "Let's roll out!"

25

Right at the two-hour mark, I parked my car in front of Olivia's farmhouse. She stood on the front lawn, surrounded by her people. My gaze locked with hers, and for a moment, I thought about smirking until my focus jumped over her shoulder to the tall, dark, and incredibly gorgeous man standing ten feet behind her. At the sight of Sam, the vice grip in my chest loosened, and I could finally draw in a full breath. Like Anna had said, he was a bit beat up, but those bruises would fade. The only thing that mattered was he was alive.

I couldn't tear my gaze off him, not as I unbuckled my seatbelt, not even as I climbed out of the car. The only thing that kept me from running to him was the feel of Maddie's hand on my forearm, holding me back.

I understood her trepidation. To get to Sam, I'd have to clear Olivia's entire pack. A pack that looked to be more like sixty people. Guess Maddie hadn't been able to count them all.

Movement next to Sam snagged my attention, and I looked to Anna and Vlad who stood side by side, their hands clasped. Anger burned in Vlad's gaze, and I knew without a doubt he'd take out as many wolves as he could when it came down to it. My mother stood next to Sam, their arms almost touching. Fear widened her eyes as she glanced between me and Olivia. Anna, Vlad, and I... we'd been through some hard times together. This wasn't their first abduction—long story—but my mother was completely inexperienced in matters such as these. Her body language emphasized her anxiety, and I was pretty sure Sam was the only thing keeping her calm right now.

Catching her eye, I offered a small smile, silently reassuring her that everything would be okay. She didn't seem convinced. So, I glanced at Sam and gave a small nod. He had no idea his parents were—hopefully—waiting in the woods surrounding this place, but he'd learn soon enough.

And speaking of, I remembered the phone stuck in my back pocket. Knowing Adrien was waiting for me to get this show on the road, I stepped forward and addressed Olivia. "You've been busy, I see. Quite the pack you've accumulated."

Satisfaction brightened her eyes. An expression I very much wanted to smack off her face. And I would when the time came. Right now, I needed to feed Adrien and his people as much information as possible.

"And tonight, my numbers will grow. Can't help but notice I outnumber you now."

For now.

A smug smile crossed her face, one that had me gritting my teeth.

"Have you explained to your people how this will go?" she asked.

"Nah." I shrugged. "You're the alpha, right? That's up to you to figure out. I fulfilled my part of the negotiations. I brought them here. Once you give me back my family, the pack is yours."

On cue, a few of my members gaped and turned to stare at me with wide expressions. I'd asked them to play along. And causing a bit of strife within my group would only convince Olivia of my true intentions.

"I never wanted this," I told her. "When Reggie died, these people came and dragged me out of New Orleans. I'm just as happy to go home. *With* my family. The question is, are you going to uphold your side of the agreement?"

Olivia snarled.

"Come on, Olivia," I prodded. "This isn't hard. I brought my pack, exactly as you demanded. And I'm relinquishing the territory to you. Hand over my family."

She considered me with narrowed eyes, her fingers drumming against her thighs. An anxious tic perhaps? Or had I pissed her off? How I wished I could peer into her mind and see what new schemes she was formulating.

I sighed and tapped my foot, allowing a bit of my impatience to show through. "Maybe you have all night, but I sure as hell don't. Release my family. Now."

"Or what?" she snapped at me. "Your pack knows you've betrayed them. You think they'll side with you if you decide to attack now?" She scoffed and spat on the ground at her feet. "I knew you were a weak alpha, but this just proves it."

Her comment hardly fazed me because I knew it wasn't true. But I pretended as though it did and let heat blaze through my cheeks. "Are you going back on your word?"

She considered this, then finally sighed and gestured behind her. "No. I promised I would return your family to you. And as much as I'd love to kill them and watch your face, I did make a promise."

Surprise had my eyes widening. I honestly hadn't expected that. Guess even villains could have morals.

Her people stepped aside, giving Anna, Vlad, my mother, and Sam room to move forward. But they'd have to pass right by Olivia, which I didn't love. My brow furrowed as I watched them move closer to her. Olivia didn't so much as breathe in their direction, but for some reason, that made me all the more nervous.

She had an axe to grind. I just couldn't picture her letting them leave without a scratch. I hadn't thought her vindictive when we'd first met, but I *had* killed her mate. Surely, she wanted a little vengeance for that?

I kept my eyes locked on her, even though I itched to watch Sam. And I was so grateful I did. The instant she moved, horror swept through me. I hadn't noticed the blade tucked into her sweater, but I noticed it now, when it came sliding into her palm. Just like I noticed her arm propelling outward.

Toward Sam.

I screamed his name, then exploded into wolf form in under thirty seconds. I practically melted from one shape to another. The instant my four paws touched down, I dug my claws into the earth and shot forward.

Sam ducked, narrowly avoiding the blade, but his movements were jilted. Slowed. His injuries, I realized. Broken bones, perhaps? Whatever the cause, he wasn't nearly as fluid as normal.

Olivia rotated and lashed out once more, and this time her knife slashed across his abdomen. Pain flashed in Sam's face as he jumped backward. In that moment, I knew the blade was silver. She'd come fully intending to kill him.

Well, I'd come fully intending to kill *her*.

And I would be the one to win.

A chorus of howls sounded from the trees, and Olivia whirled around. Shock, confusion, then rage colored her face when everything clicked in that head of hers.

She spun to me, her face contorted with fury. "You lied!"

How I wished I could spit back a sassy retort.

Instead, I rumbled back what I imagined was a witty reply, then leapt into the air, paws outstretched and jaw gaping. I only needed one second to snap her neck. Just one measly second.

And for a moment, I thought I might get it, when something massive slammed into me, riding me to the ground. We collapsed to the soil, our limbs tangled. One of Olivia's people had leapt between us. He threw an elbow at my neck, one I barely avoided with a quick duck and a hard bite. He cursed when my fangs sunk into his forearm. I shook hard, shredding through muscle and bone, then unlatched my jaw and hopped backward.

Blood streamed from the wound, and while he was distracted by the sight of his muscles and tendons—things that had probably never seen the light of day before—I lunged forward and tore out his throat.

I didn't pause to take that in. I couldn't.

Instead, I bolted into a full sprint and went after Olivia again. She and Sam had continued their little dance, with him attempting to keep her from stabbing him. Meanwhile, Vlad and Anna were neck-deep in their own battles, while my mother stood off to the side, fear rooting her feet to the ground.

I glanced over my shoulder and silently rejoiced the minute Adrien's wolves flooded the field like a plague of locusts, entering the battle. They engaged with Olivia's people, taking the heat off me.

I pressed onward. She swiped out with the blade, catching Sam's arm. The skin split, and the sight of his blood enraged me. I attacked. I barreled into Olivia's legs and took her out at the knees. We spilled to the ground with a groan and a grunt, her arm connecting with my windpipe. I choked on my breath but refused to let that slow me. Not when we were here, at this moment. Not when I could finally end things.

She scrambled off me and dropped into a fighting stance, the blade turned inward against her forearm. I eyed her, anticipating her next move. As she'd said, Cole and Anna had trained me to fight. Twenty bucks said she'd had Corbin teach her some moves—what intelligent villain wouldn't?—but it seemed doubtful that anyone had trained her as thoroughly as me.

I remembered Cole's lessons. How he'd taught me how to fight—and kill—both in human and wolf form. The way she bounced on her toes, the way her shoulders kept moving, she clearly had a plan in mind. What she didn't account for was Sam.

He closed in behind her, as quiet as a mouse.

I kept my focus on her and off him, so not to give his position away. Then I purposely glanced to either side of Olivia, noting anyone who might be a threat. Luckily, Adrien's wolves had engaged all her people, and one by one, were killing them off. Their death sounds would haunt me for the rest of my life, but I couldn't let that slow me.

Deciding it was now or never, I bunched my muscles beneath me and sprang forward.

Olivia snarled and feinted back. But she also dropped her shoulder, cataloguing her next move. I hit the ground in front of her and adjusted my position, sailing under her knife the second she lashed out with it. My shoulder collided with her middle, and down we went. The instant we landed, I slapped each of my front paws on her arms and pressed them into the soil.

Then I stared into her eyes.

The fear shining within gave me pause.

This woman was my sister. Was I so coldhearted that I could kill her without a second thought? She was just another of Reggie's casualties. He'd changed her, nearly killing her in the process, then welcomed her into the pack without offering her any of the same accolades he'd given me. He'd ranked her below me, given her nothing. Not that he'd given me anything, per se. But I hadn't been as affected by that as she had.

"Please," she whispered, tears forming in her eyes.

My heart broke as I stared at her. Maybe I didn't have to kill her. Maybe I could give her the same choice she'd given me. Give her the chance to leave. Except she'd come back. I knew that without a doubt. She'd return in search of revenge. And I refused to put myself—or Sam and our child—in that position.

But could I do it? Just lean down and rip out her throat?

Sensing my hesitation, Olivia reared up, knife in hand. And she thrust it forward. I caught the glint of the silver, saw the serrated edge heading right for my belly.

Fear and horror washed over me, and I froze.

An instant before she could stab me, Sam appeared. He plucked me off her with one hand, and with the other, he grabbed the blade, twisted, then slammed it home in her chest.

Shock widened her eyes and her mouth parted, but no sound came out. Nothing other than a raspy wheeze as the silver punctured her chest. He'd stabbed her in the heart. There'd be no surviving that. And call me callous, but suddenly, I didn't care. She'd nearly stabbed me! Nearly killed my child. I never should have hesitated.

Sam gripped me with both hands and hauled me into the air as though I weighed nothing. A darkness shadowed his face, and his eyes shone with his wolf. The hard edge of his jaw told me how close he was to losing it as he inspected every inch of me.

I wriggled in his grasp and licked his nose. It was the only way I could think to show him I was fine, that she hadn't so much as nicked me.

Relief loosened his features, and he tucked me against his chest, his arms banding around me. Even though I couldn't quite breathe, I didn't complain. This was exactly where I wanted to be. He wasn't the only one who needed reassurance. Though he wasn't showing it, I knew he was in pain. I could sense it.

"You're okay," he whispered in my ear, as though trying to convince himself. "You're okay."

I nodded, then fidgeted in his arms until I could see the battlefield.

Everywhere I looked, my people stood. Some were bloodied and bruised, but Olivia's people were the only ones littering the ground. All dead, from the looks of it.

"Sam..." came a soft voice.

He turned, still refusing to release me, and spotted his mother striding toward him, mercifully clothed. She must not have fought, probably on Adrien's orders.

I licked Sam's cheek, then wiggled until he put me down.

When he finally did, I nudged him toward his mother before I went in search of my own. She stood next to Anna and Vlad, her arms wrapped around her middle. They spoke in hushed tones, but when I approached, my mother dropped to her knees and flung her arms around my neck.

"I was so scared," she whispered in my ear. "Are you okay?"

I nodded and gave her a small lick as well.

"Ew, Lucy," she said, though it lacked gusto. She wiped her face, then rested her head against mine. "Anna told me what happened. About the house and everything. Is everyone okay?"

I gave another nod, unable to do much else until I shifted back. I didn't want to though. Shifters were an easygoing bunch when it came to nudity, but I wasn't quite there yet. I'd been raised human, and standing naked in front of your future in-laws wasn't something people did. My pack was one thing. Sam's family was a whole other.

Thankfully, Maddie and I had packed spare clothes in the car, compliments of Cole. Not that they'd fit me, since none belonged to me, but it was better than strutting around naked in front of this many people.

I looked at Anna and Vlad and raised my brows, which likely looked hilarious in wolf form.

"We're fine," Anna said.

Vlad scoffed. "Fine? You nearly burned to death today."

She had. I nosed her arms and waited for her to show them. But her skin seemed unblemished.

"Werewolf blood," she told me. "It packs a punch. I'm fine, I promise."

Vlad growled—a sound I was very familiar with.

Anna leaned into him and rested her head against his shoulder, her arms going around his waist. "I really am okay. A bit tired, but nothing a little rest can't cure."

Come to think of it, I was tired too. And craving a bath. A long one.

I couldn't believe we'd done it. We'd won. Looking back on it all, it felt like it'd taken an eternity to reach this point. But we *had* done it. Olivia and Corbin were dead, as were their pack members. No one was left to cause more trouble. And hopefully now, the alphas would keep better track of their people.

Sam, Adrien, and Elena strolled over. Adrien remained in wolf form and strode up next to me, butting his head against my shoulder. I gave him a once over, surprised to find his fur stained with blood. I just hoped it wasn't his.

"Everyone's okay," Elena said. "A few scrapes, but nothing that won't quickly heal." She tipped her head back to gaze up at Sam and she smiled. "You two did it. It's over. And you're free now to live your lives. How's it feel?"

A true smile spread across Sam's face.

For the first time in months, he looked carefree. Happy. Content. And my heart warmed at the sight of it. He had nothing else to worry about now. There was no one left to harm either of us. His mom was right. We were free. And boy, did it feel good.

Sam dropped to his knees and tucked me against his chest, resting his head against mine.

"I love you," he murmured, his voice still a few decibels below normal.

I couldn't say it back, but I uttered a sound that I

thought mimicked his intonation well. So well that everyone burst out laughing. Except for Adrien, who chuffed out something a bit more wolfy sounding.

"As we have no house to return to, may I borrow someone's phone to make some arrangements for us?" Vlad interrupted. "While the sun is still hours away, we need a safe place to sleep."

"Here," Elena said. She pulled Adrien's phone from her back pocket and offered it to Vlad. They must have decided to let her handle the communications instead of using the fanny pack.

Vlad thanked her, then dialed a number he must have memorized. He turned away from us and immediately started speaking to someone.

"What about you guys?" Elena asked. "Do you plan to name a successor and come home to New Orleans?"

That'd been the plan the last time I'd spoken of it to Adrien and Elena.

I squirmed out of Sam's grip and turned to face him, my gaze boring into his. I knew he understood when he kissed the tip of my nose.

"No, we're staying."

The battlefield went quiet, and I glanced back to find my entire pack watching us with rapt attention. I'd never told them about Sam's and my conversation a few nights ago. That I'd been considering staying as the alpha.

After returning to the car to shift and dress, I returned to Sam and took his hand, locking our fingers together in a show of support.

"I know the last few months have been trying," I said to my pack. "But in that time, you all have come to feel like family to me." I faced my second in command. "Cole, without you, I'd be dead. No doubt about it. You've been a steadfast supporter of me, and without you, I would never even consider taking up the mantle as an alpha. I admit I had a moment where I suspected you might be a spy for Olivia"— his eyes shot wide at my proclamation—"but clearly that was unfounded."

"Uh, right?" He glanced around nervously, causing a few of our members to chuckle.

"After everything we've been through, I believe this is a decision that we all should make. This is your pack, your family, as much as it's mine. If you don't want me to be your alpha, I will respect that choice, and I will appoint Cole as my successor."

A few gasped, including Cole, who seemed stunned by this news.

"But if you want me, I'd love to remain your alpha. I won't forcefully take the position. I respect you all too much to do that to you. This must be your choice." I squared my shoulders and prepared myself for the worst-case scenario. "So, on that note, let's take a vote. Majority wins. Do I stay or do I go? Hands up if you'd like me to stay."

I waited with bated breath, and my heart started to break when it looked like no one intended to raise their hand. But before the despair and grief could fully settle in, arms shot up all over the place. One after another. Every single person in the pack had raised their hand.

And I was absolutely going to cry.

I bit back my tears and gave a weak laugh. "Wow. That's... amazing. I just..." I garbled out a few unintelligible words, unable to convey my emotions in this moment. I fanned my face to dry my tears, then chuckled. "Sorry, pregnancy hormones."

Laughter spread through the group.

"Well, so be it then," Cole said, his arm still jutted in the air. "To our alpha!"

"To our alpha!" they all cheered back.

26

ONE YEAR LATER

Today was my wedding day.

My *wedding* day.

And I could barely believe it.

I hadn't been there when Anna and Vlad had planned theirs, so I hadn't realized how much planning went into organizing an event like this. For twelve months, Sam and I had undergone meal planning, seating arrangements, political discussions, invitation decisions, you name it. Every day came paired with some new issue. It'd gotten to the point where I'd started fantasizing about Sam and I running away to some remote tropical island to elope.

Somewhere warm. Quiet. Peaceful.

Just us and our family and friends.

But no. Because I was the Alpha of the Mississippi Pack, and Sam, the former heir of the New Orleans Pack, we were told an elopement wasn't appropriate. Nor were we allowed to invite any humans who didn't know about the existence of werewolves. Our dream of a quick, small wedding had been shunted aside, and in its place grew this uncontrollable nightmare.

But we'd *made* it. And that was all that mattered.

I stood in front of a floor-length mirror and swayed side to side in my gown. I hadn't wanted anything too extravagant, and thankfully Anna had listened to my requests. We'd opted for a strapless column gown with a pleated bodice that emphasized my figure. It, and the shapewear I wore beneath, hid what remained of my baby belly. Fabric-covered buttons adorned the back in a timeless row, ending at the edge of the sweeping train. Simple but classic, and it suited me well.

Anna had done my hair and makeup earlier in the day. After a few trial runs, we'd decided on a loosely curled half-up style, secured with pearl pins.

A gentle knock on the door pulled my attention away from the mirror.

"Come in," I called.

The door swung open, and I wasn't surprised when a blonde head popped in. Anna's startling blue gaze settled on me, and a wide grin broke out on her face. She stepped into the dressing room, clad in a gorgeous bronze dress fit for my maid of honor, with a beautiful baby girl bouncing on her hip.

My beautiful baby girl.

I couldn't stop myself from tearing up at the sight of my precious daughter snuggling my best friend. The two had bonded instantly after her birth, so much so that Sam and I had named her Annalise. But whereas Anna looked like the sun, with her blonde hair and blue eyes, my daughter reminded me of the night. She'd been born with a head full of raven black hair, just like her daddy. Her eyes were still blue, but Meredith thought they might turn green eventually.

"I think this little one is looking for her mama," Anna said, gazing lovingly at my little girl, who wore an adorable white dress to match me.

I crossed the room and pulled Annalise into my arms.

"Hopefully she doesn't spit up on you," Anna

said, laughing. She'd meant it as a joke, but with this little monster, there was a good chance of that happening.

"Maybe grab me a blanket, just in case."

Anna darted to Annalise's baby bag and pulled one out, draping it over my chest and shoulder. I repositioned Annalise and watched as her eyes immediately closed. Ah, nap time. No matter who she bonded with, she'd only sleep on me or Sam.

"Oh shit," Anna said, snickering quietly. "Do we risk moving her? You're due to walk down the aisle in like five minutes."

I bit back my own laugh to keep from startling her awake. Of course she'd fallen asleep just as I was expected to get married. "No, it's okay. She can just walk down the aisle with me."

Anna reached for the blanket, but it was wedged between us. Because of course it was.

"I could pull really fast?" she suggested.

"It's fine." I shook my head, laughing at our circumstances. But sometimes we had to adapt, a lesson I'd learned after becoming a mother. I could risk waking her, but it'd also risk her having a complete meltdown. Or I could go as is. Sam was her father, he'd understand. In fact, he'd probably love it. The man was head over heels in love with his little girl. And she had him wrapped around her little finger.

"You ready then?"

I glanced back at the mirror once more, then nodded. I was presentable and ready to go. No point delaying matters.

Anna chuckled at Annalise, then led me to the door. Together, we stepped out, only to find my mother standing in the middle of the hall, waiting for us. Warmth lit her face when her gaze dropped to my sleeping daughter.

"Well, guess this is happening," my mother said.

"Mm-hmm. Is Dad here?"

Her expression faltered, but she nodded. They still hadn't resolved matters between them, and I was beginning to wonder if they ever would. My mother had made it unequivocally clear that it wasn't any of my business and to back off. Considering I had my hands full running a pack and raising a daughter, I'd done exactly as she'd asked.

"Alright, then let's do this," I said.

We turned a final corner, and I approached a set of closed doors. My father stood next to them with a beaming smile, alongside Maddie, who I'd asked to be a bridesmaid. They both looked so good, Maddie in a dress identical to Anna's that accentuated her hair and eyes, and my father in a gray suit, complete with boutonniere.

"Hi, sweetheart," he murmured. During our wedding rehearsal, I'd taken his elbow and let him walk me down the aisle, but that couldn't happen now, thanks to the beautiful little bundle tucked in my arms.

He gazed down at his granddaughter, then leaned in and brushed a light kiss against her brow. Thankfully, Annalise kept snoozing away. Noise and touches never bothered her, but if I dared move her, she'd wake up, ready to raise hell. I'd rather that not happen today.

Once he straightened, my father offered my mother a polite smile, then turned and placed his hands on the doors. "Ready?"

I was more than ready. I would have married Sam on the spot after he'd proposed, but everyone convinced us to have the proper thing. To invite all the alphas from all over the country. To build connections and relationships. To grow our community.

My father threw open the doors, the sound of violins playing music reaching my ears. My eyes, however, tracked right to Sam. Dressed in a dashing tuxedo, he outshone everyone else in the room.

Including me. Our gazes met, and a flush of heat spread across my skin. I'd never met anyone who could steal my breath like he did. And from the look of adoration and love in his gaze, clearly he felt the same.

The gentle touch of my father's fingers against my elbow told me Maddie and Anna had finished walking down the aisle, and it was now my turn. With every step, my smile grew until my darn cheeks started to ache. I'd expected my pulse to quicken or my stomach to twist with nerves, but instead, it was the opposite. I felt confident and steadfast in my decision to marry Sam. He was my soulmate. My best friend. My everything. With every fiber of my being, I knew he was the only one for me.

When we reached the end of the aisle, my father shook Sam's hand, then took the nearest empty seat.

Sam beamed down at our daughter and chuckled. "Why am I not surprised?"

I brushed a gentle kiss against her brow. "We can marry you together."

"I love you," Sam said. "So much."

"Alright, save it for the vows," came a teasing voice.

I laughed and lifted my head to find Cole

standing at the podium. We'd asked him to officiate the ceremony, and he'd happily agreed.

Adrien stood next to Sam as his best man, and beside him, Vlad took on the role of groomsman. Neither Anna nor I had expected that development. But the two had merely shrugged. Perhaps they didn't dislike each other as much as we thought anymore.

We took our places before Cole, who began his speech. We'd heard it all at the rehearsal, so instead, I focused on Sam and Annalise. Strange, the twists life took. When I first learned that Sam was my mate, I'd run for the hills. The thought had utterly terrified me. But even that hadn't scared me as much as the thought of having a child. Today, I couldn't imagine my life any other way. This beautiful baby girl wrapped in my arms meant the world to me. As did her father. For them, I would do anything. Just as I knew Sam would do the same for us.

"You may now recite your vows," Cole said, gesturing to Sam.

My mate turned to me with a smile that melted my heart. "Lucy, I love you more than words can say. The night we met, my world changed. I'd never pictured myself loving someone as wholly as I do you. You're my person. The other half of my soul.

My reason for existing. The flame that burns in my heart. And I vow to do everything in my power to keep that flame alive. To keep our love burning, even in the darkest and coldest of nights. From now until our dying days."

My god... this man.

Tears filled my eyes, but I couldn't wipe them away, not when my hands were full. But because he was *Sam*, he grabbed his pocket square and gently dabbed my eyes for me. I gave a weak laugh and thanked him. Couldn't ruin my makeup now, could we?

"Your turn, Lucy," Cole said.

How could I match that? "Sam..." I considered my words, then decided to just let it all out. "When we first met, you terrified me. There you were, this beautiful, wonderful man, telling me we belonged to each other. Back then, I didn't understand what you meant. But I do now. Thanks to you, I know what it means to have a soulmate. Because I feel it. I feel you. You bring so much joy and happiness into my life. You taught me what it means to truly love and be loved. Without you, I'd be lost. Today, we aren't just marrying, we're binding our souls together. Because we belong to each other—of that, I have no doubts."

Smiling, Sam cupped my face. "You are incredible. And you astound me every single day with everything you've accomplished. But even without me, you *would* survive. Because you're too strong and wonderful to ever be *nothing*."

This time, my tears slipped down my cheeks. And I didn't care. Anna could fix my makeup later. "I love you," I whispered.

With a wink, Sam leaned in and murmured against my lips, "I know."

The instant we kissed, the crowd quietly cheered, purposely keeping their voices down so not to wake Annalise. It made me laugh that so many alpha werewolves and vampires quieted themselves on behalf of a little person not yet six months old.

"We can exchange rings later," Sam suggested. "When Annalise is awake."

Cole laughed and nodded. "Fair enough. By the power vested in me by the State of Mississippi, I now pronounce you husband and wife. Feel free to kiss—again."

Sam did exactly that, his hot mouth landing on mine with zero hesitation. We'd agreed to keep it tame, for the sake of public propriety, but I couldn't resist. I slipped my tongue into Sam's mouth for a quick French kiss, then grinned when I leaned back.

"Ladies and gentlemen," Cole called out, "may I present to you, Mr. and Mrs. Wolfman."

The shock on Sam's face nearly had me laughing.

"Kidding," Cole said. "Anna told me to say it."

Her snicker behind me told me she'd indeed been in on it.

"Now, let's get out of here and let this baby sleep in peace," Cole finished.

As everyone stood from their seats, Sam leaned in and kissed me again, his gaze dropping to his daughter. After a moment of staring at her, he lifted his head with a wicked gleam in his eye. "Wanna start practicing for a second one?"

Oh, hell yes.

EPILOGUE

WHAT AN INSANE JOURNEY, HUH?

The last few years of my life have been wild. But you know what, I don't regret any of it. Because it led me here. To my happy place. To Sam and Annalise.

As for everyone else...

Anna and Vlad eventually returned to New Orleans. While Anna and I will always be best friends, New Orleans is her home. In her words, *it's where a crazy vampiress like me belongs*. We visit each other frequently. And by frequently, I mean once every two weeks or so. Anna refuses to stay away from my daughter for too long. *Have to teach her how to be a star*, Anna says.

My mother returned home to Perish. She and my

father are speaking, but they haven't reconciled yet. She opened a new Vampires Anonymous location in Perish, which has been helpful for the few located there.

Maddie has officially joined my pack, and I love her to pieces. She reminds me so much of Anna in her youthful, pre-vampire days. She's adjusted to the role of sister and aunt well, and any time she isn't out hunting naughty vampires, she drops by for family time. The happiness I see in her means the world to me. She's finally found her place.

My pack is doing quite well. Everything has settled, and we've never been stronger. We've also been maintaining relationships with the other packs, continuing the video conferences and whatnot. A few of my members have even developed individual relationships with members from the other packs. It's made things interesting, that's for sure. Some have suggested we reveal ourselves to the humans, but many aren't willing to take that step. The time will come.

Sam and I are deliriously happy. Annalise is the apple of our eye, and we're working toward baby number two. Sam wants at least two more children. I'm considering it. Our biggest surprise was entering Annalise's room one morning to find her running around in her crib in wolf form. So our little girl is officially a wolf-born.

I haven't met any more family members, but Maddie sometimes talks about seeking out the others. I told her I'd support her, but I'm happy as things are, with just the two of us.

She's been a bit bored lately. Looking for some excitement.

Who knows, maybe she'll find some.

As for me, I'm content living my best life. No more adventures for me.

Love ya,
Lucy

SMITTEN WITH THE VAMPIRE KING SNEAK PEEK

THIS WAS A BAD IDEA.

So very, very bad. I mean, one bed? Seriously? It made sense, considering Jaden and her fiancé had purchased this cabin to escape the rest of the world. But it would have been nice if she'd mentioned the whole one bed situation when I'd first asked to use this place. Though, I suppose I couldn't blame her. I hadn't been entirely truthful about the situation.

I certainly hadn't told her I'd kidnapped the King of Vampires.

Just like I hadn't told her he was my mate.

Heck, she couldn't even remember meeting him. Or that she'd witnessed me turn into a werewolf. This whole situation was quite messy, really. I *could* have just let Chris stake Gabriel and be done with him. It wasn't like I knew anything about him other than the fact that we were destined to be together. But who believed in destiny and fate these days? Not me.

Instead, I'd clubbed him over the head and rendered him unconscious right before sunrise, leaving him at my mercy. Thankfully, I kept my car stocked with plenty of blankets and tarps—common inventory when one was a slayer. I'd wrapped him up, tossed him in the back, and blazed a trail here. Somewhere safe.

Or so I'd thought.

Nibbling my bottom lip, I turned to study the vamp—correction, the damn fine vamp—in question. He lay stretched out on the four-foot-wide couch, his long ass legs dangling over the farthest armrest. Wavy, dark, shoulder-length hair framed his aristocratic face—like a painting brought to life. Even unconscious, he was the definition of cold beauty. And I knew from my own experiences that he was hella powerful. Likely more so than any vampire I'd ever faced before. But that didn't make him invincible.

"Okay..." I whispered to myself before taking a spin through the tiny cabin. "One bedroom. One bed. One couch." A couch that neither of us would comfortably fit on, considering I was five-foot-nine and Gabriel was six-foot-three.

Or we could take opposing shifts. He could keep watch at night, and me during the day, to make sure no one burned him alive. Sounded pretty boring, but hey, we'd do what we had to keep him safe.

No need to share a bed.

At all.

Ever.

Right?

About the Author

 Kinsley Adams is a thirty-something-year-old author who stopped counting when she turned twenty-five. When she isn't writing uproariously hilarious romantic comedies, she's raising her womb-gremlin with the hopes that he might one day become the world's first Supreme Leader (and yes, *Debbie*, that's a Star Wars joke). You can find her and her books online at kinsleyadams.com.

If you enjoyed this book, please leave a review! Your support and feedback are greatly appreciated. And be sure to sign up for Kinsley's newsletter at kinsleyadams.com/newsletter for updates on new releases, sales, and more!

Also by Kinsley Adams

www.ingramcontent.com/pod-product-compliance
Lightning Source LLC
Chambersburg PA
CBHW020250030726
47499CB00001B/144